MUSKRAT HILL

MUSKRAT HILL

EASY JACKSON

FIVE STAR
A part of Gale, a Cengage Company

GALE
A Cengage Company

LIBRARY OF CONGRESS CATALOGING-IN-PUBLICATION DATA

Names: Jackson, Easy author.
Title: Muskrat Hill / Easy Jackson.
Description: First edition. | Waterville, Maine : Five Star, [2020]
Identifiers: LCCN 2019023492 | ISBN 9781432866044 (hardcover)
Subjects: GSAFD: Suspense fiction. | Mystery fiction.
Classification: LCC PS3610.A3496 M87 2020 | DDC 813/.6—dc23
LC record available at https://lccn.loc.gov/2019023492

First Edition. First Printing: February 2020
Find us on Facebook—https://www.facebook.com/FiveStarCengage
Visit our website—http://www.gale.cengage.com/fivestar
Contact Five Star Publishing at FiveStar@cengage.com

Printed in Mexico
Print Number: 01   Print Year: 2020

MUSKRAT HILL

CHAPTER 1

There was little chance of him recognizing me. His face had been splashed for years in magazines, newspapers, and newsreels, so when I looked out the upstairs window of the hotel I had been dumped in and saw him stepping from a new Studebaker, I knew immediately who he was.

My husband had abandoned me the night before in a tiny burg somewhere between Fort Worth and Amarillo. After years of watching him waste both our inheritances and losing an only child in a railway accident, all I had left was a note saying goodbye and twenty dollars he didn't know about. But he couldn't take the memories in my heart of our son or of a hometown that now sat at the bottom of a lake. Nostalgia for Muskrat Hill had, of late, almost overwhelmed me, along with a desire to know more about my past. My sweet mother never told me the full truth, and the only two people left who possibly could were a U.S. senator in Washington and a fifty-year-old country music legend.

After seeing him alight from his car and enter the hotel, I went back to my iron bedstead and sat down on the faded quilt to think, trying to remember everything I could about Kittrell Robertson.

He stood taller than average, not heavy, but by no means slight. He had graying dark hair, a straight nose, light blue eyes, and full, wide lips. Unlike many country musicians who purposely dressed like hicks, he wore well-cut suits, expensive cowboy hats, and handmade boots. The custom-made suit he had on when he alighted from his car had been light blue with dark blue piping around the sleeves and shoulders.

His deep baritone and ability to move an audience had made him the envy of his peers. He was known as a kind, generous man given to fighting when he had been drinking too much. He employed a heavy, overweight manager whose job was to make sure he didn't, and to protect him from the constant stream of Depression weary people eager to put a touch on him.

He also had an eye for pretty young women and three ex-wives to prove it. I wore my dark hair long simply because I couldn't afford to bob it, and I was slender, but being ten or eleven years younger than Kittrell Robertson still didn't make me young. The violet print dress I had on had been purchased before the stock market crash. At the time, I regretted spending so much money on it, but it was of excellent quality, and unlike the flapper dresses then in style, it fitted at the waist, managing years later to still look decent and not too unfashionable.

I racked my brain trying to think of how to approach him. I could give my maiden name and know he would see me. But he might not tell me the secrets about my past I wanted to know.

I closed my eyes, and an image of his parents popped into my brain. Pope Robertson had at one time been the most famous Texas Ranger in the state but had retired to run a grocery store in a small town. Kit resembled him, except his father's hair had been gray when I knew him. He, too, had been a kind man, extending credit to poor people when no one else would. I remembered someone sneaking up on him once as a joke, and the look in his eyes when he whirled around had frightened me. Even as a child, I realized there was much more to him than just a kindly grocer.

Kit's mother had been several years younger than her husband—a lovely woman with full lips, graying blonde hair piled high on her head, and lively blue eyes that always seemed to have an impish streak of humor in them. I, along with every-one else who ever got close to her, adored her. Sitting with my eyes shut, I could see them once again, as they were back so long ago.

I opened my eyes. It was as if Kittrell Robertson's parents had told me what to do.

The five and dime was still open. I hated to bust my twenty, because once broken, it would soon be gone. But my chances of interviewing a United States senator were almost nil, as was any hope of ever running across Kittrell Robertson again.

Kit's manager looked me up and down with experienced eyes, and I grasped my Big Chief tablet and pencil tighter to my chest, meeting his cool gaze with my own wide dark eyes. "I'll ask him," he said, and tromped heavily up the hotel stairs.

In less than two minutes, he returned. Pointing with his thumb, he told me to go on up.

With my heart in my throat, I walked up the stairs and knocked on the door. A deep voice told me to come in.

I turned the knob, struggling to keep from shaking. The room was larger than mine, containing two overstuffed chairs that had passed the bloom of newness many years previously. I almost turned and fled, but Kit came forward, holding out his hand, and I knew no matter what, I would stay.

"Miss . . . I'm sorry, I forgot the last name," he said.

"Please, just call me Giselle," I stuttered, unwilling to lie about my first name. It wasn't that uncommon, and it would take a stretch for him to connect it with a little girl he had known thirty years ago.

"Please, have a seat," he said, indicating one of the chairs.

I glanced on the bed and saw a sheaf of official looking papers.

"Divorce papers," Kit explained in a dry voice.

"I'm sorry," I said.

"Don't be," Kit said. "She was a bitch and the next one will probably be worse. I've already instructed my lawyer to show her the photographs of her and the lawn boy locked in naked clutches if she asks for too much money."

He sounded so disgusted, I felt sorry for him. I gave him a sympathetic smile and sat down, perching on the edge of the cushion, trying to look like a professional writer.

Kit smiled briefly in return and sat down easily in the other chair, crossing his long legs and leaning back. "My manager said you wanted to write a piece about my father for *Real West* magazine."

"Well, yes," I said. "I don't have an assignment. I'm new in this field and hope they will accept it."

He smiled and nodded. Emboldened by his attitude, I plunged on. "Actually, I was hoping you could tell me about his last big murder case, the one you helped him solve."

Kit tensed and straightened in the chair. "What do you know about that? It never appeared in the newspapers."

I swallowed and let a lie cross my lips. "The daughter of the sheriff in Sulfur City told a friend of mine about it. I was hoping you could tell me."

Kit sat without speaking for so long, I was afraid he was going to ask me to leave. "I've never spoken to anyone outside of Muskrat Hill about it," he said. "I was afraid if I told it, it would get twisted and cheapen a memory that means a lot to me."

I sat without answering, pressing my lips together and hoping.

He looked away. "But my life is so dismal right now," he said, "maybe if I did tell it, it would help." He turned back to me. "I think this is a dry county, but can I get you a glass of water? It's a long story."

CHAPTER 2

I don't know how boys are today; my ex-wife won't let me have hardly anything to do with ours. But back then they were brutal. The oldest boys picked on the next age group. In turn, they harassed us. We wrestled with each other constantly, trying to build up enough muscles and skill to fight the older boys off.

My particular nemesis had all the hallmarks inbreeding and poor nutrition leave behind—bad teeth, shallow, sickly skin, and a skinny, almost bent, frame. But Scut Tabor had knuckles as hard as doorknobs, and for some reason, he delighted in hassling me.

A bunch of us were down by the river that day. Only Whitey, my best pal, stood with me, his little freckled face pinched in concern. I took little notice of him, however, because my eyes were riveted on Scut.

"Your old man's a has-been, you chunk of turd," Scut taunted. Turning to the other boys surrounding us, smug satisfaction filled his flat, pale eyes when he saw the bloodlust on their faces. "Everybody says that," he said, looking back at me.

I felt my fingers clenching into fists and my face smoldering in an anger I couldn't control. Of course, that just made Scut goad me that much more.

"Your parents are so ancient; I don't even know how they managed to spawn you."

"Maybe they found him under a cabbage leaf," another boy

said with a laugh, but Scut, the leader of the pack at the moment, didn't want to share the glory.

"Nope," he said. "If his old man bent down to look under a cabbage leaf, he'd never be able to straighten back up again."

The boys hooted with laughter, and as if in one mass, they moved closer. Scut, too, took a step forward.

"Or maybe he just adopted you from one of those outlaws he caught," Scut said. "He's so old now, he couldn't catch a one-legged prostitute in a rundown whorehouse."

The round of raucous laughter set me blazing in shame, but gratified Scut, who spun back to me, thinking of something else.

"Hey, maybe your mama . . ." he began.

I rushed him, knocking him to the ground. My fists pummeled into Scut as hard as they could, but he pushed me away.

"Fight, fight!" the boys around us yelled in excitement. A few of the older boys yelled, "Come on, Scut, get him! Get him!"

I was used to Scut beating on me whenever he took a notion. However, this time, I barely felt his blows. I kept punching, vaguely aware it wasn't Scut I was fighting, but the destiny that had given me a father in his sixties—a father who breathed heavily and tired easily, a father who would never play ball or join in foot races. The fevered exhilaration of the boys who were egging Scut on to massacre me did not drive me to fight harder; it was anger at the God who had given me a mother in her fifties who would never bear me brothers or sisters, a beautiful woman people liked but whispered about behind her back. With every blow that fell from Scut, I struck back at my fate in a hard fury.

For once, my clouts landed. The fickle ravings of the mob began to shift to my side. I managed to get Scut down and straddle him. Grasping his tangled hair, I beat Scut's head up and down against the ground until he began to cry, blood gush-ing from his nose and mouth.

"Make him eat dirt, Kit! Make him eat dirt!" the screams around me ordered.

I forced a handful of dirt into Scut's mouth. He relented after a second or two, closing his mouth and swallowing. I felt Whitey's hands upon my shoulders, pulling me back.

"Come on, Kit," Whitey said. "Come on, it's over, let's go home."

As I stood up, I realized my face was wet with tears. Sobs wracked my throat, and mucus was running from my nose. I wiped my face with the back of a dirty hand and let Whitey lead me away.

With all anger spent, Whitey and I walked the trail back to town. We said nothing about the fight at first, neither one of us quite believing it had happened. Instead, we kicked a couple of rocks, stopping to pull long stems of grass to chew on.

After a minute, Whitey spit his out. "What do you think he was going to say about your mama?" he asked.

I shrugged my shoulders. "Don't know," I said, and began kicking through the grass, feeling the blades catch between my toes. I waited for Whitey to say more, but he didn't. Whitey never talked about his parents and what went on at his house. If something was going on, nobody knew about it, but Whitey never wanted to go home. It was tactfully understood between us that I would do what I could to see that Whitey didn't have to and not ask why. Maybe Whitey figured what went on in the Robertson house wasn't much his business either.

We were almost upon the diamondback before we realized it was there. It was the sound that awakened us, a rattle so loud and scary we froze. I stared at Whitey; Whitey looked at me, and together we raced away, making a wide arc around the coiled snake.

I took the lead, and laughing with fright, turned to see Whitey catching up. Looking at Whitey instead of watching where I was going, I stumbled on a rock and fell. When I rose on all fours and looked up, I saw a sight even more terrifying than that of a rattlesnake in the middle of a path.

In front of me lay the body of a young woman, flies buzzing around her surprised and lifeless eyes. Her mouth drooped open, blood droplets coming from a tongue that had been slit like that of the snake. I jumped up, and together Whitey and I stared with gaping jaws.

I'd never seen any creature so badly mutilated. The bodice of her dress had been ripped open, one breast removed and thrown casually aside. An ear hung by its lobe, flies sitting in the coagulated blood. Cuts were all over her torso, neck, and face.

Whitey tugged on my arm. "Let's get out of here," he said in a trembling voice.

"Pop," I whispered. "We have to tell Pop." I started running toward town with Whitey behind me.

We had entered the woods when I caught sight of a man on horseback, and I thought my racing blood would gush out of my nose and ears in panic until I realized it was Asa Jenkins, our town marshal. I turned to Whitey and yelled, "It's the marshal!"

We raced toward Asa so fast, we scared the big mahogany bay he rode. "Whoa, now," Asa said, calming the horse. "Boys, what is it?"

We couldn't speak, but stood fearful, gasping for breath. When we were able to tell him, Asa reached down and pulled both of us onto the back of the big bay. Breathing in relief, we explained the exact location, and with no more comment, he pushed his horse in that direction.

With my face at Asa's back, I thought he smelled, dressed, and talked just like any other white man in his thirties who didn't smoke or drink and led a somber life. But there was no mistaking the marshal was half Comanche. It showed in his coloring, in his chiseled features, in the way he held his muscular body. Asa guided the horse without effort to where we found the dead woman.

After that, it became a jumble to me and probably to Whitey, too. People appeared almost out of nowhere, staring, gawking, wondering and getting closer and closer until Asa had to push them back. He asked for a blanket, and someone removed one from a horse and handed it to him.

Asa covered her, and rising, he faced the crowd. "I have to go for Pop Robertson. Stand away from the body, and don't let anyone touch it. Pop needs to see it just the way it is."

A few of the younger men looked doubtful, but no one contradicted him. Asa told Whitey to stay put; Pop would want to talk to him. Whitey clearly wanted to ride back with us, but nine-year-old boys weren't encouraged to speak their minds in Muskrat Hill, and Whitey remained silent.

I rode to town without speaking, with Asa so preoccupied, he barely noticed he had a boy behind him. We were halfway through the woods west of town when Asa looked around and asked, "Where's Blackie?"

"Pop had to put him down day before yesterday," I replied, missing the constant companionship one-eyed Blackie gave me before he got ill. "He was whimpering in pain so bad Pop didn't have a choice, but Mama cried and cried until Pop told her if she didn't stop, he was never letting us have another dog."

"Don't worry," Asa said. "He'll take in the next stray somebody drops off on him." He paused and added, "Your mother is too kindhearted."

The way he said it made me wonder if Asa meant the dog or something else. We reached the clearing, and as I looked at the small bustling town of Muskrat Hill, I thought every detail of it appeared sharper than it ever had before. The train was at the station, puffs of black smoke belching as it rocked ever so slightly back and forth as if telling everyone, "I won't be here long, so hurry up." The big doors to the livery stable were open, and I could see the giant blacksmith's hammer pounding up and down on an anvil. The marshal's small office with its tiny one cell that hardly ever had an occupant stood near it. And beside it, the somber funeral parlor with its gilded gold lettering on the door. At the far edge of town was the slaughterhouse and pens. The horses in the stables made more noise than the animals Big Oscar, the butcher, killed with quiet efficiency. It seemed odd to me that Oscar Sorenson was the gentlest of men, while Mr. Petty, who took good care of the horses at the stables and could calm any vile-tempered stallion, was sour and unpleasant to his human customers.

Pop's large general store with its clean lines and sparkling whitewash sat at the edge nearest the woods. A wagon had pulled up to the front, overloaded with burlap sacks filled with flour and beans and all the other staples the town relied on. Pop, with his silver hair and trimmed gray mustache, stood on the high porch beside the wagon bed with paper and pencil in hand, counting merchandise and comparing it to that on an invoice.

While Asa wore a black suit and a gray brocaded vest every day, in the summer Pop favored white suits and light-colored vests. He stood now in his shirtsleeves with a spotless white apron tied around his waist. A man of tallish height with a solid build, he never bothered with a hat unless he was going to be out in the sun for a long time. Then he put on an expensive Stetson that cost more than half the merchandise in the store.

While Pop stood by the wagon, marking on his paper, a salesman wearing a dark suit and derby hat was busy pulling women's undergarments out of a suitcase, talking in Pop's ear faster than a train rolling down a steep grade. Pop bent an ear toward the salesman to show he was listening, but his eyes stayed on the wagon as he continued to count bags of flour.

When Asa slowed the horse, I slipped off, my feet running toward Pop as fast as they could. I stopped short and looked up to Pop, again unable to speak of the abomination I had witnessed in the meadow. Pop glanced down at me, his sharp blue eyes taking in my tattered appearance with one glance, but he said nothing and continued listening to the salesman chatter and the wagon driver's desultory comments while the young deliverer in the back of the wagon moved sacks for him to tally.

"Now this is absolutely the latest style," the salesman said, unabashedly holding up a woman's corset. "Every woman who walks in the store will want one of these."

"My wife usually handles that," Pop said without looking at him. "But she's in the back trying to convince one of her old maid friends that life is still worth living even if you don't have an old man farting in your bed at night."

"Say, Pop," the driver said, stopping to spit a stream of tobacco over the side of the wagon. "Did you hear about that robbery near Houston? One of those little towns down there where everybody raises sugarcane? Some slick stranger talked the bank president's wife into showing him the safe and then he left her trussed up like grandma's old hen at Sunday dinner."

"That's not my line of business anymore," Pop said.

The wagon driver continued his monologue as if Pop had never spoken. "Got clean away with nary a trace," he said, spitting again.

Pop glanced at the salesman. "Too bad you don't have something in there for pains in the neck," he murmured.

His comment was lost upon the wagon driver, who had a habit of never listening to anything but the sound of his own voice, but the salesman took Pop literally. "As a matter of fact, sir, I do," he said, rummaging through his suitcase.

17

"Folks down there is all up in arms about it," the laconic wagon driver continued. "The banker is offering a re-ward and is so mad at his old lady, he won't even sit with her in church."

The salesman drew out a corset made of metal. "It's the newest thing on the market. Guaranteed to straighten the spine, relieve neck pains, backaches, drooping bladders, and loose bowels."

Pop looked up from his invoice and asked the driver's young assistant, "What about the beans?"

"They're right here, Captain Robertson," the young man said, nimbly stepping to the front of the wagon, pushing aside flour sacks so Pop could count bags of pinto beans. As Pop began to mark off the beans on his invoice, a dawning of recognition came over the salesman's face.

"Robertson?" he said. "You're Pope Robertson! The sheriff who captured the Dawson gang!"

The salesman stood staring at Pop in respect and admiration, something I was used to seeing when folks found out the man selling them groceries had once been the most famous lawman in the state of Texas. Pop gave a short laugh and brushed it aside as usual. "I haven't been Pope Robertson in a long time, sonny."

The train whistle gave a long sharp trill, and the salesman pushed the metal corset into Pop's hand. "You keep it for now, Sheriff Robertson. I'll come back in three weeks. Just keep the corset, Sheriff. I've got to catch the train." He made a dive for his suitcase, still babbling in excitement. "Goodbye, Sheriff Robertson, thank you. Thank you."

Pop looked at the corset in his hand and grimaced. He dismissed it and watched as Asa dismounted and walked forward. Before Asa could say anything, the wagon driver interrupted. "Hey, lookee yonder coming up the street. It's Mayor Foster. Ain't he a coxcomb to beat all?"

I turned to see the mayor of Muskrat Hill walking in our direction, a large-framed man whose dandified clothes cost even more than Pop's. He owned hundreds of acres of prime farmland, but since his wife disliked living in the country, they kept a house in town they stayed in almost exclusively. It suited him very much to be the mayor, although as far as I knew, no election had ever officially put him in office.

"I heard his brother Melvin hired a housekeeper," the gossipy wagon driver said. He spit again and continued, "I figured she'd be so ugly she would start trying to tree coons round about midnight, but they say she's not a bad looker. I didn't know Melvin had it in him."

Pop paid no attention to him, but motioned to his assistant. "Take it around to the side and unload it."

"Sure thing, Captain," he said. He hopped over the sacks and got into the wagon seat, taking the reins from the older man. After he urged the mules to the side of the store to unload in the storeroom, Pop looked at Asa and spoke.

"Do you boys want to tell me what's the matter or do I have to guess?" he asked.

Asa removed his hat and through habit beat the dust from it on his pants. "Kit and Whitey found the body of a dead woman on the river road this afternoon, Pop."

Pop's forehead creased in immediate concern. "Who is she?"

"I don't know," Asa said. "Pop, somebody did a job on her. I've never seen anything like it. I've got to have your help, Pop."

Pop gave a heavy sigh. "Asa, I haven't been a lawman for years."

"I know, Pop!" Asa said. "But this is beyond me! You don't know what I'm up against."

He took a breath and started over. "Look, Pop, I can handle a few drunks on Saturday night or a domestic squabble, but this is . . . this is way beyond anything in my experience."

19

Pop remembered me and looked down. "Son? Are you all right?"

I could barely nod. Pop patted me on the back. "Go inside, tell your mother what happened and bring me my hat and jacket."

"Yes, sir," I answered, grateful for a direct command.

I opened the door and went inside; walking through the lengthy store stacked to the ceiling with anything anyone in a thriving little town could imaginably want. I walked past the high counter on my right, the lower counter following it, past the round table and chairs where men gathered to talk in the afternoons when it grew too hot to work. I pushed aside the bright curtain that separated the store from the living quarters. I could hear my mother's voice, soft, gentle, talking to a friend. Pop had a deep voice with a cadence so distinctive and demanding of respect, that once heard, was never forgotten. My mother's, however, almost always sounded lovable and unassuming, yet often full of gentle humor. I followed it to the back, to the kitchen, where she sat beside Miss Maydell who at thirty was the town's old maid.

I was so quiet, they didn't realize I was there, and I stopped to listen to their conversation.

"I love him, Dolly," Maydell said, surprising me with the passion emanating from her skinny, pale face with its small, tight mouth and worried little button eyes. "He wants to meet in the woods. He says he wants to keep it a secret, a delicious secret just between the two of us for now."

My mother gave a small sigh and got up to refill Maydell's cup from a pot on the stove. Her slender body moved with grace despite a slight limp that caused her to drag one leg. Standing by the stove, she pushed back a strand of the gray-streaked blonde hair she wore loosely pinned on top of her head. Turning around, her wide dark blue eyes looked with concern at her friend, and her full pink lips that were usually always smiling pressed together briefly, as if she wanted to say something, but wouldn't.

When she did speak, she kept her voice kind. "That doesn't sound good, Maydell."

"Oh, I know it doesn't, Dolly," Maydell said. "But I love him so much! I get weak way down deep inside me when he's around."

"Maydell, that kind of love is what got me this game leg," my mother said. "Loving is easy. Finding a man you can also admire and respect is a lot harder."

"You're so lucky," Maydell cried. "You have Pop."

A strange look came over my mother's face. "Yes," she answered. "But I haven't always . . ."

I wanted them to keep talking. I wanted to hear more about the man Maydell was meeting in the woods, to find out how my mother had gotten a bum leg, anything to keep from having to tell her about the body in the meadow.

CHAPTER 3

My mother turned and caught sight of me. "Kit!" she said. She jumped up and examined my eye. "Have you been in another fight?"

I nodded and put my arms around her waist, burying my face beneath her chest. She hugged me and stroked my hair. "I won," I muttered.

She stopped stroking in surprise. I never won. "Did you tell Pop?"

I shook my head and in a halting voice, told her about stumbling onto the body of the strange woman.

"Marshal Asa wants Pop to look at her," I ended.

Perturbed, she nodded, and with Maydell following, she hustled me to the front of the store, and it was she who picked up Pop's hat and jacket from the rack by the front door. We hurried outside to find Asa and Pop in an argument with the mayor. Proud of his wavy salt and pepper hair, the mayor believed himself to be more handsome than he really was, his nose being a little too bulbous and his cheeks being a little too flat. Now, however, his face was an ugly red, although he clammed up when he saw the women.

"Son," Pop said. "Go to the stable and fetch my horse."

"Yes, sir," I said. "May I take Gastor, Pop?" I asked, hoping my father would let me ride our old mule.

"Yes, get a move on."

The mayor looked at me and ordered, "Fetch my horse, too, boy."

I nodded, saying, "Yes, sir," again before running for the stables.

Mr. Petty wanted to know why Pop wanted his horse saddled, and I had to go through the entire story again. A small man, he pushed back his wide-brimmed hat while he listened, showing the whiteness of his forehead. The watery eyes underneath his bushy gray eyebrows and the chapped mouth beneath his big handlebar mustache creased in frowns as I told him what we'd found. Mr. Petty watched his language somewhat in the presence of women, but he didn't care what he said in front of little boys.

"Probably just some goldarn whore stirred up some man so he couldn't take it no longer. Goldarn women," the little man said. "Get on out of here. I'll bring your father's horse around. You sure he don't want the buggy?"

"Yes, sir, he said the horse. And Gastor?" I added timidly, for I was a bit afraid of Mr. Petty.

"Hell, I'll put a bridle on him. It ain't so far you can't ride bareback. Now get on out of here, and let me tend to my business."

"Yes, sir, Mr. Petty," I said. "And Mayor Foster's horse, too, please, sir."

"That blowhard can come get his own goldarn horse," Mr. Petty said, "Danged ole splayfooted crib sucker."

I left with Mr. Petty's grumblings fading in my ears. The grown-ups were still knotted in a tense group when I returned. My mother looked upset as the men talked and speculated. Pop stopped to glance at me, and I explained that Mr. Petty would bring the horses around. I'd done my part; if Mr. Petty didn't want to bring the mayor's horse, they could argue it out.

Mr. Petty arrived on his own horse, leading Smokey, my

father's gentle old blue dun, Gastor the mule, and the mayor's palomino, that was in fact, a beautiful horse, but as my father once commented, "Built to parade, not to work."

I waited nearby while Pop got on his horse. If it bothered the man who had once thought nothing of staying in the saddle for fourteen hours a day for weeks on end that it now took a while to get on one, it didn't show.

Once in the saddle, taking a deep breath, my father looked down at my mother. "Dolly, it will be all right."

She nodded, and the five of us turned to leave town. Before we arrived at the spot in the meadow, another five had joined us.

The crowd stood away from the body as Asa had ordered, and when the people saw Pop, their murmurings stopped. I slid off the mule and went to him, holding the reins of the horse in my hands, ready to assist Pop if he needed me. With the crowd silent and staring, Pop got down, saying, "Thank you, boy. Leave the horse and the mule over yonder underneath that tree."

I nodded. That meant Pop didn't want me to stand back, but to return to his side. I led the animals to the tree, tying Gastor to a low limb. Smokey had been trained to stay in one spot as soon as his reins hit the ground, but Pop hadn't had any luck training hardheaded Gastor.

Pop crouched on one knee and pulled the blanket off the woman. He shook his head in dismay and began the task of examining the body and the ground around her. He was silent and intent for so long, the crowd began to murmur again, their voiced thoughts and ideas becoming increasingly louder and more violent the longer they looked at the horror in front of them.

"It was probably one of those Mexicans what lives on Tortilla

Flats," a voice said. "Mexicans love knives; everybody knows that."

Another man stared at Asa in hatred. "It's the doings of an Injun!" he said. "And here we've got a half-breed marshal running our town."

Asa colored, but did not look up and continued to sit on his haunches, watching Pop. A slight little tenant farmer who barely eked out a living for his wife and nine children jumped in front of the crowd, waving his arms.

"It was one of those black cotton pickers what done it! Plain and simple!"

"Hush! All of you!" the mayor said. "We don't know who this woman was. It was probably a drifter who is long gone by now. So stop it right now."

The crowd looked rebellious and toned it down, but only a little. Throughout their speculations, Pop had continued his search for clues in silence without appearing as if he heard them. When he stopped and turned to Asa to speak, a sudden hush came over the onlookers.

"See this?" Pop said, pointing. "Her head's bashed in. That's what killed her. All this carving was done immediately afterward. That's the reason there's not more blood. There's practically none on the breast. That was done last." He shook his head again. "The final indignity," he muttered.

He began to rise, and I came nearer. He straightened and told Asa, "I don't think she was killed here." He pointed to the ground. "There's no sign of it. I think she was killed somewhere else. The body, the breast, they were dumped here later.

"Listen to me," Pop said, turning to the crowd. "She was killed before she was mutilated. A renegade Indian would have sliced her, watched her suffer, and then killed her. And besides, there are no more of those kinds of savage Indians around. The same goes for a Mexican. A Mexican bandit would have slit her throat, not bashed her head in. A Negro outlaw might have bashed her head in, but never would have bothered dumping the body way out here—he would have run away rather than take that risk. We could be looking at the work of a sadistic white man, so don't go off half-cocked pointing the finger."

"That's right," the mayor butted in. "I think we should just forget about it. It was strangers and nothing to do with us."

Pop sighed and gave a slight shake of his head in disgust. "We'll send for the sheriff. In the meantime, if you hear of anything, let Asa or me know about it." He looked at me. "Fetch my horse for me, please, sir."

I ran for the horse and brought him back. Pop, again breathing rather heavily, looked at Asa. "I'm stove up from kneeling so long," he said. "Give me a leg up, will you?"

Asa nodded and helped Pop onto the horse. From behind them came a snicker. I turned to glare at Scut and the other boys, but it was an older teenager who was grinning. "That's Muskrat Hill for you," he said to a friend, throwing his voice so everyone could hear. "We got a half-breed marshal and an old fart that can't even get on his own horse by hisself to solve our crimes for us."

Pop stared him down. "You think I'm too old, do you? I can still shoot your foot off and call it an accident."

Asa stepped forward. "Break it up people. Somebody got a wagon? Let's get this body back to town."

Whitey rode with me on the mule back to town. With the fate of the dead woman now resting in Pop's and Asa's hands, Whitey and I felt lighthearted and could give in to the excitement it generated in Muskrat Hill. The town was abuzz with it, in every building and up and down the street. Later, after leaving the horse and mule at the stables, we followed Pop back into the store. Pop took off his hat and hung it by the door, but before he could get his jacket off, my mother was there to help.

"Pope?" she asked.

He shook his head. "She wasn't anyone anybody knew, Dolly. I don't know why she was dumped here."

As my mother hung the jacket by the hat, Pop looked at Whitey and said, "Whitey, go home and eat your own mother's cooking for a change."

Whitey and I exchanged glances. I shrugged and Whitey left. My mother hugged me. "Are you okay, son?" she asked.

I nodded and followed Pop as he went behind the counter. "Play a game of checkers with me, Pop?" I asked.

"Not now," Pop said. He opened the cash register and began counting the day's take. He stuffed it into a bag and carried it through the curtain to the safe we had in the living quarters, just like he did every day. We were back in our routine. With a sigh and shake of her shoulders, my mother threw off the nightmare of murder. She picked up an opened envelope and withdrew the letter inside, looking over it with interest. Returning to the back of the counter, Pop began to look for his ledger.

"Pope, I got a letter today from my cousin Clara Grace. She said she's coming here to live with us. She thinks we need to be saved from Methodism and return to the mother church." She stopped talking and pointed to a shelf the ledger rested on. "It's right there," she said.

Pop grabbed the ledger, and she continued with her story. "From reading between the lines, I think Cousin Ralph and Willie Mae are asking her to leave. Oh, Pope, she doesn't have anywhere else to go."

Pop exploded in an uncharacteristic tantrum. "I'm old and I'm tired, and I don't want to be bothered with a bunch of kids or crazy relatives, or a gabby corset salesman! I want to be left in peace!" He threw the ledger down and added, "As a Methodist!"

He stormed to the back of the store, realized he forgot the

ledger, came back, snatched it again, practically growled at us, and stalked to the back, ripping aside the curtain that separated our living quarters with such violence, I thought it would tear. I took a deep breath and turned to my mother. She shrugged her shoulders, shook her head, and stared at the whirlwind Pop had left behind.

Pop had calmed considerably by the time supper was put on the table, but neither of my parents seemed to want to discuss the dead woman. Pop didn't skirt the issue; he just plunged headlong into another one.

"I do not like your family, Dolly," Pop said, stabbing a slab of cornbread and slathering it with butter. "They mistreated your mother, and they neglected you when your parents died."

"Now, Pope," my mother said, pouring him a glass of buttermilk. "You know Auntie and Uncle instigated that when Mother left the church to marry Father. And they've been gone for years. I say let bygones be bygones."

I shoveled in food, looking from face to face, not daring to interrupt for fear I would miss important information. Most of my friends had no interest in knowing anything about their parents, but I realized without even thinking about it that mine operated on a different level.

"And have we heard anything from these kinfolks of yours in years?" Pop countered. "No, until they want something, and then we get a letter saying because some cousins Ralph and Bobbie Lou can't stand her . . ."

"Willie Mae, Pope, Willie Mae."

"Whatever, because they can't stand living with your crazy cousin Clara anymore, they think it ought to be our turn." Pop stuffed the last bit of cornbread in his mouth, chewing it while nodding his head in righteousness.

"She's not crazy, Pope. Just eccentric, that's all. Eccentric."

"Dolly!" Pop swallowed hard. "The nuns wouldn't even have

her in the convent."

Stymied, my mother pressed her lips together and thought. "Oh," she said, "that's just because she's so independent and outspoken."

"Independent? And she's coming here to mooch off me?"

"She has nowhere else to go, Pope," my mother pleaded, her lips puckered full and her eyes wide.

"Don't look at me like that, Dolly!"

Something occurred to me. "Mama, Pop, who will take care of me if something happens to you?" I blurted.

"Oh, honey," my mother said. "You could just take your pick. Anybody in Muskrat Hill would be glad to take you in."

"Don't worry, son. I," Pop said, looking at my mother, "have decent relatives not far from here who would be glad to help you and your mother if anything happened to me."

That satisfied me until another thought popped up. "What about Whitey? Would you take care of him if something happened to his parents?"

Pop turned to my mother and raised his brows. "Don't we already?"

"Pope," my mother chided. She smiled, her busy thoughts turning to housekeeping. "We'll turn the parlor into a bedroom for Clara Grace. No one ever sits in there anyway," she said with a happy nod of her head.

In a turnaround of moods, Pop sat quietly watching her, and she caught his look. I could see the considerations of her mind turning away from their previous domestic track as she stared at Pop. A glazed and empty look came into her eyes. It was as if all thought had fled her brain to be replaced with a breathless craving that I didn't understand. She looked at Pop as if she wanted something from him that she had to have. "Pope," she said in a husky and confused voice.

Pop rose, went to her, putting his hand on her shoulder. He

bent down and kissed her cheek, something much more than a peck. I thought it was almost as if he wanted to take a bite out of her and eat her.

"Pope, thank you. Thank you for everything," she said in a small grateful gasp, taking his hand and kissing it. "You are so good to me." When she let go of his hand, he gave her a brief and tender caress before moving away.

She looked at me for a second as if she didn't know who I was, and I had the feeling I had intruded on something private between them. As I wondered why my mother felt so grateful to Pop, she rose, back to her usual self. "Oh, Kit, darling, hurry up and finish eating," she said, gathering the dishes. "The store is going to be crowded tonight with people wanting to talk about that poor unfortunate woman."

Soon afterward, Pop sat at the round table in the rear of the store, picking his guitar and softly repeating the words to an old tune his father had taught him.

"You say you love me but only give me a corner of your heart," he crooned in an absentminded kind of way.

I watched and wished as I often did that my father would teach me to sing and play. Pop kept promising one day he would. My mother walked by, exclaiming, "Oh, that song always makes me so sad." Pop immediately went into a series of complicated licks that I was sure I could never learn anyway.

The marshal walked in, and Pop stopped playing. "Any word from the sheriff?" he asked.

"Not yet," Asa replied. "The man I sent hasn't come back yet. Maybe they plan on returning in the morning."

A knock came at the door, and Big Oscar, the butcher, stuck his head in.

"We playing tonight, Pop?" he asked, showing his mandolin.

Pop called out, "Yeah, Oscar, come on in."

Oscar came in and sat down, his massive frame hanging over

the sides of the chair. He didn't seem to notice or care, but immediately began to tune his mandolin. Another soft knock came to the door. My mother went to the front, opened the door, and gave a look of surprise when she found Harmonica John standing in the shadows.

"Is it all right if I play tonight, Miss Dolly?" he asked with a polite look on his velvety black face, only his grizzled hair betraying his true age.

"Of course, John," she said, opening the door wider and standing aside to let him in.

Soon after that, the store became crowded with musicians and onlookers, most of them men who walked right in and didn't bother to knock. They sat in chairs crowded around the table toward the back and filled the stools by the counter; some even sat on the counter. Everyone came, from the mayor in his fancy suit and gray derby hat who often laughingly admitted that the only thing he could play was poker, to the poorest sharecropper in his sweat-stained homemade cotton shirt, bringing a fiddle that had been passed down in his family and that was so well thought of, he would have sold one of his children or his favorite dog before parting with it.

A few women accompanied their husbands, but they headed straight to the living quarters, crossing the threshold without a pause to sit in the kitchen and gossip. There was very little strumming and singing that night, and the kitchen percolated with speculations about the dead woman. However, Pop refused to allow name calling or finger pointing to get started. Every time an obstinate, dark look came over someone's face, Pop called for another song, or he changed the subject. He repeated several times that until they knew more, conjecture was useless. That did not stop the women in the kitchen.

Whitey and I played outside in front with the other children most of the night, but often passed through the store to get drinks of water from the kitchen. On nights when it wasn't so pitch dark, we could get water from the pump on the side of the store at the horse troughs and not have to risk being yelled at for running through the store. But that evening, hardly anybody noticed us.

Twice my mother had me fill up the big crock in the store with water and make sure Pop's glass was full. As usual, toward the end of the evening, when the crowd had thinned out, she sat in a chair beside Pop and listened to him sing and play. A few times, she got up to do various things in the store, but she always stayed near the sound of his voice.

After everyone had gone, Whitey and I lay on the floor playing checkers by the table, listening while Pop and Mama began to talk, forgetting there were two boys nearby. There was none of the heavy tension that had been in the air at supper. My mother told Pop what the women said; my father repeated some, if not all, of what the men talked about. They speculated about the murdered woman for a good while, and then moved on to small town gossip.

"That greedy onion-head wants Fergus Miller's place so bad he's gone to the courthouse so many times to look at the title, he's probably got it memorized," Pop said. "All the while bragging about what he would do if he owned it. Old Man Miller just sat there and never said a word."

"He's got all the farmland he could possibly want already," my mother said.

"Yes, and he got the woman who came with most of it, too," Pop replied. "I can't feel sorry for him. He married her for that land and now he's got it and her. Did she come in here?"

"Oh, Pope, you know Louella hardly ever steps foot in here. And you know that doesn't break my heart."

"Hmmm, woman," Pop said. "Just what would break your heart?"

"You know you're the only one who could ever break my heart, Pope," and she bent forward to kiss him.

Whitey wouldn't look at me. He pretended to be more interested in checkers. I wondered if he also had a warm feeling inside of him just sitting there listening. Before I could ponder it too much, Pop broke the happy bubble I was in.

"Dolly," Pop said, rubbing his hand on her arm. "Be careful. I don't want to frighten you, darling, but we don't know yet what we're dealing with." He paused to look at the front door. "It may be that it was just an evil wind blowing through Muskrat Hill that we'll never see again." He turned and looked back at her. "But it may not, so be careful."

CHAPTER 4

Whitey ate breakfast with us the next morning, but said he thought he'd better go home to check on his mother. It wasn't much later a tall, thin, ghostly pale young man opened the door of the store, sticking his head in and calling to Pop, "The body's ready, Pop, if you want to have another look at it." Horace Dubois hadn't been in Muskrat Hill long, but he already called Pop by the nickname almost everyone used, except he said it in a Southern drawl tinged with the slightest of French accents.

Pop had only been fronting and dusting merchandise and was glad for an excuse to stop. "I'll be right there, Horace," he replied, taking off his apron.

I had been doing the same thing on the lower shelves and was just as keen to quit as Pop. I immediately asked, "Can I go, too, Pop?"

Pop looked at my mother. "Dolly, do you care if the boy goes?"

She looked at my eager face and nodded, saying, "I'll finish the dusting."

I regularly attended funerals at churches and graveyards in Muskrat Hill but had not seen the interior of the undertaker's parlor. The heavy burgundy velvet curtains, the ornate urns, the varnished and highly polished wood that shone in somber brilliance impressed and frightened me. Pop and I opened a door in the rear of the room and found the mayor and Marshal Asa waiting in the middle of another. The undertaker stood nearby stroking his black goatee with a bony finger. The men were so used to seeing me shadow Pop, I don't think they even noticed I was there.

"Sheriff come yet?" Pop asked Asa.

Asa shook his head. "He sent word. 'Tell Pope once a ranger, always a ranger.' He wants you and me to handle it."

"I thought as much," Pop said. Muskrat Hill sat almost on the county line, and the sheriff preferred to think of it as being in a no-man's-land that did not require much of his interest.

Staying behind Pop, trying not to attract any attention that would get me scooted out, I gave a quick look around as we approached a casket resting on two sawhorses. The stark, unfinished room with its exposed studs looked disappointingly different from the front of the undertaker's establishment. When we reached the casket, the undertaker gently removed the lid. I peered from behind Pop, wanting to take his hand, but too embarrassed to admit I was scared. Looking at the young woman, I exhaled a soundless breath of relief.

The undertaker had sewn her back together with tiny, precise stitches. Her hands now folded neatly across the front of her demure dress, which had been washed, ironed, and mended. With her eyes closed and mouth shut, she looked rather like a pretty doll that someone had painstakingly stitched back together after a tomcat had gotten hold of it.

"Her clothes look ordinary enough," Asa commented as we stared down at the body.

The undertaker bent forward. "Here." Pulling up the sleeve of her dress, he said, "Let me show you something," and he held out her bare arm.

I leaned forward, seeing tiny marks up and down her flesh.

"She hasn't been using drugs long," the undertaker said.

The mayor put on his most belligerent scowl. "That settles it," he said. "There aren't any morphine users around here. She was a stranger who came in on the train. Whoever she was with killed her and left on the next train."

"We don't know that for sure, Julius," Pop said.

"Let it drop, Pope!" the mayor said, surprising everyone with his fierceness. "Don't use this as your last chance for glory. And another thing, times have changed, and you can't go around threatening to shoot off the feet of young men."

"Julius, Asa has a duty to the people of Muskrat Hill to investigate this crime, and he has asked for my help," Pop replied. "Now shut your trap about it. And times haven't changed so much that I have to put up with a mouthy know-it-all."

Asa turned to the undertaker. "Thank you," he said. Looking at the mayor, he added, "I think we've seen enough."

The mayor gave Pop another glare before following Asa, but it had lost most of its antagonism, drained by something else I didn't understand. Pop made to leave, but the undertaker took his arm, holding him back. "Could I speak to you alone for a minute, Pop?" he asked in a low voice.

Pop nodded and indicated that Asa and the mayor were to go on. He didn't look at me, thankfully, and I stayed. When the mayor left and Asa shut the door behind them, Pop asked the undertaker, "All right, what is it?"

"She had intercourse before she died, Pop," the undertaker said. "But it can't get out that I looked, or the men in this town will try to kill me if they think I ever peeked into their wife's tunnel of love whether she was dead or not."

Pop nodded. "Was it rape?"

"I don't know; I'm not that good of an undertaker."

"Well," Pop continued. "Was she torn or bruised?"

"No," the undertaker said. "But there is something else. Her hands are smooth, meaning she didn't do housework or labor of any kind. It doesn't look like she's ever had a baby, but her nipples are tough. I think she was a prostitute, Pop, regardless of what her clothes look like."

Pop looked down at the young woman, pondering what the undertaker said. Looking up, he turned, putting his hand on my shoulder, and began to guide me to the door. "Thank you, Horace," he said as we left. "You've done an excellent job, but no one will know from us just how good of an investigator you are," and he squeezed my shoulder to indicate I was to keep my mouth shut about everything I heard.

Asa stood outside leaning against a post, waiting for us. The mayor had disappeared. Pop briefly told Asa what the undertaker had said.

"A prostitute?" Asa questioned dubiously. "The only prostitutes around here are at Miss Effie's place in Sulfur City. The sheriff there hasn't contacted me about any missing girls."

"He would, too. All Effie has to do is mutter 'shit' and his pants turn brown," Pop said dryly. "We'll wait a day or two. If it's one of her girls, she'll send him over." He gave a brief pause. "Asa, I want you to wire the prison in Huntsville to see if they've had any escapes."

Asa stared at Pop. "The prison? Pop, you don't think . . ."

"I don't think anything at this point," Pop interrupted. "All I know is this is the kind of behavior that was just beginning back then. Just do it. And in the meantime," he said, trying to lighten the mood, "we can piss Julius off by going around asking questions."

We were walking back to the store when Pop's eye was caught by a glimpse of someone behind the undertaker's establishment. As he peered into the alley between the funeral parlor and the jail, Pop put his hand on Asa to stop him. A short, stocky bald man disappeared through the back door of the funeral parlor.

"Who was that?" Pop asked.

Asa shook his head. "I don't think I know. Surely not someone from around here."

"Let's go back," Pop said, and we turned and reentered the funeral parlor.

"Horace," Pop called.

He appeared almost immediately. "Yes?" he asked.

"We saw a man walk into the back door of your business. Middle-aged, maybe older."

"Oh, yes," Horace said. "That's my new gravedigger, Bruno."

"When did you hire him?" Pop asked. "I don't believe I've seen him around town before."

"A few days ago," Horace replied. "He said he was a drifter, but had heard that I needed an assistant here. He doesn't mind manual labor, and he has some carpentry skills. He's quite willing to work for room and board with only the occasional need for monetary remittance."

Pop and Asa looked at one another. Pop turned back to the undertaker. "If he just came here a few days ago, we'll have to talk to him."

"Ah, yes, I see," Horace said. He turned to fetch Bruno but paused when his eyes lighted on me.

"I don't know how clearly you saw him," he said to Pop. "But Bruno's face was disfigured in an explosion. He's rather frightening to look at, but harmless, I assure you." He slipped back into the other room, and after a moment, returned with his new helper.

I was glad he had prepared us, because I might have let out a yelp otherwise. Bruno stood in front of us, stout and muscular, with one half of his face a scarred-over pulp. With that and his shaved head, he looked like a circus sideshow freak.

"Pop, Marshal Asa, this is Bruno," the undertaker said in his peculiar drawl. "Bruno, this is Marshal Asa Jenkins and Pope Robertson with his young son, Kit. Everyone calls Captain

Robertson 'Pop' around here. He owns the general store, but at one time he was quite the famous lawman. They are inquiring into the murder of the young woman brought in yesterday."

Bruno nodded, one of his eyes clouded and unseeing, the other seeming to pierce through Pop.

"Bruno," Pop nodded in greeting. "Because of the murder, we must ask questions that would otherwise be none of our business. I hope you understand. What is your full name?"

Bruno looked at the undertaker and made strange hand signals. The undertaker turned to Pop. "His name is Bruno Nieman," he said. "I should have told you that although Bruno's hearing is excellent, his vocal cords were destroyed. I've been teaching him the alphabet for the deaf."

"The deaf?" Asa asked.

"Yes," Horace said. "My parents were deaf, and they sent me to school to learn it so I might communicate with them."

Pop nodded and again spoke directly to Bruno. "Did you come into Muskrat Hill on the train?"

He nodded, and Pop continued. "Where did you hear that Horace needed an assistant?"

He signed the answer to Horace while I watched, fascinated by their communication.

"San Antonio," Horace translated. "One of my former colleagues must have told him. That's where I lived when I came to Texas from South Carolina."

It went on like that for some time. Bruno admitted he had hopped the train at San Antonio and jumped off just before it reached Muskrat Hill. He had the money to pay for the ticket, but he didn't like people staring at him so he hid in an empty car. He hadn't seen the young woman and didn't know who she was.

Almost the entire time they talked, I had the feeling that Bruno was sizing me up also. I, in turn, was fascinated by this ugly, cruel looking man. Yet even as I saw his features as hard and pitiless, I remembered that Horace had called him harmless.

"Thank you for answering our questions, Bruno," Pop was saying. "We may have more later on, I'm sorry."

Bruno nodded, turning immediately and leaving the room.

"Much obliged, Horace," Pop said.

After we took our leave and stood on the sidewalk once again, Pop shook his head. "Asa, I've dealt with a lot of men in my time, and I would swear that man just got out of prison. He's familiar to me, but I can't place him. I've seen hundreds of outlaws, and he may have been one of them."

"We have a man who arrives in Muskrat Hill, and a few days later we have a murder," Asa said. "It doesn't look very good for him."

"Yes, yes, I know," Pop said, beginning to walk back to the store. "But why stay when you know you will be the prime suspect?"

Early the next morning, Whitey and I played checkers on the round table at the back of the store while we waited for Pop. Whitey wasn't much good at checkers, and there were often times I lost to him on purpose just so he'd keep playing. Marshal Asa came in and greeted us, asking where Pop was.

"He's taking a nap," I answered.

"A nap?" Asa asked in disbelief. "First thing in the morning?" He looked at the curtain and began to walk toward the living quarters.

"I wouldn't do that," I warned. "Pop don't like to be interrupted when he's taking a nap. He asked me and Whitey to watch the store." Whitey nodded his head in agreement.

Asa stopped, still doubting my word when the faint sounds of bedsprings squeaking came through from behind the curtain. Asa's mouth dropped open slightly. He said, "Oh," and turned and walked back to the table. "Believe I'll wait here after all," he said, and took a chair next to Whitey.

He watched the game while Whitey and I continued to play. In a little while, I looked up at the curtain and saw my mother coming out wearing a smile, her face radiating quiet happiness. She saw Asa and said, "Oh, hello, Asa." Turning to Whitey and me, she added, "Thank you, boys, for watching the store."

We nodded and she walked to the front of the store, humming a little tune. If she hadn't had a bad leg, I thought she might have floated like an angel. Asa must have thought so, too, because he watched her, his eyelids growing heavy and secretive, his breath coming out harder and faster.

Pop came out, adjusting his belt. He caught the expression on Asa's face, and he said sharply, "Asa! If I ever see you looking at my wife like that again, I'm kicking your nose up your forehead."

Asa's face flushed, mortified with embarrassment. He jumped up. "I'm sorry, Pop. Let's get going. Let's go. We need to get a move on."

Asa's discomfiture restored Pop's good humor, and he smiled, heading for the front door while Whitey and I quit our checkers to tag along. "Just hold your horses, I've got to stop by the slaughterhouse and give Big Oscar the day's meat order," Pop said over his shoulder.

Asa didn't reply but waited edgily for Pop to put on his jacket and hat.

"You are the most impatient Indian I have ever met," Pop teased as we went out the door. "I thought Indians were supposed to be able to sit without moving for hours while they waited for their prey."

Asa gave the door behind us a firm shut. "Well, I didn't think palefaces your age could still take those kind of early morning naps, much less have a wife who looked like she enjoyed every minute of it, heap 'em great white horn dog."

Pop gave a grin and a shrug, enjoying Asa's grouchiness. "I'm an exceptional paleface," he said.

"Well, I'm an exceptional red man," Asa retorted.

"That you are," Pop agreed.

"Pop," I asked as we walked along the wooden sidewalk to the slaughterhouse. "What's a horn dog?"

"Something I will explain to you later," Pop said. "In the meantime, keep your mouth shut and your eyes and ears open. That goes for you too, Whitey."

I murmured "Yes, sir," and Whitey said, "Yes, sir, Captain Robertson."

We ran ahead of the two men to the wide double doors of the slaughterhouse, holding them open so Pop and Asa could go in first.

Whitey and I hated the smell of the slaughterhouse and the multitude of flies it attracted. Even as it repelled, it also fascinated, and we walked a few steps away from the men, our eyes wandering over the interior. I thought it looked like a dark cave—dead skinned animals hung from hooks, and piles of hides and bones lay everywhere. I couldn't understand how a nice man like Mr. Sorenson could work in such a place, but Pop said everybody had to make a living.

"Riding the plains as a Ranger, I had to butcher deer, mules, antelopes, buffaloes, anything I could to stay alive," Pop had said. "During the war, we skinned rats and ate them when we couldn't find anything else. As a boy, my mother thought life wasn't worth living if I didn't bring in dressed squirrel three times a week. Besides, I own that slaughterhouse, and I'm glad I've got a good man to run it."

Mr. Sorenson must have felt something of the same way about Pop. Once when Pop stepped out of the store, someone commented that Texas Rangers exaggerated everything they did. Mr. Sorenson had set him straight. "You don't know the half of what that man's been through," he shot back, and I wondered what Pop had experienced, because he rarely spoke of it.

The train whistle blew; Whitey and I moved closer to the men, which now included the mayor. Mr. Sorenson was explaining something to Pop.

"It may be nothing, Pop. I may run across that knife later, but I could have sworn I left it over there with the others."

The mayor turned to Pop.

"I'm asking you again to just let this drop, Pope."

"Oscar kills these animals more humanely than how that woman was murdered, and you want us to just let it drop?" Pop retorted.

Drops of perspiration were forming on the mayor's forehead. He removed a silk handkerchief from his pocket and began to wipe his face, the garish red and gold print standing out vividly against his pasty face. Despite his obvious agitation, he shook his jaw in belligerence. "You always have to have your way, Pope," he said. "That's been your problem as long as I've known you."

Before Pop could reply, a man stuck his head through the doorway.

"There's an old maid raising hell out here on the train platform," he said.

"That would be Clara Grace," Pop said, choosing to ignore the mayor.

He refused to be hurried, however, and the man at the station was coming out of the store when we arrived. He gave Pop a vinegary look and said, "You owe me one, Robertson."

At the door, we heard a clear, strident voice coming from inside the store.

"Muskrat Hill is a ridiculous name for a town."

"Oh no, Clara Grace," my mother's reply floated outside. "It's named after an old Indian legend. The muskrat dove into the ocean that covered the world and brought up the first soil, and this is it."

"Fiddlesticks," Clara Grace replied. "Two drunks down by the river saw a beaver and thought it was a muskrat."

I didn't know what I thought Clara Grace would look like, perhaps like Miss Maydell, and I was unprepared for the beautiful woman in her early thirties who stood by my mother in the store when we entered.

Tall and slender, Clara Grace had dark, luxurious hair piled high on her head. Every feature in her face was perfectly formed, from a small straight nose, full lips, to wide, ice blue eyes. But that beautiful mouth was set in a firm frown, and the lovely eyes that were shaded by thick dark lashes held nothing but criticism for the rest of the world.

"Pope," my mother said, looking relieved to see us. "You remember my cousin Clara Grace. Clara Gra—" she began, but was cut off.

Looking at Pop with her lips pressed firm, Clara Grace said, "You have no doubt read my letter, Edmund, and know why I'm here."

"Don't call me Edmund," Pop said. "I know it's my middle name, but don't call me that."

She gave him a frosty stare. "I refuse to call any mortal man 'Pope,' " she said. She turned and examined Whitey. "Dolly, why is this boy so pale and thin? No one in our family has that many freckles." She looked up. "Dolly, you aren't feeding this boy enough."

"We feed him plenty," Pop muttered under his breath.

My mother came forward and gently placed me in front of Clara Grace. "That's Whitey, Kit's friend. This is Kittrell."

Clara Grace stared at me and then looked Pop up and down.

"Humph!" she said, looking away. "Dolly, tell me again why you gave him such a strange name."

"It's an old family name," my mother soothingly explained. "It's been in Pope's family for generations."

Clara Grace snorted at this explanation, but before she could fire off a suitable reply, her eyes caught sight of Asa, who had been standing there like a cigar store Indian that had been struck by lightning.

"Dolly!" Clara Grace exclaimed. "This man is an Indian!"

"Well, yes, Clara Grace," she replied. "This is . . ."

"You allow savages to frequent this establishment?" Clara Grace demanded.

Pop had enough. He threw up his hands. "I'm leaving," he said. "You handle her, Dolly."

Whitey and I exchanged glances and hurried after Pop and Asa.

Pop and Asa took the buggy, and Pop allowed that Whitey and I could ride behind them on Gastor. This time, Asa did question him.

"Do you think it's for the best, Pop?" Asa asked. "Taking boys along on a murder investigation?"

"I've already had it out with Dolly, and I don't want to have it out again with you," Pop said. "I'm not a young buck. I'm an old mossy-horned stag. If something happens to me, Kit's going to have to grow up fast. I want to teach him what I can while I'm still here. And if Whitey's parents don't want him tagging along, they can keep him at home for a change."

Asa nodded, and this time it was I who refused to look at Whitey.

Our first stop was a tiny house built of homemade bricks and shaded by small chapote trees. While Pop and Asa gave greetings to two men in serapes and wide straw hats, Whitey and I watched a woman surrounded by little girls cut up an armadillo.

She laid it on its back, and with a sharp knife, slit it from throat to tail and then across from shoulder to shoulder. As she skinned the legs and shoulders and began working her knife close to the shell, I turned to one of the girls in dark braids who stood about my size.

"What's she going to do with that armadillo?" I asked.

She looked at me like I was stupid and made a motion of bringing her hand up to her mouth.

"Eat it?" I asked incredulously.

Pop caught my question and said, "She'll gut it and soak it in vinegar and salt water first. You can eat just about anything that way—possum, coon, javelina."

While Whitey and I looked at one another with raised eyebrows, Pop turned his attention back to Asa and the two men in serapes.

"We had nothing to do with the murder, Señor Pope," the one with a big mustache said.

"That's right, Señor Pope," the other said, hissing his words a little because of his missing front teeth. "We would have never used a knife that big or that dull. We heard all about the cuts. We know what kind of knife was used—a big, dull one."

They both looked at Asa in undisguised contempt. The mustached one spat on the ground and stared at Asa. "It was a knife like an Indian would use."

CHAPTER 5

That evening, Clara Grace sat at the supper table looking as if she disapproved of everything while my mother tried to maintain conversation. Pop went to bed early. Bruno, Horace Dubois's disfigured helper, dug a grave by the light of a coal oil lantern.

The sheriff from Sulfur City in the next county over hadn't come to claim the dead woman. We buried her in the cemetery on the highest point near the town, situated by the forefathers so mourners could see approaching hostiles. No hostiles came that day, just the curious. I tried to talk my mother into cooking an armadillo, but she refused. "That is something you can get Pop to show you how to do outside, preferably far away."

Two telegrams arrived, answering the ones Asa had sent. One from the Rangers saying because of budget cuts, they couldn't afford to send anyone, and the other stating the Deputy U.S. Marshal was down with typhus. Both telegrams strongly suggested that Pop and Asa handle it on their own, despite Pop's lack of official status.

If it upset Pop and Asa that they had been left high and dry by the county sheriff, the Deputy U.S. Marshal, and the Texas Rangers, neither man complained about it.

They had hoped someone attending the burial might have an idea who the woman was and how she got to Muskrat Hill, but no one admitted knowing anything. Although the murder had generated a buzz of excitement, after the immediate horror had worn off, a complacency settled over the people of Muskrat

Hill. As far as they were concerned, it was one stranger killed by another stranger somewhere else. Muskrat Hill just happened to be the dumping ground for the body.

Nevertheless, Pop and Asa did their duty. Pop didn't try to hide his disgust at the lack of clues and evidence. After the funeral, he sent me to tell my mother he would be home for dinner soon, before he set out again to the farms and ranches surrounding the meadow where the body was discovered.

I found my mother in what had been our parlor, speaking with Clara Grace. When I delivered Pop's message, she nodded and said, "I'll have dinner on the table directly. You watch the store for now, please."

"Yes, ma'am," I said, but lingered to take in the changes she had made in the room. The uncomfortable sofa had been pushed back and a bed brought in to take its place. The photographs on the mantel were the same, and I stopped in front of them. Staring at me from one was a slender, handsome man who had my mother's big eyes. "Is that my Uncle Thomas?" I asked.

The frown on Clara Grace's face showed just what she thought of Uncle Thomas. I wondered what he had done to make her feathers so ruffled. My mother answered in the affirmative, saying, "Now, Kit, remember this is Cousin Clara Grace's room now, and don't come running in here whenever you feel like it."

I wanted to reassure her she had little fear of that happening, but instead I replied, "Yes, ma'am," again and went back into the store.

Luckily, people didn't expect much from me, and most were happy to sit at the back table gabbing with anyone who happened in while they waited for Pop or my mother to return. When Pop had a clerk working for him, he kept the store open at noon. If not, he shut it down. I expected dinner to be as inhibited as supper the night before. I forgot Pop couldn't be constrained for long. I had a feeling my mother was worried what Clara Grace might say when she found out I was accompanying Pop on a murder investigation. Surprisingly, Clara Grace acted as if it was not only the most natural thing the world, it was almost my duty. Relieved, my mother began to chatter about other things.

"How is Mr. Petty's lumbago, Pope?" she asked.

"Lumbago?" Pop said, looking puzzled. "Tull has lumbago?"

"Yes, don't you remember? He was complaining about it the last time he was in here. Kit, don't eat so fast. You'll ruin your digestion."

"Tull complains about everything," Pop said. "I never listen to him."

My mother turned to Clara Grace. "Mr. Petty runs the livery stable across the street. He's a very nice man."

"Tull?" Pop said, as unbelieving as if she had said Genghis Khan. "Tull Petty? He's a lot of things, but I wouldn't say nice was one of them."

"Yes, he is," my mother pronounced, leaning forward and giving him a look. "He's a very nice man," she repeatedly firmly. "And then there is Mr. Dubois who is the local mortician. I've only seen him a few times, but he is a very nice-looking gentleman with impeccable manners."

"Horace the stick?" Pop asked incredulously. "He's over six feet tall and barely weighs a hundred and twenty-five pounds after he's been caught in a downpour."

"He's young yet," my mother countered. "With a wife's good cooking, I daresay he will build up into a fine specimen of a man."

"And," Pop rejoined, "I guess you'll say next that Bruno isn't too bad either."

"Who is this Bruno?" Clara Grace demanded. "I thought he

was just a gravedigger."

While the grown-ups were engrossed, I surreptitiously helped myself to large helpings of everything I could within my reach. My cheeks puffed out like Whitey's as I stuffed another biscuit in my mouth.

"I haven't met Bruno," my mother said primly, not paying any attention to me. "He has not yet come up to this end of the street. He is Mr. Dubois's helper. He's slightly disfigured, but I'm sure he is a very nice man or he wouldn't be working for Mr. Dubois."

"Slightly disfigured?" Pop blasted. "Half his face looks like melted wax. And Dolly, he might be the killer!"

"He's not a killer," my mother said. "Why would he kill that poor girl and still be hanging around here? It's not going to be somebody from here. It's not." And she looked around the table as if she wanted to believe it.

That afternoon, we found the mayor talking with Mr. Petty inside the livery. The mayor wore clothes that looked as if they belonged on a man attired for a soiree or a night on the town. At least that was from my perception of the illustrations in the magazines and newspapers we received. My mother said his wife read those same periodicals and made him dress that way, but Pop said he enjoyed looking like he had a date with Queen Victoria.

Mr. Petty, dressed in the oldest, cruddiest clothes imaginable, grumbled about readying our horses and buggy but fetched them immediately, grouching the whole time about all the work he had to do and how people just expected him to drop everything to wait on them hand and foot. When Pop stepped outside to talk to the foreman of a nearby ranch, the mayor acidly asked Asa what he was doing dragging an old man all over creation for anyway. "Pope is too old for this foolishness," he said. "His facilities aren't what they used to be either; everyone knows that. There's no way he can be anything but a hindrance to you."

My fists clenched, but I knew better than to contradict an adult in Muskrat Hill. To my surprise and Asa's, I didn't have to. Mr. Petty unexpectedly spoke up. "You better shut the . . ." and he said a string of curse words to the mayor I had never heard before. "If this murder gets solved at all," Mr. Petty said, "it will be because Pope Robertson was there to do it."

I felt overcome with pride. I took it for granted my mother believed he was the best lawman who ever walked the earth, but when I heard Pop praised from another adult, especially one as grouchy and hard to please as Mr. Petty, it meant something.

There was no denying, however, that the investigation was taking its toll on Pop. He was tired all the time, and even Asa, usually so considerate, sometimes forgot it.

We stopped at Old Man Miller's place, a small one-room cabin at the edge of the forest with a hill in front of it and a cliff behind it. "Fergus," Pop said. "We've come to ask you if you know anything about this girl who was found murdered."

"Get down, Pope, get down," Mr. Miller said, nodding a head covered in long gray hair and smiling from behind a foot-long beard the same color except for the tobacco and coffee stains that had dribbled into it. Old Man Miller believed in taking a bath once every three months whether he needed it or not. "I heard about it in town, but I can't add nothing new to the pot; I don't know a thing."

"We better be getting on, then, Mr. Miller," Asa said.

Pop glared at Asa. "We'd be happy to rest a spell and maybe drink a cup of coffee with you, Fergus," he said.

Whitey and I slid from Gastor's back and went around to the buggy. Asa reluctantly got off his horse. Mr. Miller led us into his sparse cabin, finding three crude chairs with rawhide-braided seats for the adults. Pop looked around the room, and it came to me then that he must from old habit be memorizing every doorway and every window. During a brief lull while Mr. Miller fetched coffee, I asked, "Pop, can Whitey and I go outside and play?"

"Please do," Pop said. "Just don't go far."

"Yes, sir," we cried and ran out the door.

We petted Mr. Miller's old mule in the corral, going to the corncrib and pulling out two ears of corn to feed him. "Let's go up on the hill and pretend we're Indians," Whitey said. "Bad Indians, not good Indians like Marshal Asa."

"Okay," I agreed, and we climbed the hill in front of the house, pretending we were going to steal Mr. Miller's mule and burn his cabin down.

"Okay," I said. "Now let's play like we're Rangers, and we have to kill the Indians who are after Old Man Miller's gold."

"Old Man Miller ain't got no gold," Whitey said. "And besides, Indians didn't care nothing about gold."

"Whitey," I said, disgusted. "Can't you just pretend?"

It was while we were crawling on our bellies to get a closer look at the cabin and the make-believe Indians surrounding it that we found the cigarette butts.

"This is kind of odd, isn't it?" I said.

"Why?" Whitey wanted to know. "They are probably Old Man Miller's."

"No, they're not," I said. "He chews tobacco. He doesn't smoke cigarettes. Why would someone be on this hill looking down at Mr. Miller's cabin and be smoking cigarettes?"

"I don't know, Kit," Whitey said. "You make everything hard."

"No, I don't," I said. "I'm telling Pop about it."

But we decided it would be fun to wrestle and roll down the hill at the same time, and I forgot all about it.

Later, as we were getting ready to leave, Mr. Miller thanked us for stopping by. "I don't get much company," he concluded, "and I sure appreciate the visit, Pope. But say, I forget to tell you something. Shep hasn't been around for several days, and that sure ain't like that old dog, not unlessen there's a bitch in heat somewheres. If you see anything of him, let me know."

"Will do," Pop said, getting into the buggy. "Let us know if you hear anything about the girl."

Despite having rested at Fergus Miller's, Pop arrived home exhausted. To make matters worse, Clara Grace met him at the door with both pistols firing.

"Edmund," she began. "Tomorrow is Sunday, and I want you to take me to a Catholic church in the morning."

"Clara Grace," he said wearily. "The nearest Catholic church is twenty miles from here, and I'll be darned if I take you. You can go to church with us. And another thing, don't call me Edmund."

I looked at Whitey and smothered a grin. My mother hurried to Clara Grace before she could reply. While Pop hung up his hat and removed his jacket, my mother drew Clara Grace aside, whispering like a fellow conspirator during the Spanish Inquisition. "Clara Grace, if you want to convert the people here maybe it would be a good idea to observe them for a while, and then plan your strategy."

Clara Grace was nobody's fool except when it came to religion. "Yes, Dolly," she agreed pensively. "Perhaps you're right."

Pop looked down at Whitey. "Whitey! Do you have a home?"

"Pope!" my mother exclaimed, and Pop rolled his eyes and shook his head. "All right. Go on with Kit and wash up for supper. For once, I'd like to come home and just sit and eat in silence and pretend I'm in a restaurant where I don't know anybody."

Whitey and I knew he didn't mean it, and laughing, we raced to the back of the store, following Clara Grace who was busy making mental charts, diagrams, tables, and graphs proving that Martin Luther had been way out of line. At the curtain, I looked back at my parents. My mother followed Pop, dragging her bad leg and planting playful kisses on his neck and shoulders while he tried to suppress his grins.

Good humor restored and able to catch a second wind, Pop opened the store again that evening for music. It began to rain, a soft steady rain that would bring lush grass. It didn't stop people from coming, especially the cotton farmers, who were always worried about their crops. At the wrong time, heavy rain could soak the cotton bolls, ruining a year's work. Violent death scared them, but the thought of a lost crop was even more depressing. However, it was too early for that. The rain stopped anyway, but while it lasted, we children played under the awning on the front porch, running in and out, oblivious to our mothers' admonishments and only slowing when the men barked, "Settle down!"

The mayor came in looking pensive and dissatisfied, followed by his brother, Melvin. But the mayor always looked brooding and unhappy when he was around his older brother. Melvin was shorter, stockier, with a belligerent chin that made him resemble a bulldog wearing rimless glasses. He was a fussy man with a wide streak of pettiness; even so, Pop always had a civil attitude toward him. Regardless, even though Pop never let it show, I sensed he didn't like Melvin and for some reason, didn't want me around him.

Melvin didn't want me around him either. He had a strong dislike of children and of almost everybody else in Muskrat Hill except for perhaps my mother.

"Dolly," he exclaimed, coming in the store. "Did you get that new crochet thread? That last thread you sold me is quite unsuitable. The doilies I made with it look like they belong in a cheap boardinghouse."

My mother hastened to assure him she had ordered a different brand. As she went behind the counter to fetch it, the mayor shook his head in resignation. "Melvin," he said, "our father would roll over in his grave."

"Don't talk to me about that beast, Julius!" Melvin said in a high-pitched voice. "He was a brute, and you know it."

"Well, you got even with him," the mayor said, and with another shake of his head, he moved away to join the other men playing and singing.

Trying to distract Melvin from his brother, my mother smiled and said, "Here you go, Mr. Foster," handing him the thread. "You haven't brought your new housekeeper in the store yet. We'd like to meet her."

Melvin gave a smug smile. "Oh, she's shy," he said, and he smiled again as if enjoying some private joke. He headed for the front door, but kept a stream of conversation running with my mother that obliged her to follow him. She stood at the door smiling and nodding while Melvin went out, still chattering. He didn't stop until he got into the wagon seat with a woman covered in shawls. Pop joined us as we watched Melvin and his reticent housekeeper drive away.

"There is something about her that seems familiar to me," my mother mused, "but I can't place what it is."

Pop looked down at her and grinned. "Maybe she's somebody you used to work for years ago."

My mother cocked her head and answered sassily, "Well, you would know more about that than I would, wouldn't you, Sheriff Robertson?"

They went back into the store laughing, but I stood on the door threshold staring at the back of Melvin and his housekeeper for a full three seconds before I gave it up and ran to play with the other children.

That night, Asa stood in the corner and only spoke two or

three words the entire evening. Every time Clara Grace walked by, his eyes followed her. As soon as she turned around, his eyes dropped to contemplate the wooden planks of the floor. Pop saw everything and knew what was going on, but made no comment. I thought Pop would rag Asa, but he didn't. Instead, when they were playing a particularly lively dance tune, Pop grabbed my mother and said, "Dance with me, darling!"

"Pope," my mother laughed. "I'm no good." However, laughing and smiling, trying to keep up with her bad leg, she let him swing her around the room. They waltzed by an open-mouthed Clara Grace who gaped in horror. "Dolly," she exclaimed. "You allow dancing in this store! With children present, no less!" She snapped her mouth shut, and unable to do anything about it, she jerked her chin and stomped to the living quarters.

Pop gave my mother an inquisitive look. "Catholics think dancing is sinful? I thought that was Baptists?"

She shrugged her shoulders. "I think she gets them confused sometimes, or else she just invents her own sins."

The undertaker, Horace Dubois, slipped in, and although he was courteous as always, he kept away from Harmonica John, and John seemed to just as assiduously avoid him.

At breakfast the next morning, I told Pop I thought Horace had been steering clear of Harmonica John and that John had refused to acknowledge Horace's presence.

"It was like they were secret enemies, Pop," I said.

Pop shook his head. "A society can make laws to see that people are treated right, but it can't dictate how a person feels," Pop said. "Nor should it try."

I didn't understand what he meant. I just knew that Horace Dubois and Harmonica John quietly disliked one another.

Clara Grace fussed and fumed, but she walked with us to church that morning. I resignedly followed Pop into the pew; the only thing I liked about church was the singing. I had to sit still without going to sleep, but I had perfected a technique of keeping my eyes open while falling into a state of semiconsciousness. The only problem came when my mouth would sometimes relax and droop, irritating Pop, and he would nudge me, whispering, "Shut your mouth; you look like a half-wit."

The mayor's buxom wife, Louella, marched to the piano and began to pound on the keys. Louella had a piercingly strident and demanding voice that caused her to be gently ridiculed behind her back. Her dark hair had turned pig-iron gray, and although she was born only a year or two before her husband, her dress and demeanor screamed "stern society matron" so loudly, she looked at least ten years older. She and my mother met at social functions, sat together at quilting bees, attended the same women's circle at church, but she was another one of those women who never sought Mama for private chitchats. This however, did not appear to bother my mother, and if I did not know her better, I would think she went out of her way to avoid the mayor's wife.

The crowd stirred, and Asa walked in from the back. He wore his gun belt as usual and placed his pistol on the pulpit where he could reach it if he had to. While he picked up his hymnal, I stole a glance past my parents at Clara Grace.

I had heard of people looking bug-eyed, but had never really witnessed it before that morning. Clara Grace paled, and she turned her head in slow motion to my mother. "Dolly," she said in disbelief, "he's an Indian preacher. And an Indian preacher carrying a pistol to the pulpit."

The mayor's wife ceased the prelude, and Asa's voice boomed out, "All rise. Let us sing hymn number one hundred, 'Nearer My God to Thee.' "

The piano keys crashed once more into song, and everyone stood, including Clara Grace with the assistance of my mother. Pop bent across her and hissed at Clara Grace. "He was called to be a minister, not to be stupid."

My mother leaned back, eyes wide with foreboding. She knew the signs.

"Nearer, my God, to Thee, nearer to Thee! E'en though it be a cross that raiseth me," the people of Muskrat Hill boomed. The Biblical verse, "the spirit is willing but the flesh is weak," was written to describe the singing in our little chapel.

"And let me tell you something else, Miss Clara Grace Know-it-all," Pop continued in a loud enough whisper that the people three rows up could hear. "That boy's mother was kidnapped and raped by Comanche warriors. She was rescued but gave the baby up to missionaries to raise."

"Pope," my mother pleaded from behind clenched teeth, still leaning back, knowing even as she spoke her entreaty was futile.

"Hush, Dolly," Pop said. "Clara Grace asked for it." He looked back at Clara Grace. "He tried living with the Indians when he was a teenager, but he didn't fit in with them any more than he fits in with the white world, but his adopted parents and his nine brothers and sisters adored him and so do we. Now if you can't be courteous, I'm going to jerk you outside and give you a cussing that will put you nearer to God than you've ever been in your life. Do you understand me?"

Clara Grace didn't even tremble. "A society should not try to dictate how a person feels," she recited coldly.

"Feel however you want," Pop said through gritted teeth. "But act right."

Clara Grace said, "Humph," with a toss of her head and began to sing in total unconcern.

Afraid to turn my head and possibly get cuffed, I felt the vibrations that meant Pop was about to detonate. From the corner of my eye, I saw Pop give my mother a look that said, "I've just about had it with her." My mother nodded and looked down at her hymnal and tried to sing. She couldn't, however, because she began to shake with repressed giggles. She shut her eyes tightly and looked as if she were willing herself to stop, but the mere effort of trying made her shoulders and face twitch that much more. Clara Grace stared at her in disapproval. Pop glared at her, but I caught her eye, and we exchanged smiles. Pop saw me and frowned as if I were a traitor to the male race, so I put my head down and began to intone as loud as I could, "Nearer my God to Thee . . ."

When I did look up, I saw Asa staring at Clara Grace, his face wearing the inscrutable mask of his ancestors.

The next morning, Asa had to wait for Pop again. "Sorry," Pop said, coming out of the store. "I know we're running late, but I still need to stop by Big Oscar's."

Asa frowned. "Another nap?" he asked sarcastically.

"No, no, no," Pop replied. "Since Clara Grace has arrived, it's called a back rub. I have a sore back and some mornings, Dolly has to give me a back rub."

"You're disgusting, you know that?" Asa said.

"Why, because I'm old? The older the goat, the stiffer the horn. Besides, one day you might be married and waking up to a beautiful woman beside you, and then you'll be disgusting every chance you get, too."

"I doubt that will ever happen," Asa said, no longer sarcastic but morose.

Clara Grace came out of the store, and Asa's face underwent an immediate transformation, turning into a wall of stone. Almost as tall as he was, she looked at him with cold blue eyes, the dark lashes sweeping down over them, and said, "Oh, it's you." Turning from Asa to Pop, Clara Grace demanded, "Edmund, you must make Kit come inside and start learning his catechism. Papa always said to start them young."

Pop waved her aside. "Take it up with Dolly. I'm a busy man." He began to walk away with Asa, Whitey, and me following.

Over his shoulder, Pop said, "And don't call me Edmund."

Clara Grace gave Pop's backside a sour frown and went back into the store.

"Making love to her would be like making love to a fence post," Pop grimaced. "They both have knotholes but are far too rigid to enjoy."

Asa opened his mouth to say something, but stopped himself.

From behind the men, I saw slight Mr. Petty doing a fast hobble up the sidewalk. Asa and Pop stopped, knowing immediately something was wrong because Mr. Petty never walked more than ten steps when he could ride.

"You better get down to Oscar's, Pope," he said in a breathless voice when he reached us. "It's bad, Pope. It's bad."

Whitey and I raced to the slaughterhouse. The big double doors were shut, and we stood on each side, waiting to open them for Pop and Asa. Taking long strides with Mr. Petty trailing behind them, they arrived in seconds. We opened the doors and followed them inside.

Pop immediately drew me near him and covered my eyes with his hand, but not before I saw Big Oscar hanging naked upside-down from a meat hook, his gut split with his intestines hanging out, his testicles removed and stuffed into his mouth. Strips of flesh had been torn from his body.

People jammed the store that afternoon, their voices so shrill in panic that children stayed near their parents, afraid of this unknown terror that was striking our previously peaceful town. Pop, who usually had control over every situation, did not even attempt to stifle or get rid of them. The mayor's face looked pale and sickly. He would look at Pop and his mouth would work as if it wanted to speak, and then he would visibly brace himself. Asa stood near Pop, unable to hide his dismay. I watched my mother try to reach Pop, but someone was always grabbing her, seeking comfort and reassurance. Scrawny Miss

Maydell dogged her steps, the worry lines around her eyes and mouth making it look as if she, too, were about to burst into tears and maybe blurt out another confession. Passing near her, one man pushed his way to the front of the mob, his flushed face wild with emotion as he addressed the crowd.

"I've lived through Indian trouble. I know what their work looks like! I found my brother with his guts split open and his heart ripped out of his chest by Comanches. This isn't something any white man would do. This has renegade Indian written all over it." He turned and glowered at Asa, and I had never seen so much savage hatred on a man's face.

"And you, Asa," he said. "You were right there on the spot when those boys found that woman."

"That's right," the man beside him shouted. "You have free run of this town, of the whole county. No one would ever question what you were doing."

The color drained from Asa's face, but it was Pop who roared back. "Shut up that kind of talk. You've known Asa for years. You know he couldn't do something like this!"

"You don't know that for sure, Pop," another man in the crowd hollered. "You've got a blind side, always partial to every crippled cur stray that comes around."

The store fell still. Mouths shut and everyone turned to stare at my mother. Someone's baby gave a cry and was quieted immediately. I didn't understand what was wrong, and I stared at my mother, usually so animated, and saw only a whitening of skin and widening of eyes in a face that looked like a china doll about to shatter. Pop broke the silence in a voice even more terrible than the screaming and shouting because it was so deadly composed.

"Get out," Pop told the man. "Get out of my store right now before I strangle you with my bare hands."

No one moved as Pop glared at this person who had insulted

us in a way I didn't understand. The man's eyes beaded and sweat broke out on his forehead; he ended the standoff by flouncing from the store.

The mayor found his voice for the first time that evening. "Pope is right," he said, his tone a squeaking imitation of its natural timbre, but even then it woke up the crowd. "Calm down and go home. Go about your business and remain calm." He began to physically shoo people from the store. A few people gave Pop and Asa shy nods as they walked past. As the last person left, Pop turned to Asa.

"Are you sure he's still in prison?" Pop asked.

"Yes, Pop," Asa replied in a voice on the verge of despair. "But he's not in Huntsville anymore. They've got him working on a chain gang in the cane fields near Houston."

"I want you to wire the warden and have him send someone out there who knows him personally to make sure it's really him," Pop said.

"Okay, Pop. If you think so."

"Yes," Pop replied. "Do it. Now."

Whitey whispered in my ear. "Who are they talking about?"

I shook my head. "I don't know." A shadow of fear overcame me. I didn't want to know the answer.

CHAPTER 6

Asa left to fire off yet another telegram. Pop planned to go out again to question people up and down the streets of Muskrat Hill. Before he left, my mother apologized to Clara Grace for walking into a rampage of murder. "If you want to leave, Clara Grace, I understand," she said.

"Of course not," Clara Grace immediately responded. "I shall not shirk my Christian duty by leaving you to face this alone."

We all knew it wasn't so much Christian duty that kept her with us, but that she had no place else to go.

Whitey and I, still scared half to death, shadowed Pop; however, no one said anything about us. The funeral parlor became our first stop.

"Did you find anything unusual?" Pop asked Horace.

Horace shook his head, his narrow skull and pointed beard giving him the look of either an aesthetic monk or a Renaissance artist's rendition of Lucifer, depending on the way the light shone on him.

"No," he replied. "Except that for a big man, he had an unusually small penis, but I don't think that will be of any help to you."

We didn't get home until late that night and were almost too tired to eat. While we poked food into our mouths in gloomy silence, my mother said she and Clara Grace had sold out of every firearm and piece of ammunition we had in the store.

"All the butcher knives are gone, too," she said.

Pop rubbed his forehead. "Somebody in this town has got to know something. What am I forgetting? I'm forgetting something."

That night, I woke from my sleep finding myself sitting bolt upright in bed with my fists clinched. Beside me, Whitey whimpered in his sleep, but stirred awake when my mother entered the room quietly, pulling a chair up to the bed.

"I just thought I'd sit in here with you boys for a while," she said, her voice soothing and soft. "Go back to sleep." Closing our eyes, we were able to sleep soundly the rest of the night.

The next morning, the walls of the store again groaned with human bodies stuffed in every corner, demanding to know what Pop and Asa were going to do.

"As soon as the next train rolls in, Asa and I are going to get on it," Pop explained. "We'll be riding the lines, seeing if any of the regulars noticed anyone or anything peculiar."

People didn't seem to know what to do, and they lingered waiting for Pop and Asa to leave. Whitey and I had already asked to go along and been refused, so we were more than a little despondent. Despite an atmosphere of uncertainty and apprehension, people grew hungry and restless, buying crackers and pickles by the handfuls. Luckily, it had not taken Clara Grace long to pick up on how the store operated, and she assisted my mother while Pop tried to reassure people that everything would be all right.

The town's old maid, Miss Maydell, came in, and I saw Pop's eyes rest on her and stay longer than usual. He left the men he had been talking to and made his way across the room to my mother.

Pulling her aside, Pop spoke too softly in her ear for me to hear, but she nodded. He returned to the other men, and my mother walked through the crowd to Maydell, stopping to speak to her. Taking her by the arm, she led Maydell to the back and behind the curtain.

I stared, wondering what it was all about. Clara Grace gave me a poke on the shoulder, and I remembered I was supposed to be fetching a can of tomatoes for a woman who didn't care how many murderers were on the loose. She still had to cook dinner.

When the women returned, someone immediately wanted my mother's assistance, and Miss Maydell was left standing alone near the back wall, a figure of emotional turmoil. She slumped momentarily, and what looked like a wave of relief crossed her face before she straightened and left the store, refusing to look in Pop's direction.

Pop and Asa caught the train and stayed gone for two days. Again, they drew a blank and had no news to report. People had faith in their diligence, however, and some of the animosity against Asa decreased. Pop remained cynical.

"If they are not picking on him," he said, "they'll be picking on somebody else."

His prediction proved true, and it began with the second biggest scandalmonger in town next to the mayor's spiteful brother, Melvin. The Widow Crenshaw had dark eyes, a tubby middle, and a querulous mouth set in a round baby face surrounded by fluffy white hair.

My mother, perturbed, glanced throughout the store, but Pop had disappeared the minute Netta Crenshaw had entered. "Netta," she began, "I don't think . . ."

"Dolly," Netta said disapprovingly, because she disapproved of everything about my mother. "We all know you think you must be circumspect because of business, but face the truth."

"It's not business; I really don't think . . ." my mother began again, but the widow was off on another tangent.

"And that handyman of his. Have you seen that monster?"

She looked round at the other faces.

At this point, my mother gave up and left the group, but she complained about it to my father that afternoon.

Pop listened abstractly and gave a heavy sigh. Turning to my mother, he said, "As much as I detest siding with Netta Crenshaw on anything, we must look at Horace and Bruno with clear eyes. They move into town, and we have two brutal murders one on top of the other." He looked at me. "Kit, come along, we're going to see Horace again."

He put on his hat and jacket, and once outside, I asked him, "Pop, do you really think the undertaker and his helper might be killers?"

"I can't see it," Pop said. "Asa's been keeping an eye on them, and he said they appear to be the most innocent of men. But I've met murderers with angelic faces before."

We stopped in front of the funeral parlor. Pop turned to me. "Remember, keep your mouth shut and only speak when spoken to," he said.

"Yes, sir," I nodded.

The door was locked, so we went through the alley to the back where Horace kept a barn containing a fancy glassed-in hearse and a stable for his horses. Horace and Bruno were sitting in front of the barn, Bruno sharpening an ax on a grindstone while Horace sat smoking a pipe.

"Hello, Pop," Horace said, rising. "Here, take my chair."

"No, keep your seat," Pop said. "We won't be here long."

Horace sat back down while Bruno slowed his grinding, looking up to study Pop and me frequently, staring at us with that one sinister-looking eye.

"What can I do for you today then?" Horace said.

"I'm embarrassed I haven't invited you over for supper, Horace," Pop said. "That wasn't very neighborly of me. Will you and Bruno dine with us this evening?"

Horace glanced at Bruno. "I would be honored to accept your invitation, but I'm afraid Bruno shuns company."

Pop looked at Bruno, returning his gaze. He nodded. "I understand. We'll expect you then," he said, turning back to Horace. "There is something else."

"Yes?" Horace asked, giving an almost imperceptibly tense pause before putting his pipe back to his mouth.

"It's about this sign language," Pop said unexpectedly. "I'd like you to teach it to me and my family if you would. I'd appreciate it if you could come over, maybe eat supper with us two or three times a week and show us afterward."

"I would be happy to," Horace said, surprised and perhaps even relieved. "But you don't have to bribe me with food."

"No, it's not bribery," Pop assured him. "We are a social family and like company."

No wonder Pop had warned me to keep my mouth shut. As much as he had complained about Clara Grace, it almost dropped open.

"Then I am twice honored," Horace said, nodding his head.

I leaned forward, dying to get a closer look at his horses. Horace noticed the yearning in my face and gave a slight smile. "Would you care to see my stallions?" he asked Pop.

Pop immediately responded yes. We followed Horace into a stable housing four slick, midnight-black perfectly matched horses. While Pop looked on admiringly, Horace talked about them, his face suffused with adoration and pride. They neighed and pranced, gluttons for the attention he gave them.

"What are their names?" I asked during a lull in the conversation, hoping just one innocent question wouldn't get me into trouble.

"This is Ace," he said, petting the neck of a particularly noble looking stallion. "I raised him from a colt and have tried to match all the others to him. He's my best horse."

Moving on, he went down the line. "These two are Nero and Nighthawk. I found Nero at a small farm in Kentucky and Nighthawk belonged to a friend of mine."

He stopped at the last stall and stared with the skin around his eyes crinkling and a small smile tugging at the corners of his mouth. The horse in the stall was full of blood, feisty, throwing his head, and pawing the ground. Yet it seemed to me he was putting on an enjoyable show for us more than anything else.

"And last, but certainly not least as you can see, is Black Jack. I had to play poker forty-eight hours straight to win him from a Mississippi gambler, but he was worth every cut of the cards," Horace said with a laugh.

"This horse will allow you to put a collar on him and pull a wagon?" Pop asked, raising an eyebrow in doubt.

Horace patted Black Jack fondly. "He'll do whatever I tell him to do," he said softly, and I envisioned him holding a bewitching power over the beast.

I held Pop's hand walking home, full of happy chatter about the horses. As we left the yard and entered the alley, I looked back to see Bruno staring at us, his face a mask of brooding disfigurement.

Inside the store, Pop told my mother that Horace was coming for supper. "He's going to teach us sign language."

"Sign language?" she questioned. "Oh, Pope, you and Kit can do that. I have so much going on right now. I'm trying to sew on Clara Grace's trousseau. I can do the towels and things and pretend they are for me, but I don't know how I'll hide the wedding dress from her."

Pop stared at her in disbelief. "Dolly! I admire your optimism, but I think you are entertaining a fantasy."

"Oh, no, Pope," my mother said. "Clara Grace is a beautiful young woman, and one of these days, she's going to realize that domineering father of hers is dead, and she can marry whoever the Lord leads her to."

Pop just shook his head. Then he gave a little grin and teased, "Did the Lord lead you to me, Dolly? I thought it was because I wouldn't leave you alone."

"He didn't lead me anywhere," she laughed. "It was more like He shoved me over a cliff. He let me fall so in love with you, I knew I'd die without you."

Pop gazed at her, swallowing and blinking rapidly. "Dolly," he said, taking a breath and becoming matter-of-fact. "My hearing is not as good as it used to be. My father was deaf when he died. The thought of not being able to communicate with you and Kit tears me up. Now please do as I ask."

She immediately became contrite. "Of course, Pope, when you put it like that," she said. "Now I can learn and have a good time without feeling guilty for neglecting other things." She reached over and hugged his neck, kissing him on the cheek.

Later, while we were alone in the front of the store, Pop handed me a folded piece of paper. "Take this to Asa's office. If he's not there, slip it under the door, but try not to let anyone see you give it to him or leave it for him, whatever the case."

"Yes, sir, Pop," I said. Asa was gone, but after looking around to make sure no one was watching, I slid the paper under the door as fast as I could.

The end of the day found my mother surrounded by bubbling pots and pans, wiping the sweat from her brow caused by pies baking in the oven. Pop came in and took one look. "Dolly! Who are you feeding? The Army of Northern Virginia?"

She turned and smiled. "That poor Mr. Dubois needs fattening up. Besides if he's going to do us a favor, we should do one for him. And we have to have enough to send him home with a plate for Bruno."

"That's all fine and good, Dolly," Pop said. "But you do realize we may be giving nourishment to a couple of deranged killers?"

"Well . . ." my mother thought for a moment. "I wouldn't want to be beholden to a deranged killer anyway." Holding a spoon, she turned and called toward our old parlor.

"Clara Grace! Mr. Dubois is coming for supper, and he's going to teach us sign language. Do you want to learn, too?"

Meanwhile, Pop was making cutting motions across his throat, but gave up and shook his head in resignation.

Clara Grace opened the door and gave my mother a suspicious look. "Why would I want to learn sign language?"

"Because it might become a mission for you, Clara Grace. Just think of all the deaf-mute people you might convert to Catholicism," my mother said, turning her attention back to a pot on the stove.

"That is true," Clara Grace pondered. She gave a glance of dissatisfaction in Pop's and my direction. She hadn't had any luck converting us.

"I will set the table," she said. "Will it be just Mr. Dubois, no one else?"

"That's right," my mother said. "Just Mr. Dubois."

Horace arrived on time and in an even fancier suit than he normally wore. He had on a silk hat, an elaborate silk tie, a suit made of some sort of thick shiny fabric, and a vest of heavy brocade. Whitey had shown up for supper, and my mother had made us wash our faces and comb our hair. She had me put on clean clothes, albeit ones patched at the knee. Whitey's clothes had even more patches than mine, many of them done by my mother at night as we slept. But she, Clara Grace, and Pop looked quite presentable, and none of them showed any discomfort in Horace Dubois's company.

Both my parents welcomed him warmly. "We don't have a formal dining room," Pop explained. "Sometimes we sit here in the back of the store, other times in the kitchen. Tonight, we'll sit in the kitchen where it's more private. But you may have to remove your jacket because of the heat."

Horace seemed perfectly at ease sitting in his shirtsleeves at our kitchen table. His manners were impeccable—polite and sensitive, yet so ingrained and flowing from him in such a smoothly understated way; he made everyone around him feel relaxed. Even Clara Grace lost some of her starchiness.

"Would you care for more mashed potatoes?" she asked politely.

He would. Without seeming to do so, he tucked in an amazing amount of groceries. My mother gave my father an "I told you so" shrug of her shoulder when Horace wasn't looking.

The undertaker habitually wore a solemn and somewhat mournful expression that befitted his profession; therefore, his dry wit and jollity caught me off guard.

"As to my vocation, I cannot complain when business is bad, and I am unable to brag when business is good," he said. "However, I can attest that as a whole, undertakers are the last people to let anyone down." Pop laughed, and it took my mother a minute to figure out what was so funny. I don't think Clara Grace ever got it.

As a teacher, Horace was articulate and patient. Jokes withstanding, Clara Grace proved to be the quickest student. Whitey and I didn't do too bad, either.

After he left that first night, my mother sent Whitey and me to bed. I was just about to drop off when I heard a faint knock at the back door. Naturally curious as to who would be calling so late at night, I got up and peeked to see who it was.

Pop had the lantern turned so low, it was hard to see anything. Nevertheless, I could make out the tall broad shoulders of Asa standing in the dark shadows of the back door.

"Nothing," Asa was telling my father in a muted voice. "He

never left the premises."

"All right," Pop said. He turned and picked up a napkin-covered plate. "Here, Dolly fixed this for you," he said, handing the plate to Asa. "She knew you'd miss your supper."

"Thank you, Pop," Asa said. "Give Miss Dolly my thanks."

"I will," Pop said, patting Asa on the shoulder. "Eat and go on to bed now."

Who never left the premises? I sneaked back into my room and falling into bed, fell instantly to sleep.

On our second lesson with the undertaker, we were able to converse using sign language. Horace requested Whitey and I address him as "Mr. Horace," instead of Mr. Dubois, which we readily did. Clara Grace asked if his people were from France, and if so, was he Catholic. He replied yes, they were, but they were Huguenots, thus the reason they immigrated to the Carolinas.

"Oh," my mother said excitedly. She tried to sign that her people came to Texas from Spartanburg, except that she had to stop and ask Pop how to spell it. Pop laughed and told her since her people came to Texas in 1821 via Kentucky and Missouri, he sincerely doubted Horace knew them.

Horace smiled kindly and signed that he was from Charleston, and Spartanburg was much further north. He explained it was a county with quite a few ruffians so perhaps that was why her family moved to Texas. Pop immediately added there were no rougher bunch than my mother's family, to which she laughingly signed, "Says you," and Clara Grace signed for so long trying to prove Pop wrong that I gave up trying to follow her. However, my mother's question gave Pop the opening he needed to ask Horace why he had come to Texas.

"Alas," he signed. "I was spurned in love." This caused him to receive quite a bit of sympathy from my mother, to which he was not averse.

"And you, Miss Dolly," Horace asked. "Do you have any more relatives besides Miss Clara Grace?"

"No," my mother signed. "I had a brother who left home and disappeared years ago. We don't know what became of him."

"In prison, no doubt," Clara Grace muttered. "Papa always said he was a wild, uncontrollable boy."

"That's not true, Clara Grace," my mother spoke, forgetting to sign. "Thomas was high-spirited, and he had a bit of a temper, but he was a sweet young man." She looked at Horace and smiled. "You remind me of him. He was such a slender boy, so kind and well-mannered. He taught me to read, and he used to let me ride piggyback and pretend he was a racehorse, the fastest and most beautiful horse in the world."

"Papa said . . ." Clara Grace began.

"Clara Grace, your papa is dead and even when he was living, he was not God," my mother said.

With her lips pressed together in a thin line, Clara Grace arched an eyebrow and gave a meaningful glance toward Pop. "Someone else I know isn't God either," she said.

"Oh, Clara Grace, I know that," my mother said with a laugh. "I don't imagine God has near the stomach rumblings in the mornings that Pope does."

"Dolly!" Clara Grace exclaimed. "Is nothing sacred to you?"

"Ladies!" Pop said, and then he signed, "Argue if you must, but do it in sign language."

My mother signed "Okay, Pope," and Clara Grace heaved a sigh, but stopped talking. Horace grinned and signed, "This reminds me of home."

I began to see Pop's wisdom. His explanation to my mother was probably true, but he had also found a way to question Horace without inciting resentment or suspicion. My mother unwittingly aided Pop with her natural friendliness and naive curiosity. Her inoffensive chatter more often than not gave Pop the opening he wanted to delve deeper.

However, there didn't seem to be much to find out. Horace had immigrated directly to San Antonio from South Carolina and worked there about six months. Pop knew the mortuary where he was employed and the man who owned it. Horace decided to go out on his own and open shop in Muskrat Hill after hearing of its possibilities from a stranger passing through. He found Bruno good company, but other than indicating Bruno must have had something of a hard life before getting off the train in Muskrat Hill, he did not know much about him.

"Wire the mortician in San Antonio and make inquiries about Horace," Pop instructed Asa later. "No, on second thought, I'll do it. He knows me."

Asa agreed it was a good idea. "But Pop, don't you think it's odd that Horace insists on hitching up studs to a hearse wagon?"

Pop grunted. "I don't think it's odd; I think it's a fool thing to do. But," he added with a wry smile, "maybe he gets tired of handling lifeless corpses and gets his enjoyment from being masterful with something exciting, who knows?"

Both men grinned. Pop looked toward the front of the store, his face becoming serious once again. "Horace may have his peccadilloes, but Bruno is another matter. If he's been bumming around the countryside, there's no telling where he came from. He doesn't leave the property when Horace comes over here?"

"No," Asa said. "Never. I don't know what to think about him, Pop. He goes to the door or the window and looks in this direction, as if he's watching the place. I can't believe it would be the millinery shop he's interested in. It has to be this store."

Pop went to the window, stood to one side, and peered toward the undertaker's parlor. "We mustn't judge by looks," he muttered. "But his coming here just as murders are committed is damning."

Chapter 7

No matter what color they were, the people of Muskrat Hill did not mind viewing other races with suspicion. They did, however, like to think of themselves as kind in other respects. Although they did not openly suggest that the disfigured Bruno should be a murder suspect, many of them took Pop aside and voiced the same thoughts about Bruno's sudden appearance in Muskrat Hill that Pop had.

Pop reminded one and all there was no evidence against Bruno other than he had come to Muskrat Hill at the wrong time. "And why would he want to kill Oscar?" Pop said. "There is no motive."

After Horace's second visit to our home, everyone in Muskrat Hill became sure he was courting Clara Grace. A few came into the store throwing arch smiles and broad hints, hoping she would reveal her feelings; others made vague warnings about flirting with the devil. Insinuations and hints were lost on Clara Grace, however. Pop certainly saw no reason to warn her—she and Horace treated one another with politeness and nothing more, much to my mother's regret.

"I guess he really is stuck on that girl back home," she mused to my father in one of their rare moments alone.

"Clara Grace is unquestionably beautiful," Pop said, peering up from his ledgers. "But she is not the irresistible siren you make her out to be."

"Pope! Of course not," she said. She absentmindedly

contemplated the curtain hanging between the store and the living quarters. "The postal clerk at the train station told Melvin Foster that Horace sends letters every week to South Carolina. One is to a girl who almost certainly is his sister, but the other is probably to his old sweetheart."

"And Melvin hasn't asked to open and read the letters so he'll know for sure?" Pop asked.

"Pope, don't be funny," she said. "But Melvin made it a point to run in here and tell me so Clara Grace would know she has competition."

"He was probably hoping Horace and Bruno . . ." Pop said with a jeer, but my mother cut him off.

"Pope! Put a lid on that!" she laughed, glancing at me. "Besides, Melvin has a housekeeper to keep him occupied now."

"Did she come in here when Melvin was talking about Horace's mail?"

"No, she sat in the wagon hunched over," my mother said. "She saw Louella Foster walking into the millinery shop, and she hunkered down so low, I thought she was going to slide onto the toeboard. But then Louella has that effect on people. Poor Asa practically hides when he sees her coming because she always wants to advise him on how to run the church."

When Pop didn't need us, Whitey and I would go to the undertaker's barn and ask to look at the horses. Either Bruno would nod his permission, or Horace would be there to give us the okay. Most of his day was spent feeding and tending to those four animals, and he didn't seem to mind our awe of them. We were fascinated with Black Jack and loved to watch him and try to pet him when he would let us. Horace would always warn us to stay away from him if he wasn't there.

"He can be a little bit of a devil," Horace said, stroking his favorite pet. "Your father told me that horse racing is frowned upon by some of the sterner elements in Muskrat Hill, but that there are frequently horse races in the next county." He stared at Black Jack in admiration and shook his head. "Ah, how I'd love to race one of my thoroughbreds against the horses here but it is considered unseemly for a mortician. It tries a man's soul to be solemn and upright at all times."

He looked down and inspected us. "Kit, you are built square and chunky, a good attribute for a boy, but not for a jockey." His eyes fell on Whitey. "But you, young man, would make a fine jockey with the right amount of training, I daresay."

"I wish we could ride your horses," Whitey whispered.

I sucked in my breath at his audacity, but Horace, however, looked amused. "Can you ride bareback? We'll put bridles on Nero and Nighthawk and see how you do."

We leapt in excitement. Horace bridled the horses and led them to his corral. Bruno opened the gate for us, and Horace led them in. "All right, *mes petits amis,* let's see what you can do."

Bruno gave us a leg up, and we were both so elated we could hardly hold the reins. After sitting a moment, trying to slow our rapid breathing, we began walking the horses around the corral while Horace grinned. Bruno stood expressionless with his arms folded across his chest, feet spread wide. We got a little braver and began to trot the horses. Pop hardly ever let me ride Smokey, and it was a pleasure to ride a magnificent horse and pretend I was a dashing cowboy.

"Kit," Horace said. "I owe you an apology. You are a superb horseman."

I reddened with pleasure. "Mr. Petty said when my Pop was young, he had the best seat on a horse he'd ever seen," I bragged.

"Ah yes, Mr. Petty," Horace laughed. "I have yet to make his acquaintance."

"He'll tell you what he thinks," Whitey said. "That's for durn sure."

Later, Whitey and I ran into the store to tell Pop about our experience. We stopped short, and to our dismay, saw my mother in tears, with Pop looking torn and aggravated at the same time.

"Of course you can do it, Dolly," Pop said. "There's nothing to it."

"No, I can't," she cried. "They know they can fluster me and get me confused! They'll lie to me. And I'll get it wrong and then you'll be mad."

"No, I won't, darling," Pop said. He turned and saw us staring and waiting. In frustration, he yelled over his shoulder. "Clara Grace! Come in here a minute."

Clara Grace came in holding the inevitable religious tome in her hands. "What is it, Edmund?" she asked. "What is so important that you have to raise your voice so loud that the people in China can hear you?"

Pop got a grip on himself, and I knew it took everything he had. "Clara Grace," he said evenly. "I have to investigate these terrible things that have happened. Dolly doesn't like to check in deliveries. Will you handle that while she watches the store? All you have to do is take the delivery invoice they give you, make sure every item is there, and then pay them and have them sign a receipt. Do you think you can do that?"

Clara Grace threw him a withering look. "Of course. I'm not a moron, Edmund," she said.

Pop paused before answering, tapping his foot slightly, audibly breathing in and out. "Thank you, Clara Grace," he said when he could get the words out without shouting.

She said, "Humph," and went back behind the curtain. As soon as it stopped fluttering, Pop pulled my mother aside.

"Dolly," he whispered, grasping her arm tightly, "do not let her say one word about religion when Ephraim Hutchins makes his delivery. He is a hard-shell Baptist who thinks the Catholic

Church is the Scarlet Woman. If she opens her mouth to say one word about the saints and infant baptism, fall on the floor, pretend you are having a fit, whatever it takes. He gives me the best prices and the most reliable delivery I can possibly get here. But I can't even own a fiddle because he won't walk into a building where there is one. The only reason he'll let himself come here is because I once strummed 'Just As I Am' to him on the guitar."

She nodded her head vigorously. Throwing herself on the floor and pretending to have a fit was something she felt she could easily handle. "Okay, Pope. I can do that."

"Thank you, darling," Pop said, and kissed her. "Come on, boys, let's hit the trail," he said, fetching his hat and listening as we excitedly told him of riding Horace Dubois's horses.

Asa met us with a telegram in hand. Pop wasted no time reading it. "It's from the mortician in San Antonio. It says, 'Horace Dubois fine man, stop, will follow with letter.' "

"That's a relief," Asa said.

"Let's wait till we get the letter before we mark his name off the list," Pop said.

With Asa, me, and sometimes Whitey in tow, Pop questioned every person who lived in town, up and down the streets from the mayor's wife, Louella, in her coldly pretentious and echoingly empty home, to Harmonica John's cluttered house, popping to the rafters with rowdy grandchildren who I enjoyed playing with while Pop and Asa talked.

"Got your shadow with you today, don't you, Pop?" Harmonica John said with a laugh when the men came outside and saw me.

"He's my right-hand man," Pop said in a matter-of-fact voice, and I felt my chest swell with pride.

Whitey and I were allowed to go wherever Pop went. The only time he hesitated was when it came to visiting the mayor's brother, Melvin. Pop looked down at us and then looked at Asa. Asa said nothing, and after a moment of deliberation, Pop said, "Come along, boys, but when we get there, mind your manners and be quiet."

Melvin Foster's small frame house stood by itself about a mile outside of town by the side of the road. Their father had left Melvin a small inheritance which he used to build something away from Muskrat Hill. The bulk of the estate, invested in land, went to the mayor, and he married into a family with even more acreage. Melvin worked in his brother's office as a book-keeper, but he liked to boast that at home, he didn't lower himself to keep so much as a scrap of paper in the house.

He met us on the tiny porch, looking none too happy to see us.

"We've got to find Oscar's murderer and the murderer of the young woman," Pop said. "We were hoping you might have heard something, Melvin, or maybe had seen something un-usual."

"I would have told you so, Pope," Melvin said, peering over his glasses at my father.

"I realize that, Melvin," Pop said, "but I thought maybe we could jog your memory of some little something that seemed unusual."

"I repeat," Melvin said. "I would have told you so."

Pop looked at Asa, took a deep breath, and tried not to give in to the irritation Melvin generated. "We need to talk to your housekeeper, Melvin," he turned back and said.

"She doesn't speak English," Melvin said promptly. "She's from one of those Germanic countries."

"Nevertheless, we must see her and speak to her, Melvin," Pop said in a firm tone.

Melvin paused before agreeing. "Wait here," he instructed. He went back into the house, staying gone for what seemed like an unnecessarily long time. I was about to lose the battle not to fidget when Melvin opened the door and came back onto the porch.

"Follow me," he said, and again he wore the same self-satisfied sneer he had when he bought the crochet thread. "And you boys keep your hands off my things," he warned.

We nodded, too afraid to even say "yes, sir." Pop and Asa removed their hats upon entering the house, with us two goggle-eyed boys behind them. I had one of Pop's old hats stuffed with newspapers inside the sweatband to make it tight enough to stay on; Whitey wore a ragged cap, and trying to act like Pop and Asa, we removed our headgear, too.

The house was made up of chopped up little rooms, and Melvin led us single file to a bedroom beside the kitchen in the back of the house. Whitey and I looked around, expecting a home as fussy as Melvin, but besides the prolific use of doilies, the house was sparse with a quiet elegance. Pop and Asa walked into a small bedroom, with Whitey and me squeezing in behind them.

In the darkened room, a woman sat in a rocking chair with her back to a heavily curtained window. Above her head, a stream of light came in from above the curtain rod, the sun shining at such an angle that it almost blinded us to look in her direction. All I could see under a white dust cap was a blurry, somewhat attractive face, with full lips in a sensuous twist.

"Ma'am," Pop said, "My name is Pope Robertson; this is Marshal Asa Jenkins. We need to ask you a few questions."

"Speaka *de Deutsch*?" she asked in a curiously flat voice.

"*Nein,*" Pop said, shaking his head.

"*Ja,*" Asa said, and he carefully spoke a sentence to her in German. Pop looked at him in surprise, but turned back to the woman when she answered, "*Nein.*" Asa asked her another question in German, but she again answered, "*Nein.*"

"*Danke sehr*," Asa said. He turned to Pop. "She hasn't seen anyone unusual or heard of anything."

Pop nodded his head to the woman. "Much obliged," and with Melvin standing holding the doorknob, we filed out of the bedroom.

"I told you so, Pope," Melvin said at the front door. "If you want to find out something, perhaps you should question my brother more closely. There is quite a bit of our father in him, I'm sad to say," and he shut the door in our faces.

Pop shook his head and put his hat back on. He raised an eyebrow at Asa, and Asa answered his unspoken question.

"My adopted mother was part German."

"You never cease to amaze me," Pop said and walked toward the buggy.

"Do you think there is something in what he said about his brother?" Asa asked.

"Maybe," Pop said. "But he's very contemptuous of Julius." When Pop reached the buggy, he stopped and looked back at the house. "That was a performance staged for our benefit, and I don't know why."

"You think so, Pop?" Asa asked.

"I know so," Pop said, "and she's not sleeping in that bedroom. There was a fine even powder of dust on top of the dresser and the nightstand."

"I thought Melvin . . ." Asa began and stopped, turning a deep red.

"Yep," Pop said. "I reckon a dog can throw a leg over either way at times."

Later, Pop and Asa caught the mayor alone in front of the store and confronted him, repeating Melvin's words. Pop said, "I think he's right, Julius. I've known you a long time, and I think you're keeping something back."

"Like hell I am!" the mayor exploded, so angry he began to

shake. "I'm not hiding anything, nothing at all. And another thing, I can't believe you'd listen to Melvin. You know how he feels about me."

"All right, Julius," Pop said. "All right! Now calm down. What can you tell us about this woman he has living with him?"

The mayor took a deep breath. "I can't tell you anything. Melvin won't let me talk to her. I guess he's afraid I'll try to steal her away, although I wouldn't. She's not much of a housekeeper if you ask me."

"Do you know where she came from?" Pop asked.

"Look, Pope, all I can tell you is that Melvin somehow hooked up with her in Sulfur City. I heard through the grapevine that she had approached some minister there with a letter of introduction, saying she was a widow and needed help. I went to talk to the minister, and he didn't know anything or else wouldn't tell me anything. I just got the distinct impression he didn't like her and was glad to see her go. But when Melvin found out I'd been asking about her, he hit the roof and started screaming obscenities at me."

"Sulfur City, huh?" Pop said.

"Yes," the mayor answered, reaching into his pocket and pulling out a blue bandanna to wipe the sweat from his face.

Pop stared. "Where's your silk handkerchief?" he asked.

"It's lost," the mayor answered irritably. "Although I think that wretched woman Louella hires to do our washing probably stole it. She swears she didn't, but she was admiring it, and the next thing I know, it was missing. She claims someone took it off the clothesline. And what in the hell does my handkerchief have to do with murder? Or Melvin's housekeeper for that matter?"

"Nothing," Pop said. "I'm just covering everything."

"Well, leave me alone and go harass someone else," the mayor said and left. But the lines of worry remained on his face as he walked away.

CHAPTER 8

I suggested to Whitey that we go to Horace's barn. We found him next to Ace's stall, leaning over the railing and staring despondently.

"What's the matter, Mr. Horace?" Whitey asked.

He turned, anxiety dripping from the top of his arched brows to the ends of his mustache. "Ace has been off his feed for several days," he explained. "I don't know what could be the matter with him. Kit, would you ask your father to look at him?"

"Sure," I said. "I'll ask him right now."

We ran back into the store, and since Pop was bent over his ledgers, working alone, we were able to explode into chatter.

"Pop," I said. "Ace is off his feed, and Mr. Horace is really worried about him. He asked if you could come look at him."

Pop stared up from his books. "It's hard enough for me to keep this store running and do a murder investigation," he said. "Tell Horace the best thing he can do for Ace is to take him to Tull Petty."

Horace was dubious about our message, but we assured him Mr. Petty knew everything there was to know about horses.

"Your father said so, eh?" Horace asked.

Both Whitey and I nodded, and Horace rather reluctantly put a bridle on Ace. Gone was the regal bearing I had first witnessed in Ace; he now hung his head down, looking tired and mournful.

We walked with Horace as he slowly led the stumbling horse

down the street to the stables. "Don't worry, Mr. Horace," I said, feeling sorry for him. "Mr. Petty can put him right."

Mr. Petty saw us coming in. He put down the bucket of oats he had in his hand and immediately went to Ace, petting him and examining him gently without being told anything.

"How long has he been off his feed?" he asked Horace, never taking his eyes or his hands from the horse.

"Three days," Horace said. "He was fine a week or so ago, and then he just gradually slacked off until he's almost stopped."

Mr. Petty continued to ask Horace questions without ever taking his attention away from the animal. When satisfied that Horace had told him all he could, he led Ace to an empty stall, all the while talking to him in a low voice.

"Don't worry, boy. You're going to stay with me a few days, and I'll have you right in no time at all," Mr. Petty murmured. He stayed with Ace long enough to calm him and get him used to the stall before returning to us.

"You been eating supper a couple of nights a week with Pope, haven't you?" he asked Horace unexpectedly.

Puzzled, Horace said, "Yes, I have."

"You stay an awful long time," Mr. Petty commented.

Clearly Horace did not understand this line of questioning. "Yes," he said. "Pop asked me to teach them sign language. He said his father went deaf, and it haunts him that the same thing might happen to him, and he will be unable to communicate with his family."

Mr. Petty nodded. "That Clara Grace is a mighty fine-looking woman."

I saw immediately where he was going, but Horace was so distracted because of Ace he did not. "Yes, she is," he replied automatically. "She and Miss Dolly have been so kind to me. Miss Dolly is a wonderful cook—a marvelous woman."

"Uh-huh," Mr. Petty answered. "Well, get the hell out of

here. I'll tend to your horse. Come back in three days. He should be well by then."

"Three days?" Horace asked, his voice giving away his doubt.

"Maybe four," Mr. Petty admitted. "Just let me do my job, and come back in three days."

Reluctantly, Horace left. We walked back with him to his place, saying hello to Bruno, who seemed to watch our every move. We left Horace there, assuring him again if Pop said Mr. Petty knew what he was doing, he did.

Before going home, we went back to the stables. Mr. Petty was rummaging through an unlocked cabinet, bringing out various vile looking bottles and pouring different amounts into a bucket.

"What is that, Mr. Petty?" I brazenly asked. "What are you giving Ace?"

He whirled around. "None of your dang business," he barked, making us jump. Holding up the big brown bottle, he said, "This here is asafetida." He looked at us and glared, "I ain't gonna tell you the rest. It's a secret." He peered at us through watery eyes. "When you're a little older, maybe I'll give you my secret formulas so they won't be lost to science forever, but right now, they stays right here," he said, pointing to his head. "Now get the hell out of here and go beleaguer some other poor old man."

"Yes, sir," we said. We stopped to pat Ace, who perked up enough to give his head a shake of goodbye. As we were leaving, we could hear Mr. Petty still muttering. "Goldang kids, worse than goldarn women, always pestering a man, wanting to know things that are none of their dang business. Goldang women are the worst. I'm coming, Ace, old sport."

While Pop and I went out almost daily, my mother began taking on more responsibility of the store, but her forte was and always had been dealing with customers. Alternately, Clara

Grace handled the vendors and deadbeats using a firm hand and a no-nonsense square of her jaw. Some began to cautiously ask if they could come back when Pop was in the store. After Clara Grace's negative response, none of them had the courage to repeat the request.

One night soon after we had taken Ace to Mr. Petty, we had just finished supper when we heard a knock at the front of the store. Pop motioned his head to me, and Whitey and I ran to the door to see who wanted in. After we saw who it was and asked him to wait, we returned to the kitchen with solemn faces.

"Well, who is it and what do they want?" Pop asked.

I looked at Whitey and back at Pop. "I think it is Mr. Hutchins," I said slowly. "And he wants to talk to you."

"What do you mean, you think it's Mr. Hutchins?" Pop said rising. "It's either Mr. Hutchins or it's not."

The women followed and peeked around the curtain, their jaws dropping as they saw Ephraim Hutchins at the front door wearing a new suit, a stiff white collar, and a tie. Whatever other seven deadly sins might reside in Mr. Hutchins's heart, gluttony was not one of them. He was on the tall side, with eyes as sharp as mesquite thorns, fading brown hair parted slightly to one side, and a wide mouth that looked like it had been drawn across his face with a ruler and a level. He stood looking restless, uncomfortable, and determined.

"What does he want?" Clara Grace asked, but my mother looked around the kitchen.

"I should have known not to turn the parlor into a bedroom," my mother said with a moan. "Quick, Clara Grace, help me clear the table and put on another pot of coffee. Do we have any cookies left? Kit, don't tell me you and Whitey ate all those cookies?"

Clara Grace looked at her as if she had taken to speaking

Mandarin Chinese. Pop pushed his way back through the curtain.

"We'll have the kitchen cleared in a minute, Pope," my mother said. "Clara Grace, try pinching your cheeks and biting your lips to put a little color in them. And take your apron off."

"What are you talking about, Dolly?" Clara Grace asked, irritated.

"Mr. Hutchins has asked permission to call on you, Clara Grace," Pop said. "Do as Dolly says."

"Call on me?" Clara Grace said. "Are you all insane? I'm not going to sit here and talk to that man like I'm some kind of simpering Southern belle. Send him away!"

Pop took Clara Grace's arm and propelled her to the curtain, forcing her to look at Mr. Hutchins. "Do you see that man, Clara Grace? He has bought a new suit, taken a bath, and spent a fortune on hair oil to look presentable for you. Do you know how much courage it took for him to possibly appear a fool coming all the way over here just to talk to you? Now do what Dolly says."

"I will not!" Clara Grace said, aghast at the thought.

Whitey and I watched, gulping in horror that Clara Grace had openly defied Pop. We looked from Pop to Clara Grace to my mother. She took Clara Grace aside and whispered lengthily in her ear. When she finished, Clara Grace's face had lost most of its belligerence, and she nodded her head. "You are quite right, Dolly," she said, and she headed for her room.

My parents exchanged glances and exhaled deep breaths. "What did you tell her?" Pop asked.

"I told her Mr. Hutchins needed saving. Maybe you'd better go out there and tell him Clara Grace needs the same thing."

Pop nodded, heading for the front of the store where Clara Grace's middle-aged bony admirer stood pulling on a tight collar and reeking of lilac water.

With Mr. Hutchins ensconced in the kitchen with Clara Grace, and my mother again lamenting she had turned the parlor into a bedroom, the four of us sat at the table in the back of the store. "Is this going to be a regular occurrence?" Pop asked. "Because if it is, I'm getting a more comfortable chair to sit in out here."

"Kit," my mother said, "Go fetch Pop a stool for his feet, please."

I headed for the kitchen, but she called, "No, don't go back there. Find one in the front of the store."

Thwarted in our desire to eavesdrop, Whitey and I played checkers while Pop read a newspaper. Asa saw the light burning and came in.

"Ephraim?" he said in a shocked voice when we told him. He sat down in a chair near Pop and looked despondent. "Hutchins is a wealthy man," he commented miserably.

"Don't worry," Pop said. "Clara Grace doesn't care for riches. She says that all the time while she's shoveling in the groceries my money buys."

"Pope," my mother said.

"Well, it's true, Dolly," Pop said.

Clara Grace and Mr. Hutchins came in, both looking mildly exhilarated. "Thank you, Miss Clara Grace," Mr. Hutchins said, nodding his head to her. He started to walk to the front of the door but stopped at the table.

"Hello, Jenkins," he said. "Seen anything of your family lately?"

Asa looked surprised. "No, I haven't been down there lately. But my sisters write me regularly."

"No, I meant your Indian brethren," Mr. Hutchins said.

Asa flushed, but answered evenly enough. "No, the ones who haven't been killed by smallpox and cholera are all in Oklahoma."

I thought it a low blow to a man who didn't even know who his own father was, but oddly enough, Pop didn't look perturbed. He merely told Mr. Hutchins it had been nice to see him.

After he left, Asa asked Whitey if he wanted him to take him home. My mother nodded her head. "You've stayed with us two nights in a row, Whitey," she said kindly. "Your mother might be getting worried about you."

He nodded and left with Asa. My mother got up and started for the back with Clara Grace. "I think I made a lot of headway with him, Dolly," Clara Grace said, showing more excitement than I had ever seen her exhibit. "He listened to everything I said, and we had a good discussion."

"Yes, Clara Grace," my mother said, nodding. She threw Pop a look over her shoulders and continued nodding as Clara Grace prattled on.

After they left, I leaned against Pop. Pop put his arm around my waist. "What is it, son?" he asked.

"I didn't like what Mr. Hutchins said to Marshal Asa," I said. "It sounded mean."

Pop laughed. "Son, Ephraim doesn't give a hoot what Asa is. He's just trying to cut him down in front of Clara Grace. Don't be surprised if he meets Asa in here again if he doesn't say something about how little money a town marshal makes."

"But Marshal Asa didn't do that to him," I protested.

"That's because Asa is as innocent and inexperienced with the ways of women as a newborn colt. If he wasn't, he'd be whispering in Clara Grace's ear right now that Mr. Hutchins's first wife was so unhappy, she jumped in a well and killed herself."

I shook my head in disgust. "I'm glad I'm a little kid, Pop."

"You'll be grown before you know it, boy," Pop said with a gentle smile. "And then you'll be doing the same thing to get what you want."

Mr. Petty wouldn't let Horace in the stables until the three days were up, but he allowed Whitey and me to peek at Ace in the meantime, grumbling all the while about kids driving a man crazy. At the same time, he glowed with pride when we exclaimed how miraculously better Ace looked. We would pet Ace and tell Mr. Petty about Nighthawk and Nero, explaining what great horses they were, and yet we knew they weren't really in the same class as Ace.

We dutifully reported Ace's progress to Horace every day. Since Bruno was always around, I became brave and started signing simple greetings to him. He insisted Whitey and I call him by his first name only. "Bruno," he signed. "No mister." The responses he gave were always short and his face, the part that worked, never changed expression. Even so, I couldn't get over the feeling he was watching me, much more so than he did Whitey.

On the third day, Mr. Petty permitted Horace to look at Ace, but told him he wanted the horse to stay one more day. Horace was so grateful for Ace's recovery, he readily acceded.

"What was wrong with him?" Horace asked, rather timorously because he, too, was a little afraid of Mr. Petty.

Mr. Petty shrugged. "This and that," he said. "You've been letting these here boys ride Nero and Nighthawk, haven't you?" he asked.

Horace nodded. "Yes," he said, bewildered at Mr. Petty's sudden attack, and his knowledge about his other horses.

"Yeah," Mr. Petty said. "And I heared how you favor that Black Jack. You done hurt Ace's feelings. He's a mighty proud horse, and he was beginning to feel a trifle underappreciated."

"What?" Horace said, mystified.

"You heard me," Mr. Petty said. "You've got to let Ace know he's your number one hoss. You've done let yourself get too involved with this here Black Jack because he's an attention grabber, but you know in your heart Ace is the king."

"Yes, er, yes," Horace said. "If you say so. I'll be back to get him tomorrow."

"I ain't letting you take this fine horse unlessen you agree to give him the attention he deserves," Mr. Petty threatened. "Let Kit and Whitey take a turn riding him every once in a while, so he don't feel left out."

"I will, I promise," Horace agreed.

Once outside, Horace patted the sweat from his forehead with a handkerchief. "Good God," he said. "Is everyone in Muskrat Hill just a little bit crazy?"

"Yep," Whitey said, nodding his head. "Just a little bit."

I didn't care how crazy the people in Muskrat Hill were. Mr. Petty had just coerced Horace into letting us ride Ace occasionally, and that's all that mattered to me. Later, I reported the exchange to Pop. Whenever I went to the undertaker's barn, Pop wanted me to tell him about it. The mayor walked in and listened to my conversation about Ace. When I finished, the mayor questioned Pop's wisdom in letting Whitey and me ride Horace's stallions.

"Julius," Pop said, "if those boys are going to be worth their salt on horseback, they have to learn how to handle anything that could turn feisty."

"I grant you that, Pope," the mayor conceded. "But letting them hang around those two men?"

"Kit tells me what goes on, and I trust him not to be led astray by anybody, including Horace and Bruno," Pop said.

"Other parents warn their children to stay away from Horace and Bruno," the mayor reminded him.

"I want to protect Kit, but I can't keep him in a cocoon, Julius," Pop answered. "And besides, a lot of that is superstition. In the meantime," Pop said, "Kit and Whitey are helping me keep my finger on what's going on in Muskrat Hill."

I didn't know whether Whitey and I were much help or not. We were wild about Horace's steeds and took every opportunity to stop by and visit them. My mother did fear that we were pestering the two men and made us promise not to go too often, but Horace and even Bruno didn't seem to mind. Horace began letting us run short races behind his barn, always with Nero and Nighthawk, sometimes with Ace. The man was an equine fanatic, taking joy in teaching us the rudiments of racing, while Bruno stood nearby. Horace said it was good for us to learn to ride bareback and Pop agreed. Pop sometimes came and watched us, but he rarely had time. When he did come, however, he took pleasure in seeing us laugh and squeal as we held on to the horses' manes and raced to the tree that marked our finish line. That they were high-spirited and sometimes difficult only added to our excitement. Asa said we were becoming more Comanche than white, and that, for some reason, pleased us enormously. Horace, however, considered it normal training for Southern gentlemen.

The day after the mayor chastised Pop, while Horace and Whitey were going over how to do a posting trot, I found the courage to question Bruno.

"How come Mr. Horace doesn't court Clara Grace, Bruno?" I asked. "Everyone thinks he is."

Bruno shrugged his shoulders and signed, "He is in love with a girl back in South Carolina."

I decided I should practice my signing, so I replied with my fingers, "Is she the one he writes to all the time?"

Bruno looked surprised, but nodded. "He is trying to get her to come to Texas and marry him," he signed. "Besides, Horace is infatuated with your mother."

My mother? My mother was old enough to be Horace's mother or maybe even his grandmother. "Pop is the only man for my mother," I signed empathically.

"He knows," Bruno replied. "He admires your father very much. It's just puppy love."

I wasn't too sure what puppy love was and didn't want to think about it. I looked at Horace and Whitey, but they were still engrossed in the lesson Horace had already taught me. I turned back to Bruno. "Bruno," I signed, "can I ask you another question?"

He nodded and instead of looking at him, I looked down at my fingers. I was so curious I couldn't stand it, but at the same time, I didn't want to see anger in Bruno's eyes in case I made him mad.

"Pop said you look like a man just out of prison," my fingers flew. "Is that true?"

I looked at Bruno's hands instead of his good eye. "Yes, I was in prison a long time," he signed.

I managed to look up at Bruno. "Why were you in prison?" I asked, switching over to speaking.

"I killed a man many years ago," Bruno signed.

"Why?"

"Because he needed it," Bruno's fingers told me.

I began to sign again. "Where were you in prison?"

"Up north. Ohio."

I looked up puzzled. "And you rode the train all the way from there to Muskrat Hill?" I signed.

"Yes," he signed back.

CHAPTER 9

That night after supper when Whitey had gone home and Clara Grace read in her room, I told my parents as we sat at the table what Bruno had revealed. Pop shook his head, lowered it, and put his hand over his forehead, still shaking his head. He stopped and looked at my mother. "Dolly, I would swear that Horace would never hurt those boys, but I do not know about Bruno."

I worried she would raise a fuss and tell me I couldn't go anymore, but I was wrong.

"Pope, why would Bruno admit that to Kit?" she asked. "He told Kit he had been in prison for killing a man many years ago and had just been released. That is the confession of a man who does not want to live a lie, not the confession of a cold-blooded, sadistic murderer. He's been kind to Kit and Whitey, and I think he deserves a chance."

Pop took a deep breath. "Yes, you're right. Kit, did you tell Whitey or anyone else about this?"

"No, Pop," I said, shaking my head.

"Then don't. Things are rough enough for Bruno and Horace as it is," Pop replied. "Be as wise as a serpent and as harmless as a dove, Kit. Treat Bruno with friendliness, but don't go off alone with him or any other grown-up."

Pop heaved another deep sigh in worry. He looked at my mother. "But why come here, Dolly? Why come almost straight from prison to Muskrat Hill?" But it was a question neither one of them could answer.

The next morning, I went into the kitchen after breakfast to take the trash bundle outside to the burn pile, a chore I had forgotten to do. It wasn't on the counter, and going to the door, I could see my mother holding it in her arms, her steps becoming increasingly slower. She kept looking around uneasily, as if she expected to be surprised by something or someone.

The door to the outhouse began to open. Fluttering in fright, my mother dropped her bundle, covering her heart with her hand. Pop stepped outside.

"Oh, Pope, it's you," she exclaimed in relief. "I had the terrible feeling I was being watched."

Pop's eyes scanned the yard and beyond. Finding nothing unusual, he went to my mother and hugged her. "Dolly, don't go anywhere alone. Don't even step outside the store by yourself at night. Clara Grace is a pain in the ass, but she came at the right time. You two girls stick together."

My mother looked up at my father, her eyes wide with fright. "Do you think it's him, Pope? Do you think it could be him?"

He shook his head. "No, darling, he's still in prison."

"But what about the other one?" she questioned. "Has he come back?"

Pop shook his head. "He disappeared years ago, Dolly," he said soothingly. "Somebody has probably killed him by now."

She buried her face in his chest, clutching him and muttering, "I love you, Pope. I love you."

He stroked her hair. "I know you do, darling."

Whitey came around the corner about that time. Pop, seeing him, turned back to me. "Kit, you and Whitey run along and play for a while; I won't be needing you just yet. And Whitey, don't be leaving your house before daylight or going home alone after dark anymore."

"Yes, sir, Captain Robertson," Whitey said.

Whitey and I walked around the store and started down the street. "Who were they talking about, Kit?"

"I don't know," I said miserably. "And Pop doesn't want me to know or he would have told me."

"Scut's got an uncle on a prison farm up north," Whitey said.

"What's he there for?" I asked.

"Stealing chickens, I think."

I shook my head. "I don't think that's him."

A group of boys had congregated near the slaughter pens. Oscar's brother-in-law had moved to town to run the business, but he lacked Oscar's friendly personality. Pop said it would be hard to warm up to anybody taking Oscar's place.

As Whitey and I neared the other boys, one put his nose up in the air and began to sashay around like a girl. "I'm Kit's crazy cousin Clara," he said in a falsetto voice. "And nothing I ever put in the outhouse stinks," he continued, pretending to delicately wave a handkerchief.

The boys laughed, and as Whitey and I grew closer, someone called out, "Hey, Kit, you think your old man is ever going to find the killer?"

Scut, kicking at the dirt, looked up and said, "Aw, leave him alone."

It astonished me to have Scut Tabor take up for me, but the other boy didn't immediately stop. "My old man says your old man is a has-been who'll never solve these crimes," he bragged.

Beside me, Whitey tensed, and I knew the other boys were waiting for me to lose my temper. I was waiting for it, too, but instead, I found myself speaking.

"My old man," I said, "will find the killer a lot faster than your old man could. Your old man couldn't find his pecker if it wasn't behind button number three on his pants."

My quick retort surprised the heck out of the boys and out of me, but a couple of seconds later, they began to roar with laughter, pointing fingers of derision at my tormentor.

"Come on, Whitey, let's go back," I said.

We headed back toward the store, kicking at pebbles in the dust. "Do you really believe your pop will catch the killer?" Whitey asked.

"Yeah," I said, sure of the answer. "Pop's like a bloodhound; nothing will stop him once he gets started."

As we neared the store, I looked toward the woods. Out of nowhere, a gloved hand appeared from behind a tree, making a "come here" motion. I blinked, and it disappeared.

Halting, I asked Whitey, "Did you see that?"

"No, what?"

I stared at the trees. "I don't know," I said. "Let's go in the store."

Pop was in the back, measuring rope for a lean old rancher.

"Sorry about that, Sam," he said. "I thought I had more rope. Dolly must have sold some."

"That's all right, Pope," the old rancher said. "I'll take what you got. Just put it on my bill."

"Sure thing," Pop said, expertly coiling the rope and handing it to him. The rancher left, and Pop walked to the front, grabbing his ticket pad.

"Pop," I asked as he scribbled on the ticket. "Have you ever seen a ghost?"

"In my younger days I saw a few ex-girlfriends who spooked the hell out of me." He looked up. "Run down to the stables, please, sir, and ask Mr. Petty to bring the buggy around. Asa should be here any minute. If you boys want to ride along, saddle Gastor."

"Yes, sir, Pop!" I said, and Whitey and I raced from the store.

Mr. Petty grumbled and fussed, just like he always did. "Was that Ephraim Hutchins duded up and going into the store the other night?" he demanded. His voice was as abrasive as sandpaper, but the hands he put on the horse were as gentle as those of a mammy for her baby.

"Yes, sir," I said. "He came a-courting my cousin Clara," I added proudly.

"Gol-durnit," Mr. Petty said. "That bastard has no call to come into Muskrat Hill and try to steal our women. That sorry s.o.b. needs to stay where the hell he belongs."

Whitey and I stared at one another in surprise. I looked back at Mr. Petty and timidly said, "Maybe you should court Clara Grace, too, sir."

I expected to have my head blown off, but Mr. Petty said, "No, she wouldn't go for the likes of me. I'm too old and crusty."

"Yeah, and she only likes Catholics," Whitey piped up, surprising me with his boldness and his knowledge of my family, although I don't know why, he knew almost as much about it as I did.

Mr. Petty turned a ferocious glare on us. "What the hell makes you think I'm not a Catholic?" he roared. "I'm a danged good Catholic and don't you forget it."

"Yes, sir," Whitey and I both muttered, backing up a little.

"I'm a danged good Catholic," he repeated. "So, she's a Catholic girl?"

"Yes, sir," I answered. "She only goes to church with us because Pop won't take her anywhere else."

Mr. Petty stroked the horse. "I could take her to St. Paul's. Would take all day. Course, I don't have nothing but a bunch of idiots who can't be trusted to watch the stables." He turned and gave us a speculative look, but shook his head. "No, you're too squirty yet." He sighed. "Women are more trouble than a family of skunks at a prayer meeting."

Whitey and I got on Gastor and tried to escape. Before we made it, Mr. Petty said, "Hey, you kids, you tell your cousin if she ever wants to go for a buggy ride, I'll take her. And don't forget to mention I'm a Catholic."

"Yes, sir," I said. "A danged good Catholic."

"That right, boy," Mr. Petty agreed. "Now get the hell out of here and tell your pa not to get his drawers in a wad, I'll be there shortly."

Asa was already inside the store with Pop, Clara Grace, and my mother when Whitey and I entered. "Pop," I responded when he spoke to me, "Mr. Petty will be here with the buggy in a minute. He said for us to tell Clara Grace that he will take her buggy riding anytime she wants to go."

"Buggy riding?" Clara Grace exclaimed as if I had said mud wrestling or bronc busting.

"Yes, ma'am. And he said to tell you he was a good Catholic," I added, holding back a giggle, but Whitey couldn't manage it, and he let out a soft one.

"Clara Grace," my mother exclaimed. "Isn't that nice?"

Clara Grace was still staring as if she didn't quite believe us. "He'd probably take you to the Catholic Church in the next town one Sunday if you asked him to," I added as solemnly as I could manage.

"Oh, Clara Grace, he could take you to church," my mother said happily. "He's such a nice man."

Pop gave a loud snort, making my mother add, "Well, a little rough around the edges maybe, but a nice man."

"Rough like a hacksaw," Pop said, jabbing Asa in the ribs.

My mother pretended not to hear Pop. Putting as much persuasion in her voice as she could, she said, "He would take you to Mass, Clara Grace."

Clara Grace's nostrils flared, reflecting the quandary she found herself mired in. She had been riding Pop constantly to take her to Mass; here was her chance, and Pop would rub it in later if she didn't jump on it. She lifted her jaw. "I can't leave Dolly alone at this time," she said. "Not with the likelihood of

Edmund running off at any minute to catch a killer. I couldn't possibly go off and leave Dolly by herself."

"Perhaps in the future, Clara Grace," my mother said, unwilling to give up on Mr. Petty as a potential beau.

"Tull Petty is nearly as old as I am, and it would surprise the heck out of me if he even knew the name of one saint," Pop said.

"Pope!" my mother exclaimed. "It's important for a woman to have suitors before she marries. It makes her feel good about herself. And besides, it will make her future husband feel like he's getting a catch."

"This conversation is totally ridiculous," Clara Grace said and stormed to the back.

Poor Asa had stood there the whole time looking uncomfortable and despondent. Pop regarded him with pity. "Come on, I think Tull is pulling up now," he said.

Outside, Mr. Petty climbed from the buggy and untied his horse from the back. Giving Asa a sour look, he said with more bluster than brains, "You try to cut me out with that girl, Injun, and I'll wipe the street with your red blood."

It was the closest I ever saw Asa to losing his temper. Not that he said anything. It was in his rigid stance, the stony expression on his face, the fire in his eyes. I half expected him to throw his head back, give a war whoop, whip out a knife, and scalp Mr. Petty on Main Street. Pop must have thought so, too. He drew near the two and spoke in a firm voice. "I'm going to tell you men something. Clara Grace has a mind of her own. She does what she wants, and there won't be any cutting out by anybody, because she's the one who makes her own decisions. Get that straight right now. Now shake hands on it and forget about fighting. It wouldn't impress her anyway."

No one moved, so Pop said, "Tull, you started it. Stick your hand out."

Mr. Petty, grumbling under his breath, put out his hand and Asa took it.

We left, heading further west, so far, my mother had felt the need to pack us lunch. Pop and Asa rode in the buggy, while Whitey and I took turns struggling with Gastor. He hadn't been so far from Muskrat Hill in a long time, and he didn't like it.

We left behind the lushness of Muskrat Hill. In front of us, the wheels of the buggy sent up little clouds of dust. Twisted mesquite trees appeared. After many miles, we stopped at a small ramshackle house made of homemade bricks and a blanket for a front door. A group of little Indian boys were playing in the barren yard with a skinny speckled pup. Recognizing a couple of them, I said, "Howdy," and slid from Gastor's back. Once, Pop had taken me there while he visited an old chief who was dying. The chief had wanted him to stay, so I spent all day playing with some of the boys who were around at the time. They nodded their heads in recognition, and it wasn't long after I introduced Whitey that we were on the ground, playing with the pup alongside them.

Two men came out of the house—one had a large scar running down his cheek and the other lisped through lips with a mouth missing many teeth; both wore old suit jackets and worn, loudly patterned pants. We played quietly; the Indian boys were just as curious as we were to hear what the men had to say, especially when they began to criticize Asa.

"I see you have come back to accuse us, you turncoat," Scarface said, "trying to pretend you are a white man."

Asa didn't put up with that kind of talk. "Look, when I was abandoned as an infant, I didn't have any Indians stepping forward to adopt me."

The two Indian men looked at one another and shrugged. "This is true," one of them said. "So, you think we had something to do with these killings just because it looks like maybe an Indian did it?"

"We aren't saying anything like that," Pop said. "And we aren't accusing you of anything. We just thought maybe you had seen something or heard something."

"We don't know anything," Missing Teeth said.

"It was probably the negrito who plays the harmonica," the other said.

"No," Missing Teeth responded, shaking his head. "He is like us, too old to get excited enough about a woman to kill her."

His friend nodded. "It was probably one of those hot-tempered Mexicans then. White men, they have no passion."

They talked for a while longer. Pop thanked them, and we got up to leave. I told the boys goodbye, and Gastor, sensing we might be going home, perked up to look lively enough for Whitey and me not to be ashamed of riding him. Just before Asa popped the buggy reins to leave, the scar-faced Indian called out to him.

"Don't forget, you are part Indian," he said.

"Don't worry," Asa answered, his face grim. "No one ever lets me forget it."

CHAPTER 10

Whitey and I entered the store before Pop and Asa did. Old Man Miller stood at the counter looking uncomfortable, his shoulders hunched in embarrassment.

"You have to sign for these groceries if you are going to charge them," Clara Grace was informing him in a firm voice.

"But Dolly and Pope never make me sign a ticket for my groceries," Old Man Miller protested.

"I am not Dolly; I am not Edmund," Clara Grace said. "You must sign the ticket."

Old Man Miller relented, and taking the pencil awkwardly in his gnarled fingers, he laboriously drew an X.

"Thank you," Clara Grace said. She wrapped his groceries in brown paper with competent fingers. He took them and left, not even noticing us as he walked out of the store. Pop came in at the same time, saying hello, but Old Man Miller merely grunted and went on his way as fast as his old bones could take him.

"What's the matter with him?" Pop asked. "Clara Grace, have you been running off my customers?"

"Certainly not, Edmund," she replied.

"Where's Dolly? And don't call me Edmund."

Clara Grace frowned at Pop with a slight look of disgust, but she answered him. "She insisted on taking Mr. Sorenson's widow some food, but she promised to be back before dark."

"I told her not to go anywhere alone," Pop fretted. "I'm worn out, and I want my supper," he added with a moan.

"Well, she'll be back in a minute, your highness. It's not that far to the Sorenson's place, and one of the church ladies went with her. You didn't invite that Indian for supper, did you? I don't want to eat at the table with an Indian."

My mother came in before Pop could answer. "What's wrong with Asa?" she asked. "He was about to come inside when all of the sudden, he turned and left."

"Clara Grace," Pop said, sounding depressed and tired, "there is a crazed killer on the loose, and all you're worried about is sitting at the table with a Methodist minister who has a tan."

He didn't wait for her to answer but walked to the back. Clara Grace called behind him, "Well, he might have lice."

"Clara Grace, Asa does not have lice," my mother said, following Pop. He plopped down in a chair at the table, rubbing his temples. She stood behind him and began to massage his shoulders.

"I don't know, Dolly," he said, looking tired and dejected. "I just don't know. Am I too old to solve this? What could Oscar possibly have in common with a prostitute traveling through that could get them both killed? Oscar's wife said he never left the slaughterhouse except to come here or go home to sleep."

She bent down and kissed his head. "You'll solve it, Pope, you always do," she answered. She turned and looked at me.

"Kit," she said, "did you wrestle with those Indian boys?"

"No, ma'am," I assured her. "We just sat on the ground and played with a little pup."

"Nevertheless," she said, "I believe you and Whitey should have a thorough wash tonight, including your hair."

Whitey's eyes got big, and he began backing to the door. "I best be getting home, Mrs. Robertson," he said. "My mama might be looking for me." And with that, he shot out the door.

My mother shook her head and, looking down at me, said,

"Kit, tomorrow, I think it would be a good idea if you and Whitey took a break from detecting and horse racing and went to the river for a swim. And Pope, it wouldn't hurt you to take a break either. You're going after this too hard."

Pop let out a heavy sigh and leaned back in his chair. "You're right. But Asa and I planned on looking over the slaughterhouse again for clues. Oscar's body was cold, and his wife said lately he had taken to leaving earlier and earlier in the mornings." Pop stuck the table with his fist. "Why was he arriving so early in the morning? He made it easy for someone to slip in there and kill him without being noticed."

My mother parted her lips to say something, but Pop didn't notice. He looked at me and said, "Your mother's right. Go to the river and swim. And see if you can't get Whitey to jump in with his clothes on. That boy is beginning to smell rank."

"Yes, sir, Pop," I said.

The next morning, before Whitey arrived, I had to haul firewood and start a fire under the washpot for my mother. She walked onto the back porch, carrying a basket of clothes.

"Have you got the fire going, Kit?" she called.

"Yes, ma'am, it's going good and hot," I said, poking it with a stick, enjoying watching the crackle and pop of the flames.

Across the yard, the outhouse began to shake, and the sounds of Pop stomping and cursing from inside could be heard coming through the door.

"What is it, Pope?" my mother called. She stepped off the porch, handing me the basket. "Throw these in the water, Kit, please, and stir them down with the stick. Pope, what is it?"

"Yes, ma'am," I said and unceremoniously dumped the clothes in the pot, the water sloshing out and sizzling in the flames beneath it. I stirred the clothes with an apathetic twist before throwing the stick down, my eyes on the outhouse, wondering where Pop had picked up such a large vocabulary of curse words.

The door flew open, and he stumbled out, his pants down and the back flap of his long johns open.

"Pope! What's the matter?" my mother exclaimed, hurrying across the yard.

"Something stung me when I sat down. Hellfire, it stings!" he said, grimacing and hopping in pain.

"Let me look," my mother said, falling to her knees and peering at Pop's white bottom.

"Where's Clara Grace?" he asked.

"Oh, don't worry, she's inside saying her prayers," my mother assured him.

"Doesn't she always have to say the rosary about the time it is to do the breakfast dishes?" he asked, propping his hands against the outhouse wall while my mother scanned his behind.

"Now, Pope, you know that's not true," she said. "You sat on a bee. Be still and let me get the stinger out."

"Ouch! Woman, be careful!" Pop said. It seemed funny to me that a man who had faced death multiple times by an assortment of vicious weapons could turn into such a baby when my mother was around. But then, I did the same thing.

Before Pop could pull his pants up, Clara Grace walked out onto the back porch. She began to screech when she saw my parents.

"Dolly! Oh my God! Oh my God!" she screamed, placing both hands to her cheeks and reeling like a drunken woman. "Edmund, you pervert! Papa always said you were a Babylonian. Dolly, how could you?!"

My mother, still on her knees, stared incomprehensively at Clara Grace. Pop, however, glared at her in fury. "Clara Grace," he hollered over his shoulder, "you shut up and go back inside before I turn around and burn something in your memory that no amount of praying is ever going to wipe out."

Clara Grace huffed and ran back into the house, with Pop shouting at her back. "And don't call me Edmund!"

Just as the bottom of Clara Grace's dress flew across the threshold, the teenage boy who had smarted off to Pop the day we discovered the dead woman came around the side of the store with a few of his friends. He saw Pop standing with his drawer flap open and my mother kneeling on the ground, and his eyes got as big as two pigs with the bloat.

"What are you looking at?" Pop yelled at them.

"Uh, nothing, sir," one of them muttered.

"Then get the hell out of here!" Pop ordered.

"Uh, yes, sir," they said and fled, almost running into Louella Foster, the mayor's portly and buxom wife.

"Pope Robertson!" she said, the feathers on her large hat shaking in indignation. "I ought to have you arrested for indecent exposure."

Pop, pulling his pants up, glared at her. "And I ought to have you arrested for trespassing."

I smelled something burning, thinking at first some of the clothes had fallen into the fire under the washpot. That wasn't it, and glancing at the back door, I saw smoke coming from the kitchen.

"Something's burning in the kitchen, Mama," I called.

"Oh, my bread!" my mother exclaimed, jumping up and running into the house.

"What do you want anyway, Louella?" Pop demanded. "I know you didn't come over here to use my privy."

"I wouldn't use your privy if my life depended on," Louella said, full of scorn. "Not with every lice-ridden piece of trash who comes to town on Saturday going in there."

"I'll have you know that privy gets scrubbed at least once a week."

Louella looked like she wanted to continue the argument, but changed her mind. "It doesn't matter. I came over here about something else."

"What is it?" Pop barked.

She looked indecisive, as if she didn't know exactly how she should word what she wanted to say. I stared at her curiously, for that wasn't like the mayor's wife at all.

"I've been hearing rumors about some of the things you and Asa are doing," she said. "Now, Pope, I want it to stop. Leave brothers out of this. Just stop it."

Pop, his anger gone and just as perplexed by her attitude as I was, said, "What are you talking about?"

She opened her mouth, but paused, shaking her head before speaking. "Just leave brothers out of this."

"Louella," Pop said. "I've questioned every person in town. Why would I not question Julius and Melvin?"

She shut her mouth and set her jaw, but did not answer. She shot Pop an angry look and turned to leave, but not before glaring at me, too.

When Pop and I walked back into the store, Clara Grace was standing beside Asa. When she saw Pop, her lips pressed in a firm line, and she sailed past him into the living quarters. Pop made a scowl, but the curtain was already fluttering behind her.

"What is this about you being a fiend and Clara Grace being afraid no man will ever want her after what she's witnessed?" Asa asked, puzzled.

"Humph," Pop muttered. "The less you know about what goes on in that squirrel brain, the better off you'll be. Come on, let's go."

Miss Maydell came into the store just as Pop and Asa were leaving. They nodded, greeting her with, "Good morning, Miss Maydell." Although habitually and almost painfully shy around men, she usually spoke. However, this time, she kept her head down and only nodded. Pop looked at Asa and shrugged as they went out the door.

I had a few marbles I thought I might want to take on our excursion to the river, but I couldn't remember where I had put them. Sometimes my mother placed them in one of the cupboards below the shelves, and I began to search on the other side of the store.

My mother greeted her cheerfully as usual. "Hello, Maydell. How are you doing today? Was that enough . . ."

Maydell cut her off. "I need a pound of coffee, Dolly," she said, her voice tense. There was something in the way she spoke that made me look up and peer between the shelves. I could see the back of her calico dress, her thin hand working nervously by her side.

"Of course," my mother answered, good-naturedly fetching the coffee. "What else?"

Maydell glanced tensely around as if trying to make up her mind. "A can of tomatoes," she said automatically. "And one of those," she said with a sudden point.

"A lantern?" my mother asked.

"Yes, on the top shelf. In the middle," Maydell said.

"Okay," my mother said and dragged a stepladder over to reach the lantern. I wondered if I should help her, but my mother was on the ladder with her back turned to Maydell before I could say anything. To my surprise, Maydell grabbed a pencil from the counter and stuck it in her pocket while my mother asked with her back turned, "This one, Maydell?"

It happened so fast, I wondered if my eyes deceived me. Of course, we had petty thieves come into the store, but to see Miss Maydell, the primmest and most proper of our customers, steal something, a chewed-on stubby pencil no less, didn't make sense.

"No, Dolly, I've changed my mind," she said once more looking around. "I want . . . I want some matches."

"Oh, okay," my mother said. Anyone else would have been angry or wondered at Maydell's sudden change of mind, but my mother had long before learned to accept people's vagaries, or perhaps she had always been that way.

As she reached for the matches, Maydell said, "You'll have to wrap this in paper for me, Dolly. I want it wrapped in paper."

My mother set the box down and smiled. "Oh, Maydell," she said. "I can do better than that for you. You remember how you were saying you wished you had another feed sack for curtains? I've got an empty one, and I'll put your things in it."

The set of her bony shoulders and jerky movements of her hands told of extreme agitation rising in Maydell. My mother looked a little puzzled, but she continued in a happy voice.

"It won't take me but a minute to fetch it. I'll . . ."

"No," Maydell interjected. "Just forget it, Dolly. Just forget the whole thing." She turned and stumbled from the store. I stood up to tell my mother about the pencil, but several customers, along with Whitey, came in before I could say anything. I promised myself I would tell her later.

Such was the regard Whitey had for my mother; he had made an attempt to clean himself. I saw a white ring across the brown on the back of his neck, but his clothes were still dirty. We met a group of boys at the river, and I screamed, "Last one in is a rotten egg!" and jumped in with my clothes on. Of course, they all followed, Whitey along with them. We splashed and played for a good while before we stripped our garments and laid them out to dry.

We stayed there several hours before hunger got the best of us and made us decide to leave. I had my clothes on before Whitey did, and while I waited, I heard a, "Psst, psst," coming from the brush. I peered into the trees and shrubs and saw Scut motioning me to come over. I looked at Whitey and found he was still taking his time, talking and laughing with some other kid. Curiosity overcame my reluctance, and I walked into the shrubbery toward Scut.

He grabbed my arm and pulled me further into the woods where we wouldn't be seen. By then I was getting scared, but trying not to show it.

"I want to tell you something," Scut said, "but you've got to promise, cross your heart and hope to die, you won't tell nobody but your old man. And that includes your little pal, you understand?"

I nodded my head, and Scut repeated, "You promise you won't tell nobody but your old man?"

"I promise," I squeaked.

He pulled a soiled silk handkerchief out of his pocket. As I stared at it, he began talking, fast and hard as if he was daring me, threatening me, to say something cheeky to him.

"My sister found it," he said. I looked up and stared into his flat face with its brown, disfigured teeth.

"My mother's been making my sister get up early in the morning to fetch the cow and milk her. Ma and Pa argue and fight so bad, my sister don't mind leaving the house before sunrise so she don't have to hear it."

I nodded, confused; that didn't explain the handkerchief or the need for secrecy.

"Big Oscar would pass our shack on his way to work." Here Scut faltered for the first time. "She started going in there in the mornings, helping him light the fire and get ready. He began giving her pennies and pieces of meat that she would cook in the woods so Ma and Pa wouldn't find out about it. I found out, though, and I whipped her until she told me what was going on. My parents—they don't know nothing about it."

The bottom of my stomach tightened, but I continued to stare at Scut, spellbound.

"She promised she didn't do nothing but sit on his lap. I

113

tried to get her to stop, but she wouldn't. She liked Oscar and said she'd divvy with me if I didn't tell. She promised she wouldn't do nothing else but sit on his lap. But lately I think . . . ," he paused and refused to say more.

"What about the handkerchief?" I managed to ask, because I knew the handkerchief did not belong to Big Oscar.

"She found it there, by the body, the morning he was killed. She went in and found him like that. The handkerchief was on the floor beside him. Without thinking, she grabbed it and ran."

I swallowed hard and nodded.

"Look, squirt," Scut said. "I know you think I'm stupid. But even I know that somebody could have stolen that handkerchief and put it there to put the blame on somebody else, see? But your old man needs to know about it."

"I don't think you're stupid; I just think you're mean," I said, surprised by my own candor. However, a pleased look came over Scut's face. He didn't mind people thinking he was mean, just so long as they didn't think he was stupid. Nevertheless, he grabbed the front of my shirt and drew me to his face.

"The man who owns this handkerchief also owns the farm we live on, squirt, and if you breathe a word of this to anybody but Pop, I'm going to waylay you when you least expect it and whale the tar out of you with an ax handle. Got it?"

My head nodded like a jumping puppet on its own accord.

"I know people are jawing about him, saying he's too old to solve these murders, and that I rode you about him, just to see you get mad. But your old man has got more brains than anybody in Muskrat Hill," Scut conceded, stuffing the handkerchief into my pocket. "Now vamoose," he said, giving me a shove. "And don't forget what I'll do to you if you blab this to anyone else."

CHAPTER 11

I didn't know how to get rid of Whitey so I could have Pop to myself. If I told Whitey to go home, he wouldn't say much to me, but he might tell someone else that something was bothering me, and it would get around. I could be harassed for months for being a worrisome titty baby.

I sat all through supper trying to act normal, all through seven checker games until my mother told us to go to bed. As soon as I thought Whitey was in a deep enough sleep not to be awakened, I crept from the room, managing to dodge my mother's questioning glances and Clara Grace's frank inquiries.

Pop and Asa were sitting on a bench in front of the store. Hiding in the shadows, I waited for Asa to leave. Meanwhile, Pop strummed his guitar lightly as he softly sang the tune his father had taught him.

"You say you love me but only give me a corner of your heart," he sang, humming a little as he played. He stopped and put the guitar down. "Asa," he said. "We need to look at motive, means, and opportunity."

"What are you talking about?" Asa asked.

"As to motive," Pop began, "I can imagine all sorts of reasons why a man would kill a woman, but why would anyone want to kill a harmless butcher before daylight when it's still too early to have money in the till?"

Before Asa could answer, the blacksmith from across the street appeared, his big, burly frame casting a giant shadow as

115

he walked toward the store. He worked out of Mr. Petty's livery stable, and although he towered over Tull Petty by at least fifteen inches, every man who stepped inside knew immediately who was boss.

"Pop, Asa," he said when he reached them. "Something's been bothering me a while that may not have a darn thing to do with what's going on, but Tull told me to come over here and tell you about it."

"Well, spit it out, what is it?" Pop said.

"My little gal had a kitten we kept in the storeroom, hoping it would kill the mice and snakes later on. Here while back, I opened the door and found someone had stomped that cat's head in during the night."

"Was it locked?" Pop asked.

"I don't know. Half the time I forget to lock it."

"I'm sorry to hear that," Pop said, stroking his beard. "It might have been boys—they can be so mean to critters sometimes, cats in particular."

"I thought about that," the blacksmith agreed. "But I went to looking for my ball-peen hammer, and it was missing, too. I didn't say nothing at first because I thought maybe one of Tull's hands had borrowed it without asking. They will do it."

Pop and Asa exchanged glances, but said nothing.

"Tull thought you and Asa ought to know about it, Pop. I got to head on home. My old lady's petrified."

"Thanks," Pop said. "Much obliged for the information. Every little bit will eventually add up to the answer."

The blacksmith departed into the night, crossing paths with the mayor.

"Well, that's solved," Pop told Asa. "The woman had her head bashed in with a ball-peen hammer and somebody used Big Oscar's own knife on him.

"It also tells us that Bruno wouldn't have arrived in town and gone searching for a ball-peen hammer when he could just use something Horace had lying around."

The mayor approached, looking subdued and pensive. He absentmindedly fingered his gold watch.

"Pope," he said, "what's this nonsense going around town about you and Dolly performing some kind of perverted sex act in public?"

"Nothing," Pop growled. "A man can't even show his wife a pimple on his butt in Muskrat Hill without somebody taking it the wrong way."

"All right, Pope, that's fine," he said, turning and walking back down the street.

After the mayor was out of earshot, Pop turned to Asa. "What's bothering him? He only spoke two sentences, and they both made sense."

Asa shrugged and my mother came out of the store carrying two mugs.

"Pope," she asked, "do you and Asa want the last of the coffee out of the pot?"

"Yes, ma'am. Thank you," Pop said, taking a cup and handing another one to Asa.

"Thank you, Miss Dolly," Asa murmured.

My mother went back into the store while the men sat drinking their coffee.

"So, Asa," Pop said, "we have one missing dog, a dead cat, a missing hammer and a missing knife, two dead people, and a mayor who is acting strange."

"Don't forget a spinster who's acting odd, too."

"Clara Grace?" Pop said. "Clara Grace was as nutty as a squirrel's pantry before she came here, and she hasn't changed."

"No, Miss Maydell," Asa said. "Miss Dolly says Miss Maydell is not herself."

Pop grunted. "Maydell is fooling around with a married man,

117

that's all that's wrong with her."

"Who?" Asa asked. "The mayor?"

Pop burst out laughing, and I could see a grin on Asa's face in the pale light. He rose.

"I'll see you in the morning, Pop, and we can start again."

Pop wished Asa a good night and watched him walk down the street. When Asa had disappeared into the darkness, Pop turned in my direction.

"How long have you been standing there, Kit?" he asked.

I came out of hiding and went to him. "Not long," I said. "There's something important I need to tell you."

Pop paused for a minute, looking at the blackness around us, and said, "We best go inside."

"Yes, sir," I said and followed him in.

Clara Grace had gone to bed, but my mother was still up. "Kit, what are you doing out of bed?" she asked.

"Kit wants to tell us something," Pop answered for me.

Even though I believed Scut's threat with all my heart, I perceived my parents as being so much of a team that it didn't occur to me to insist on telling Pop alone. I don't think it would have occurred to Scut either.

Pop led us to the table in the back of the store, and we sat down. I pulled the handkerchief from my pocket, placing it on the table next to the coal oil lantern and in a hesitant voice, repeated what Scut said.

Pop sucked in his breath, and my mother said, "Oh, my. Oh, my." For a minute, Pop remained silent. Then he took a deep breath, moving in his seat. "Kit," he said, "I want you to repeat word for word everything Scut said to you and every look and gesture he gave. Word for word."

"Yes, sir, Pop," and I told the story again, this time trying to remember every detail. Pop and I went over and over it until we were both sure I hadn't forgotten anything.

My mother sat silent during that time, staring at the flickering shadows the lantern made. When we finished, she looked up with round sad eyes at Pop and in a voice full of misery, told him the worst of it.

"Pope, Scut's sister is ten years old."

It was as if she had struck him. He almost gasped, again taking a deep breath. He put his fingers on his eyebrow and muttered, "Oscar, Oscar."

"When I talked to Oscar's widow," my mother said in a voice catching with emotion, "she cried and confessed that she hadn't let Oscar, er," she paused to look at me. "She'd been making Oscar sleep in another room. I was going to tell you, but I haven't had time and then I forgot. I'm not excusing him, but . . ."

"Don't say any more, Dolly," Pop said. "Just don't say any more." He shut his eyes and leaned his head back. "I must look at this objectively," he murmured. He opened his eyes and said almost to himself, "We now have a drug-using prostitute and a child molester. Is it the work of some religious maniac out to purge the countryside of sin?" He turned in his seat and looked at the curtain separating the store from the living quarters, but almost immediately shook his head and turned back around.

"Thank you, Kit," he said, dismissing me. "You've told me something very important. I don't need to tell you to keep quiet about it."

"Yes, sir," I said, getting up from the table.

"Are you going to tell Asa that the mayor's handkerchief was found at the scene of the crime?" my mother asked.

"I don't know," Pop said. "Like Scut, I think it was planted there. Julius loves his possessions too much to leave them lying around, even if he had stomach enough to carry out such a heinous crime. This opens all kinds of possibilities. Who hates Julius enough to try to implicate him in a crime or was it just something thrown in to get us off the trail?"

My mother looked at me in sympathy. "Go to bed, son. Let Pop worry about it. You've done all you can do, and a good job you did, too."

Up until then, I don't think I realized how much I loved my parents.

The next day, Pop and Asa again had to question all the neighbors living around Scut's family so it wouldn't look like they were being singled out. Being careful not to let any undue curiosity show, they learned Scut's parents were so busy fighting with one another, they had little time for their children and most of the time, didn't know where they were or what they were doing. The older ones were supposed to work in the fields, but escaped every chance they got. The younger ones were slow and prone to mischievousness that evoked more pity and aggravation than anything else. They all knew Scut's sister was in charge of finding the cow and milking her, but other than that, nothing. She was a secretive little girl. It was almost a certainty her parents didn't know what she had been doing.

"How is it they have a milk cow?" Pop asked, for almost every child in Texas was raised on canned milk despite the number of cattle in the state. The answer was simple enough. The cow belonged to the mayor's wife, but she didn't like caring for it or milking. Nevertheless, she was partial to cream and butter. She let them have all the milk while she occasionally took the cream.

When Pop and Asa did find Scut's parents separately and questioned them, they were careful not to say a word about Scut or any of the children. Scut's parents merely confirmed their neighbors' opinion of them.

Pop had to question Scut's sister, but he was determined to keep it a secret. As Pop explained, if her parents found out what had been going on, it would be a mortal embarrassment to them in the community, and they would probably beat her. It called for a ruse with Clara Grace as a participant, and although she didn't mind interrogating my every move, she went along with what my parents asked without showing the least curiosity as to why.

My mother grimaced and let a mound of dirty dishes pile in the sink. Scut's parents usually came into the store on Saturdays, our busiest day. My mother stayed in the back, and when people asked where she was, Clara Grace made vague comments about "female problems," thereby promptly stopping all further inquiries. Just in case one of my mother's more persistent friends insisted on checking on her, my mother was forced to lie in bed all day, pretending to be sick. Pop roamed back and forth so he could be seen without having anyone really know where he was at any given time if they chose to recall it.

With my mother absent and Pop not working steady, I had to help Clara Grace. People expected the grocer to get what they wanted and set it on the counter until they were ready to pay, or in our case, most likely charge them until the crops came in. Clara Grace handled the payments while I fetched groceries and helped carry them to waiting wagons.

Despite never being fully accepted by the women of the community, almost every one of them who came in asked about my mother. Most were kind and solicitous, except of course, the Widow Crenshaw. Her husband had been dead ten years, and she still hadn't gotten around to moving his clothes out the chiffonier, but everyone else fell under her censure, my mother in particular. "Ailing?" she said with a frown. "She was fine yesterday."

"It came upon her all the sudden," Clara Grace answered in a tone that did not invite further questioning.

The widow sniffed and moved away. When she left, Pop came out from behind the curtain and watched her leave the store. "It will be all over town in ten minutes that your mother is in bed playing sick to get out of work," he said.

At noon, while Pop was eating dinner in the back with Asa, Melvin came in with his housekeeper, her big breasts flopping around the band of her skirt like two bags of heavy sand. Melvin practically pranced around her.

"I heard Dolly is ill," Melvin said in a voice vibrating with excitement, almost exaltation. "Nothing serious I hope?"

"No," Clara Grace answered. "She thought it would be better if she rested today." She looked past Melvin and saw Mr. Petty entering the store. "Kit," she said. "Watch the front. I have to take care of a necessity; I'll be back shortly." She left, hurrying to the back and past the curtain.

Mr. Petty walked toward me, throwing a sideways glance of disapproval at Melvin's housekeeper. "Where's your cousin?" he asked when he reached me.

"She'll be right back," I said. "She had to shake the dew from her lily."

Mr. Petty made a face. "I can't be in here long. I just came in to say howdy."

"I'll tell her," I promised. He walked away from me, but seemed hesitant to leave the store.

Netta Crenshaw returned, and with chin stuck out, her eyes searched the store. She saw me and gave a snort before heading in my direction. I wanted to turn and run, but I was the only family member left in the front of the store. The mayor came in, saw his brother, and ducked behind a shelf on another aisle.

The Widow Crenshaw reached me. "How is your mother? Where's your father?"

"Mama is still resting, and Pop is eating dinner, ma'am," I said, squirming a little and hoping she would leave.

She huffed, but stared at me. "You boys need to be watching those mustang grapes," she said so loud and querulous her voice could be heard all over the store. "They should be ripening soon. I'll pay three cents a pail, and not a penny more. And that pail better be full to the top, do you hear me?"

I nodded my head, my eyes darting around the room for an escape. She turned to follow my gaze and caught sight of Mr. Petty.

"What's Tull Petty doing in here in the middle of the day?" she demanded.

"He came in to say hello to Clara Grace," I said.

"He's just spinning his wagon wheels in the mud. Is that Melvin Foster's new housekeeper?"

Before I could answer, she marched away to accost Melvin and his housekeeper. Mr. Petty saw her coming in his direction and decided it was time to make an exit. He gave another glance at Melvin and his housekeeper on his way out, making a quick roll of his eyes and a grimace before leaving.

Melvin either didn't notice or didn't care. After wittily sidestepping Netta Crenshaw's questions, he walked around the store, talking in spurts to anyone who would take the time to stop and listen to him. His housekeeper followed him, her full lips still and silent, her eyes and hair almost hidden beneath a calico sunbonnet. Melvin did not bother to introduce her, but was keenly and gloatingly aware of the curious glances she received.

Scut's mother and father had come in during Netta's harangue at me. Oddly enough, considering the features of the rest of the family, Scut's father was a nice-looking man. Taller than average, he had a straight nose and a firm chin. Scut's mother, however, was a reedy woman with a stoop and a narrow, thin mouth. Scut's sister was with her, along with various younger brothers who wore blank expressions on their faces and had mouths that sagged open. Scut's sister was small for her age with long dirty blonde hair, the same narrow face as her mother, but her eyes duplicated Scut's look of wary intelligence.

Scut's father joined into conversation with some of the men, while his mother and sister walked to the counter. Clara Grace, having returned, eyed them coolly as she did everyone. "Mrs. Tabor," she said. "Dolly has been feeling poorly, and I haven't had time to wash the dishes. The store has been so busy. I'll pay a nickel if your little girl will go to the back and wash our dishes."

Mrs. Tabor brightened in surprise and greed. Clara Grace looked her in the eye and spoke without a qualm. "But she has to keep her mouth shut about it," she said, "because I don't want women in this town gossiping that I'm so lazy I can't keep the dishes washed."

She agreed to it immediately. Clara Grace pressed a nickel in the mother's hand and told the girl, "Kit will show you the way."

I led her to the back and the dishes. When I left to man my post at the curtain to make sure no one entered, she was filling the sink from a kettle of hot water on the stove.

Loitering at the rear of the store, I hoped no one would decide to call out for me to run an errand. Our last clerk, a lover of dime novels, had polished his glasses, donned fresh cowboy duds, strapped on a shiny new pistol, and left. He had found Muskrat Hill too tame and went looking for excitement in the wild and woolly West. Since then, until Pop could hire someone, to have help with the heaving and loading, he traded tobacco and goods with the cowboys who hung around the store front looking for jobs. All of them preferred work on the back of a horse, but didn't mind helping Pop out as long as it wasn't considered permanent. Even Asa toted sacks for customers when the need arose and he was around. I was still too little to do much toting, but it amazed me the tasks grown-ups could find for dawdling boys to do. I half expected the Widow Crenshaw to return with a list of chores.

A group of men sat at the back table, watching the front of the store where Mr. Tabor, Scut's father, and his brothers stood. One of them spit into a nearby spittoon and, indicting Scut's slow-witted brothers with his head, said, "That's what happens when generations of cousins intermarry."

Melvin happened to be nearby, and he snorted. "Cousins! More like brother and sister. Well, half-brother and half-sister anyway."

The old man who spoke looked up and said, "Melvin, you don't know what you are talking about."

"I certainly do," Melvin said. "His father sneaked over the fence to see his cousin's wife enough times. I know very well which cousin sired who."

The old man grunted and shook his head, while I wondered if there was any gossip anywhere in Muskrat Hill that Melvin didn't know about. It made me kind of sick to think about Scut's parents. My parents were old, but at least they weren't brother and sister.

After parading up and down the aisles of the store a few more times, Melvin bought a few stock items and left, an arrogant smile on his face when he shut the door behind him and his housekeeper. Several men made rude comments and were promptly shushed by their wives.

In the back, Pop interrogated Scut's sister while my mother stood nearby, helping her with the dishes. Pop said later the girl wanted to escape, but since she was up to her elbows in soapy water wearing my mother's apron, she couldn't really make a quick getaway.

He did not question her about her relationship with Big Oscar—that was a dead horse best forgotten. But he did ask her what she had seen that morning, if she ever felt they were being watched, if she ever saw even so much as a shadow when entering the slaughterhouse. The door had been locked the first time she went on the morning of the murder. When she returned later, the door was unlocked. All she saw was Big Oscar and the silk handkerchief lying on the floor next to his protruding eyes; she knew of nothing else except that she wanted the handkerchief back.

Pop wouldn't let her have it, so my mother gave her a jacket of Clara Grace's that had become too small. It would not excite comment; clothes were passed around in Muskrat Hill until they became so worn they landed in a rag pile. She seemed satisfied—a jacket she could wear in the open was better than a silk handkerchief she had to hide.

CHAPTER 12

The next morning, Pop rummaged through a display case, calling to my mother, "Dolly! Did you sell one of those folding knives I ordered from Louisiana?"

"No, maybe Clara Grace did. Did you see one on yesterday's receipts?"

When he answered in the negative, she offered to ask Clara Grace about it.

"Don't bother," Pop said. "She probably got it out to show someone and forgot to put it back, and somebody got off with it." He shook his head. "She chases off the regulars being so persnickety and then lets stuff walk out of here without noticing it."

My mother furrowed her brows. "Clara Grace and Kit said almost everyone living around Muskrat Hill was in here yesterday, Pope. Even Mr. Petty and Mr. Hutchins stopped by. She wanted to stop and explain to Ephraim about the saints, but she didn't have time. And I think she ran and hid from Mr. Petty. It was hard for her to keep up with everything in any case."

"Oh, forget it. It was probably one of those dim-witted little brothers of that wretched girl," Pop grumbled. "That's trash for you. Don't have enough sense to get out of the rain, but can swipe something faster than I can spit hot pudding out of my mouth."

I remembered Miss Maydell. Had I dreamed the incident of

the pencil? Miss Maydell wasn't trash. And Scut was trash, but he had enough intelligence and gumption to disapprove of his sister's activities and bring in an important piece of evidence. My brain was all mixed up, and I decided to keep quiet about Miss Maydell in case I was wrong about what happened. Surely a nice spinster like Miss Maydell wouldn't steal anything so trifling.

Pop straightened up from the counter. "I've got to have a talk with Tull Petty, and I don't want to," he muttered, but he didn't elaborate, and I don't think my mother heard him.

As we went out the door, Pop got caught by an old bachelor who lived several miles from town on a small ranch. He must have shaved sometimes, because I never saw him with a full beard, but I never saw him clean-shaven either. Even when he came into the store expressly to doff his disreputable hat to Clara Grace and say, "howdy, ma'am," with one gotch-eye leering upward at her. But he liked kids, so I liked him, too.

"I'm telling you, Pope," he was saying. "Them hogs is missing."

Pop sighed. Folks in Muskrat Hill let hogs run loose in the woods to fend for themselves in the summer. Come fall, there would be a community-wide roundup and hog killing time. For somebody to complain they were missing didn't make a lot of sense.

"I've been a-keeping my eye on them," the old rancher explained. "There's a big old sow—I done give her my notch, two on top, one on the bottom of the left ear, that's my special notch."

"Everybody knows that," Pop said. "They'll turn up." He began to walk toward the stable.

"But they's missing, Pope. I'm trying to tell you. I been watching them on and off for weeks, and all the sudden like, they's disappeared," he said, following Pop and me to the stable.

"Look," Pop said. "I'll put the word out and keep my eye out for them, but I've got to work on this murder case before I can start chasing down stray hogs."

"Oh, I knows that," the rancher said. "You're too old to be chasing down hogs, anyways, Pope. I just be telling you so you can keep an eye and an ear open about them."

"Thanks for the vote of confidence," Pop said, getting into his buggy.

"Another dead end," Pop moaned as we went on our way to question field hands, forgetting all about stolen pocket knives and missing hogs.

"At least we know now why Oscar was down there so early," Asa said.

"Yes, and we know it is someone who is keeping a close watch on the comings and goings of this town," Pop said.

"Did Dolly scold the girl?" Asa asked.

"No. You know Dolly," Pop answered. "She just gave her a hug and told her that right now she needed to be preparing for her future. If she wanted to be married, she should learn to keep house and be a pleasant person to live with. If she wanted to teach school, she should study hard. It bounced off of her. All she was concerned about was the jacket Dolly gave her."

Whitey hadn't shown up that morning. Sometimes I didn't see him for days, and then he would appear, looking thinner, paler, and more pinched than ever. Since it was just me, Pop wanted to give Smokey a rest and use Gastor to pull the buggy.

Mr. Petty endeavored to stay on my good side so he could pump me for information about Clara Grace. Therefore, he threw a little hay in the back of the buggy so I wouldn't be quite so uncomfortable bouncing around with feedbags, ropes, and various things Pop thought necessary for any trip. Adults didn't think too much about the comfort of children back then, and I didn't think about it either. Just being with Pop and Asa on an excursion was enough for me. I took the scenery around us for granted—the masses of serene, leafy trees on one side of the road and the rolling hills covered in rows of cotton on the other side meant little to me then. I was on the lookout for birds and rabbits and foxes.

While I sat hoping to see a hawk grab a snake and fly off with it, Asa and Pop debated whether or not to reveal to the mayor that his handkerchief had been found next to Oscar's mutilated body.

"I don't think it would do any good at this point," Pop said. "He would make hot denials, and then he would try to run to earth whoever found the handkerchief. We have to protect that little girl and her family."

Going with Pop in his detective work forced me to look at him in a new way. He was an old man, yes, but a man whose aged, experienced eyes could sweep a room and remember years later where every window and door were situated. He had a sixth sense that told him when someone was nearing us, and he unconsciously never sat with his back to a door or window if he could help it. The pioneer spirit and ranger grit never died in him.

When he interviewed the field workers, I discovered yet another side to Pop.

Pop had Asa stop the buggy on a small rise overlooking a cotton field blanketed with verdant lush leaves, the bolls just beginning to show white. Laborers dotted the fields, clutching long handles attached to wickedly heavy hoes. The men wore baggy cotton pants while the women dressed in long, faded calico skirts. Everyone wore long-sleeved cotton shirts, sweated down and sticking to their glistening black skins. They sang as they worked, their rich voices sounding strange and wonderful to my ears. In front, nearest the road, a large man with skin the color of velvety chocolate would sing a verse, and then the others would repeat it. As I watched, I learned he not only led the singing, he set the steady, even pace for the rest of the workers—the swings of the hoes were as graceful as their singing was harmonious.

"Asa," Pop said. "You better get out here and wait. I think we'd have better luck if a marshal wasn't right there with us."

"You mean because they wouldn't want to talk to an Indian?" Asa asked.

"No," Pop answered. "I mean you arrested one of them for stealing chickens on Christmas Day, and he's still mad about it. He thinks you ought to have overlooked a man stealing a Christmas chicken."

Asa scoffed at this. "From a widow with five children?" he grumbled. "But all right, I'll stay here." He handed Pop the reins and got out. As soon as Asa had alighted, I scrambled over the seat so I could sit by Pop.

He snapped the reins, and we lurched forward, heading downhill. He pulled the buggy to a halt in front of the row the big chocolate-skinned man was working. Seeing Pop wanted to speak to him, he stopped chopping cotton and walked toward us. The others ceased their singing, but continued to work, for show anyway. The longer the buggy sat there, the longer the intervals between the strokes of the hoes.

"Mr. Pope, how you be?" the big man said with a grin when he reached the wagon. "Is this here your young'un?"

"Yes, sir, this is my boy, Kit," Pop replied. "How are you, Moses?"

"Tolerable, Mr. Pope, tolerable," he replied with a laugh.

While Pop talked to Moses about the murders, I let my eyes wander back to the workers. In one of the rows of tall cotton plants, a man came up behind a woman who had her back turned to him. Wrapping long powerful arms around her, his hands grasped her breasts and squeezed. Moving his hands down, he lifted her skirt, pulling it over her back. His pants went down without a fumble.

Naturally, I had seen animals copulate, but had never witnessed humans doing it. As the man behind her thrust repeatedly with his head thrown back in ecstasy, I saw her look in our direction from under heavy lids as her body rocked back and forth.

I yanked my head back to Pop. Moses was saying, "No, sir, Mr. Pope, we hadn't heard a thing. Hadn't seen nothing, hadn't heard nothing."

Pop glanced at the two field hands humping in unrestrained lust, but he didn't say anything about it or even flicker an eyelid. Moses, however, began yelling when he caught sight of them.

"Hey now, yonder! Quit that!" He turned back to Pop. "Don't pay them no mind, Mr. Pope. That man, he been looking at that woman's backside for three hours now and can't help hisself."

Pop made a motion with his hand that it didn't matter. The lovers stopped almost as fast as they had started. While pulling down her skirt, the woman looked again at Pop slyly from the corners of her eyes—as if she wanted to make sure he had been watching. I looked from her to Pop, realizing she was trying to convey something to him. With a child's simplicity, I clearly understood she had wanted Pop to see her, had wanted him to know the same thing was available to him. But Pop's face remained unreadable, although I instinctively knew he was as aware of her as I was.

"Well, Moses," Pop said. "If you hear or see anything, I'd be much obliged if you'd get word to me."

"Sure thing, Mr. Pope," Moses said, standing back from the buggy. Pop turned the buggy around, and Moses gave the mule a smart slap in farewell, smiling and saying "goodbye" to Pop and me.

We had only gone a little way when his deep voice floated

back to us. "What's the matter with you, niggers?" he said. "You know white folks don't hold with those kind of goings-on."

Someone made a comment we couldn't hear, and the other workers burst into laughter. In a moment, they began to sing again.

I looked at Pop that day in a way I had never seen him before. I had never realized what a handsome man he was. He wore nice, clean, well-cut clothes that fitted him perfectly. Underneath an expensive hat, his hair and beard were washed and neatly trimmed. He didn't use chewing tobacco like so many men, so his mouth was free from brown spittle. He was in no way flashy, but because he exuded confidence, courage, and an inner light that very few men had, he made a strikingly fine-looking gentleman. I saw how attractive he could be to women, and also how much a quarter from him would mean to a poor woman working in the cotton fields. And I realized it wasn't just the Negro woman in the field. Other women had undoubtedly behaved in a similar manner in front of Pop, maybe not so blatantly but similarly nevertheless.

It struck terror in my soul, to think that my father might betray our tight family with someone else. I didn't know what to say to ask for reassurance. Looking at Pop, I spoke with a timid heart. "Mama would like their singing."

Pop looked down, his eyes scanning my face, and he read my mind. He put his arm around me and hugged me. "Yes, she would, son," he said. "Yes, she would." And I knew then I had nothing to fear.

My mood lightened, and I happily got into the back of the buggy when we reached Asa so he could get back in. Pop and Asa had only just begun to discuss the case again when we came across a fallen dead tree in the road. Pop started to let out a curse, but paused, scanning our surroundings with narrowed eyes instead. We got down from the buggy, and Asa said we'd better move the log instead of trying to go around it. Pop agreed, and I offered to help Asa unhitch the buggy. When we were almost done, I looked around for Pop.

He stood next to the base of the toppled tree, staring at it and into the woodlands beyond. I walked to him.

"What is it, Pop?" I asked.

He looked down at me and pointed to the earth around the rotted tree roots. "Somebody stood here and pushed it over," he said. "You can see where the ground is packed down and heavily indented. They tried to brush their footprints over, but turn around and look at the grass going back into the woods."

I rotated and stared, but didn't understand what I was supposed to be looking for.

"See that light streak going through the grass?" Pop said. "That means a man walked through there recently."

"You mean somebody did it on purpose, Pop?"

He nodded. "Just to devil us, I imagine. It might be someone Asa arrested for some minor incidence here while back who thinks he's getting even."

He continued to stare at the tracks. "If I was rangering and looking for a man," he muttered. "I'd first go up and down this road to see if he backtracked out before I'd go crashing into those woods." He glanced at the sun, which was already heading for its bed, and shook his head. "No use trying now; it's probably nothing but somebody trying to be aggravating."

We could hear Gastor neighing and stomping the ground belligerently, so we returned to Asa.

"He's balking, Pop," Asa said. "He didn't want to back up. Can you hold his ear while I tie the rope around the log?"

Before Pop could reach him, Gastor kicked a hind leg, landing a glancing blow on Asa's wrist.

Asa didn't let out an oath, but grasped his hand in pain. Pop grabbed the skin around Gastor's neck with one hand and gave his ear a jerk and twist with the other. "Asa, let Kit do it," he said. "Just tell him what needs to be done. And Kit, stay away from those hind legs."

"Yes, sir," I said, and hastened to the mule, being especially leery of his hoofs.

This time, Pop cursed when Gastor lived up to his name, and the air became rank with fumes. Asa and I caught the first whiff, but the wind blew it in Pop's face as he was forced to stand in one place, holding onto Gastor's neck and ear.

"Loop the traces through here, will you, Kit?" Asa said, trying not to breathe deeply. I seized the traces and following Asa's instructions, tied the rope to them. Pop had taught me a dozen ways to tie knots, so I knew how to do that. Pop grumbled and Asa grunted, but to me it was just another adventure—at that age, maybe even better than watching a woman bending over to be humped.

"Gastor," Pop said. "If I'm ever able to catch a deep breath, I'm going to give you a cussing you'll never forget."

Nauseous fumes notwithstanding, stout Gastor soon had the log out of the roadway, and we were on our way once again.

Besides pestering Pop and Asa to solve the killings, the inhabitants of Muskrat Hill went about their daily routines as usual. Since it was reasoned that the murders were done either at night or in the early morning hours, we children were free to roam anywhere in broad daylight.

The day after questioning the field hands, Asa left to serve subpoenas. Pop stayed busy checking out leads. It was always a case of someone hearing a rumor, Pop finding out it was a false lead, and later, being unable to confirm where it had started.

"I swear," Pop said. "Sometimes I think someone is spreading these stories just to keep me running around in circles."

Whitey came back into town after being gone several days. He never offered any explanations, and I never asked. It didn't occur to me to seek him out at his house—he had never indicated in any way he wanted me to.

I had finished my chores, and before my mother and Clara Grace could think of something else I needed to do, I asked permission to go outside with Whitey. We shot out the door and began walking down the street. A group of girls were playing hopscotch on the other side, so we crossed the road to purposely ignore them while we walked by. I started to pick up a rock to chunk at one of them to get their attention, but I wanted to brag to Whitey about my adventures with Pop. When I finished with that story, I told him a little bit about who had come in the store Saturday.

"Let's go check the grapes now, Kit," Whitey said when I repeated Netta Crenshaw's demands.

"We might as well," I said. "Because if we don't, she'll complain to my mother about it."

Our favorite place to pick grapes was an abandoned farmhouse sitting on property owned by the mayor. The ruined shack, consisting of crumbling rock and old mortar, rested at the bottom of a hill in a little clearing. Near it, tangled grapevines as big as my arm hung down from trees and ran along the ground. We topped the hill, looking downward. The windows and doors were missing, and half of one wall was gone, and at first, we didn't see anything but green grapes.

"Kit!" Whitey said. "Lookee yonder, there's something hanging from the doorframe."

We ran across the tall grass, trying to avoid the web of vines. Stopping, we peered from a distance into the abandoned house. Grass was growing inside its disintegrating walls, but a string hung from the doorframe and tied to the bottom of it, a shiny new knife flickered in the bright sunlight. Hypnotized, we began to walk toward the glittering dream of every little boy. I stopped and put my hand on Whitey's arm—it was the knife from the store.

"Wait a minute," I said. "Something's not right. I think that's the knife stolen from the store. And why would anybody hang a brand-new knife up there like that anyway?"

"Who cares?" Whitey said. "Finders keepers. Let's get it."

He took a step forward, but again I stopped him and pulled him back. "No," I said. "We better get Pop first."

Whitey stuck out his lip and stared at me mulishly. He argued with me, and I began to doubt my instinct. I hesitated. What would Pop do? Pop wasn't afraid of anything, and I wanted to be like him more than anything in the world and have him proud of me.

My nostrils became aware of a putrid odor emanating from inside the shack. The wafting stench cleared my brain. "Whitey," I said, "there's something dead in there."

We took a few steps closer. Below the knife was a brown hump.

"Look at the size of that hog," Whitey said.

"He's sure enough dead, though," I replied.

The bloated hog lay inert, eyes glassy and staring. On its side, someone had carved POPE in big letters.

Whitey jumped back, the freckles on his face popping out on his whitened skin. "Let's get out of here!" he yelled, and scrambling through the grapevines, we ran all the way back to Muskrat Hill.

CHAPTER 13

We arrived at the store panting. Pop was behind the counter, listening to Harmonica John. We paused, knowing we weren't supposed to interrupt grown-ups while they were in conversation. We felt what we had to say was important, but before I got the chance to butt in, my mother walked up and pointed to a crate next to the shelf.

"Kit, would you and Whitey stack those cans of peaches on the shelf for me, please," she said. "And put the crate in the storeroom when you are finished."

I looked at Pop. "But . . ." I started, but stopped. "Yes, ma'am," I said, giving in, and leaned down to remove the cans. Whitey and I shoved the peaches on the shelf as fast as we could, keeping our eyes on Pop.

He moved to a stool behind the shorter counter and gave a little groan as he sat down.

"The rheu-ma-tis getting to you, Pop?" John asked as he stood on the other side of the counter.

Pop nodded and took the lid off a jar labeled "Liver Treatment" in florid Victorian style that contained nothing more than a laxative concoction. Using a spoon, he measured out amounts into little pieces of paper and wrapped them. "It gets to everybody sooner or later, John," he said.

John nodded. "Sometimes a man just don't want to get out of bed of a morning."

Pop nodded sympathetically. He and my mother were used to

138

being sounding boards for everybody's problems.

"Sometimes, Pop, I don't think life is worth living. That woman of mine, she just gets skinnier and meaner every day. I told her I like me a big fat woman, and she just clamp her mouth shut tight."

"Women will do what they want; that is true," Pop commiserated.

"That's right. That's right," John said. "And grandkids. I told my old woman, I said, we raised our children, how come we have to raise theirs, too? I'm so tired, Pop. Sometimes I'm so tired; I just want to quit breathing."

"I feel that way myself many times, John," Pop said, nodding and continuing to fold his little packets of powder.

"Say, did somebody have a big barbeque?" John asked, changing the subject. "I smelled hog meat cooking for miles. Almost smelled like they was burning them."

Whitey and I paused, staring at one another.

Pop's hand stopped in midair. "That's odd. Somebody was in here complaining about missing some hogs."

I picked up the empty crate, staring at Pop. Whitey followed me as I went behind the counter. I opened the door to the storeroom, placing the crate inside, all the while listening as Pop continued.

"Which direction did the smoke come from?"

"South. South of my place," John replied.

We walked around the counter and stood behind John. Before I could say anything about the hog, the door opened and the mayor entered. Seeing him, John said, "Goodbye, Pop," nodded to the mayor, and left. The mayor ignored us and immediately began in on Pop.

"What's his hurry?" the mayor demanded, taking a stool and sitting down across the counter from Pop. He gave the constipation powders a distracted glance.

139

"He figures Muskrat Hill isn't too safe a place for him to spend time in," Pop replied.

"Pope," the mayor began, "I'm telling you . . ."

Pop interrupted him. "Julius, hold off a minute." He looked at us. "What is it, boys?"

"Pop, you know where me and Whitey sometimes go to pick mustang grapes?" I began, barely able to contain my excitement. "Over there by that old abandoned shack?"

"That's my place," the mayor said.

Pop nodded. "Slow down, boy, take a breath."

I obediently took a deep breath. Wetting my lips, I looked at the mayor and back to Pop. "Whitey and I went out there, and we saw a knife, Pop. I think it's the one missing from the store. It was just hanging from a string in the doorway."

"I saw it first!" Whitey blurted.

"You didn't try to get it, did you?" Pop asked.

"No, sir," I said with Whitey agreeing. "And something else, Pop. There was a dead hog in there. A dead hog with your name carved on it."

"My name carved on it?"

"Yes, sir. It had P-O-P-E carved on its side."

Pop rose. "I better see what this is all about."

"Can we go, too, Pop?" I begged.

"No, not this time."

"Pope," the mayor interjected. "These boys are probably just imagining the whole thing."

"No, sir," I said adamantly. "We are not."

"Watch your mouth when you are addressing your elders," Pop admonished automatically. He turned to the mayor. "My boy is not a liar, Julius, and he's not stupid. If he said there was a knife dangling from a doorway, and a dead hog inside, there was."

Blood drained from the mayor's face, making him look ill

and nervous. He waved aside Pop's statement, but said nothing.

Pop turned to us. "Boys, you know we have a murderer on the loose."

We nodded and he continued. "And you know that it is entirely possible somebody saw you and put the knife there to lure you into that shack, don't you?"

We didn't know it until then, but we nodded.

"For right now, until I can check this out, keep your mouths shut about it. *Comprendre?*"

"Yes, sir," I said, nodding, along with Whitey.

"Later, I'll want you and Whitey to go around town warning your friends to stay out of deserted places."

"Pope!" the mayor said.

Pop raised his hand to halt the mayor and continued speaking to us. "When I get back, you'll have to tell them if they see something that looks too good to be true, leave it alone. And that Marshal Asa and I said to stay away from abandoned buildings or anywhere else somebody might be hiding. But don't breathe a word of this until I get back, after I've seen what's going on."

Whitey and I nodded solemnly.

"Now run along," Pop said. "No, wait a minute. Take these powders to the Widow Crenshaw." With skilled, wrinkled fingers, he wrapped the small packets up in a larger piece of brown paper, handing the package to me.

"Tell her I said to take one a day; if she takes any more than that, she'll be on the shitter for a week. No, don't tell her that. Your mother will get upset. Just tell her not to take more than one a day, or she will have disastrous results."

"Yes, sir, Pop," I said.

"Hold on," he said, walking to the counter where he kept the candy. He took a bag and filled it with peppermints, handing it to me.

"Take this and stay out of trouble until I get back. And be home before dark."

"Thanks, Pop!" I said. "We will."

"Thanks, Captain Robertson!" Whitey said.

"Pope, do you think that was wise?" we heard the mayor say as we walked to the door. "Scaring children like that? You're blowing a minor incident way out of proportion."

"Julius, I don't care if it's minor or not. If I can make them be aware and watch out, maybe I can prevent a tragedy." He raised his voice and hollered. "Dolly! I have to be gone for a little while. Can you watch the store?"

"Yes, Pope," she called from the back. "Go ahead; I'll be up there shortly."

After we left, we spied a group of boys loitering down the street. Whitey whispered, "Hide the candy until after we go to the widow's house."

I nodded and stuffed the bag into my pocket, hoping it wouldn't make too much of a bulge. I carried the package containing the powders nonchalantly under my arm, concealed enough to make the other boys wonder what it was, and at the same time, not look as if I was trying to hide something.

Our ruse worked. When we passed them, they pumped us as to what we were carrying. We were able to satisfy their curiosity, and at the same time, hide our true treasure. Once past their prying eyes, we scooted over to the widow's as fast as we could.

We halted in front of her small board and batten house, breathing heavily, but happy. The widow had a short, black wrought-iron fence around her yard, and we could see her throwing mash to her chickens in the back.

"Here Emily, here Henrietta," she twittered, "come to mother."

I pushed open the gate and called, "Mizz Crenshaw!"

She turned with a start. "What is it? What do you boys want?"

she demanded. Even feeding the chickens she dressed from neck to shoes in a dark bombazine dress edged in lace so aged it looked like it had been stained in tea.

We drew closer, and I handed her the package. "Pop sent me with the liver powders you wanted. He said not to take more than one a day."

She took the package containing the powders, her small mouth making a frown. "I wanted Pope to bring them to me personally," she grumbled. "I don't think he should have trusted my medicine to two scruffy little boys."

"He's busy at the store right now," I said, trying to be polite.

She peered down her nose at me. "Did you check on those grapes?"

I exchanged glances with Whitey. "Yes, ma'am. They're not ripe yet."

She nodded, looking me up and down. "Humph," she said. "I guess you look like Pope well enough."

She sounded like this disappointed her for some reason, but I didn't want to take the time to find out why.

"Yes, ma'am," I said. "We have to be going. And remember, Pop said to only take one a day." With that, Whitey and I shot out of the fence like two jackrabbits on the run laughing and giggling.

We found a deserted barn and scrambled to the hayloft. Kneeling down, I pulled the bag of candy out in anticipation. But when I opened it and looked inside, something made me pause. As I sat staring at the peppermints, I thought about Pop walking amongst those ankle-grabbing grapevines. The dead hog had been a malevolent and evil sign. I knew Pop had given us the candy to keep us out of possible danger. Yet at the same time, it didn't feel right to leave him alone out there.

What would Pop do if he was a little boy in this situation, I asked myself. I didn't know what Pop would have done, but I knew what my mother would want me to do.

"Kit! What's the matter? Come on, let's eat!" Whitey said impatiently.

"I don't feel much like candy after all, Whitey." I gulped and handed the bag to him. "You take it. You can have my share." I stood up.

Whitey stared at me. "You're going to check on Pop, aren't you?"

I nodded. "Yeah, but don't follow me. There's no sense in both of us disobeying and getting into trouble."

Whitey nodded, his eyes drawn again to the candy. My parents tried to restrict my appetite for sweets, but Whitey almost never got any, and then it was only one little piece at a time.

"Go ahead, Whitey," I said, heading for the ladder. "Pop wanted you to have it."

I avoided town, creeping back to the hilltop where I could look down upon the shack, unconsciously imitating the way I thought an Indian would sneak up on someone. I could see Pop's horse, Smokey, and the buggy. With the help of a cane he disliked using in town, Pop was making his way to the front of the shack.

The knife had disappeared. I wanted to stand up and yell that it had so been there, but I remained crouched. Pop didn't act surprised or disgusted not to find the knife; instead, his eyes searched the doorframe. He stood back and raised the cane. With one quick motion, he took a swipe at something I couldn't see, and in the next instance, a ball-like object shot across his face, causing my muscles to jerk in fright. I took a deep breath and stared. Pop found it and picked it up; it looked like a round rock with sharp sticks tied around it in sinew so they protruded from it. Pop tossed it aside and carefully entered the house.

I moved as silently as possible so I could keep him in view

through the opening of the tumbled-down wall. Pop walked slowly around the inside of the shack, waving the cane to and fro in front of him, but nothing happened. Standing still, his eyes swept across the building, looking at everything in it intently. He stared for a long time at the rafters, afterwards searching the walls and ground. Stopping, he put his foot down on something, and I heard a sharp pop, almost like the crack of a whip. Fifteen hog heads and twice that many testicles fell from the rafters in one swoop, dangling from rawhide, tongues protruding from between wicked tusks. I jumped, almost wetting my pants, but Pop barely flinched. He made his way through those rotting, stinking heads with their unseeing eyes and stepped outside once again.

I wanted to run to him, but my body remained rooted to the hilltop. I wasn't as smart as Pop and knew I could trip off any kind of booby trap down there. All I could do was to watch and hope nothing happened to him.

He made his way around the shack, carefully surveying where he was going, looking down and around. He paused and again swung at the ground with his cane. This time an arrow flew from a bush, hitting the shack wall and bouncing harmlessly to the ground. Pop walked to the bush the arrow came from, pushing the branches aside with his cane. I couldn't see what he saw, except that there was no one there, and I realized it was not a person, but another rigged trap. Pop left the bush and kept walking in short, careful steps. It didn't occur to me to cry out, "Pop, get away from there and let's go home!" but I was terrified all the same.

I was so scared, I couldn't move. I didn't dare say anything for fear of causing him to whirl around and get hit by something. As I watched dry mouthed, Pop found a trail behind the house that led closer to the trees, and he began to follow it. Near the trees, he stepped on a large flat rock and an explosion went off that sounded like a rifle shot. Pop jumped to one side, and when he did, he fell into a hole, his hands grabbing at a nearby grapevine as he slid into its depths.

"Pop!" I stood up and screamed as he disappeared. "Pop! Are you all right?" I tried to see in the hole, but I was too far away.

I couldn't hear a response if there was one, so I started scrambling down the hill. I followed the wagon trail and the path Pop made without thinking; it was only later I realized I had done the right thing.

Reaching the pit he had fallen into, I heard sounds that made my blood freeze. Looking down, I gasped. Pop dangled over the hole, hanging onto the grapevine with both hands. He looked up at me. "Kit!" he cried in horror. "What are you doing here?"

I didn't answer because I was staring at what was beneath him as he hung with only a grapevine between them and him. Someone had made a pit of sharp, pointed, slender posts and had thrown in rattlesnakes that were twisting and hissing, rattling their tails angrily. To fall meant agonizing death. "Pop!" I said. For some reason, I thought about Harmonica John and the conversation of earlier in the day. "Don't give up, Pop!" I began to cry.

"Oh God, you're already here in this death trap, boy," Pop moaned. He paused and said, "Now listen to me, Kit. Listen to me carefully. Follow the trail back to Smokey and the buggy. Don't step off of it. Unhitch Smokey and grab the rope out of the buggy. Did you see the way I came? Can you follow my footsteps in the grass and the faint trail?"

"Yes, Pop!"

"Then bring Smokey and the rope to me, but don't step away from that trail."

"Yes, Pop," I said, jumping up.

"Watch your step, but keep talking to me, son," he said, his voice becoming hoarse. "Let me know you're all right."

I ran back to the horse and buggy, all the while screaming, "I'm okay, Pop, I'm okay." My fingers fumbled with Smokey and the buggy, causing me to sob in frustration. I kept at it until I got the horse unhitched and could grab the rope. I continued to call out to Pop while I led the horse, assuring him every time he asked that I was following his trail.

"I'm here, Pop," I said when I reached him, blubbering again when I saw what an effort it was for him to hang on.

"Hush, now," Pop said. "Listen to me; take the rope and tie three stout knots in one end about a foot apart. You remember how I taught you. Throw the knots down to me and tie the other end to Smokey, just like you did with Gastor. You hear me?"

"Yes, sir," I cried, trying to find the end of the rope and tie the knots.

"Hurry, Kit," Pop urged. "I can't hold on much longer. This grapevine may not hold."

I nodded, throwing the knotted rope down to him. I ran, threading and tying the traces just as Asa had instructed, thanking God Mr. Petty had put Smokey on the buggy. There was no way Gastor would have gotten close to those rattlers, but Smokey stood like a statue while I groped with the rope.

"I got it, Pop!" I cried.

"All right," Pop said, breathing heavily. He grasped the rope and held on to it and the vine. "Walk him forward slowly, boy."

I ran back to the horse and urged him onward. He seemed to know the fix we were in and what he was supposed to do. The rope moved by inches, and gradually Pop came with it. As soon as I could, I raced to help him, pulling and tugging with all my might.

"Pop," I cried when he was out. Clutching him as he lay on the ground, I began to weep.

"You did good, boy," Pop said, patting me. But his voice sounded weak, and he was fighting for breath. Nevertheless, he took out his pistol, rolled over, and fired four shots into the pit, killing the rattlers. He collapsed again on the ground beside me.

We lay there for some time, both of us too scared and exhausted to move. Pop shut his eyes. When he opened them, he said, "Kit, get on Smokey. I'm going to lead him back to the buggy, following the same trail. You sit there and be still. Let me handle him, and don't let anything spook you."

"Yes, sir," I nodded and got on the horse.

Pop, still holding the cane, led Smokey back to the buggy, taking every step with care. I watched the ground as closely as Pop did, but we passed again without incident. Once at the buggy, I slid off, and Pop, taking a deep breath of relief, continued his instructions.

"I want you to sneak back to town, Kit, and bring me a shovel. Don't let anybody see you. You hear me? Don't say anything, and try not to let anyone see you. Slip into the storeroom and get a shovel. If your mother or Clara Grace catches you, think up a lie. Tell them I said you and Whitey could use it to dig up buried treasure. Anything, but do not tell anyone where I'm at, you hear me?"

"Yes, sir, I won't tell."

"Leave it at the top of the hill. Don't come back down here."

"But, Pop . . ."

"No buts! Do as I say. Leave the shovel and go back home. Tell your mother that I said I was coming home late, and you don't know where I'm at. Do you understand, son? I don't want anyone to know about this."

I nodded, loathe to leave him, but he gave me a little push and warned me again to be careful.

It seemed that all the games Whitey and I had played prepared me for that trip. There was hardly an Indian alive who ever went into Muskrat Hill so stealthily and swiftly. Having Whitey catch me somewhere along the way was my biggest fear. I could handle my mother and Clara Grace, but Whitey already knew Pop might be in trouble.

The stockroom adjoining the store was kept unlocked during the day. I was used to the cats that darted in and out looking for snakes and mice and didn't think anything about it when a black one streaked by me as my hand reached for a shovel. Grabbing it, I crept back to the doorway, peeking out, looking right and left, before slipping away toward the rear of the building. I rounded the corner and bumped into Asa.

I froze in place but couldn't stop my heart from pounding.

"What are you doing, Kit?" Asa asked quietly.

My teeth bit my bottom lip. Surely Pop wouldn't care if I told the marshal. Asa could help Pop. "I . . ." began, but stopped. Pop had said nobody. "Whitey and I are going to dig for buried treasure."

"With a brand-new shovel?" Asa asked. He stood so still it was impossible to read what he was thinking.

"Yes," I replied. I could think of nothing else to say.

He stood contemplating me. Several seconds went by before he stepped aside and let me pass. I didn't waste time, but streaked away, hoping I looked like I was in a hurry to play yet another game with Whitey.

Pop was again brandishing his cane in the grass around the shack when I got back.

"Pop!" I called, raising the shovel for him to see. He turned and waved to me. I placed the shovel at my feet, the thought occurring at the same time that I should hide again and watch.

Pop knew that. "Kit, you have to go back," he hollered. "If you don't go home, your mother will send the cavalry out looking for us later on. Now go home and stay there. Don't tell your mother or anyone else where I am. Just say you don't know where I was going, but I said I would be home late. Now move it, boy!" he ordered.

The harshness in his voice forced me to obey, and I reluctantly left. On the way home, the jolt of what happened sunk in and fear overtook me. I couldn't cry, and I no longer cared if anyone saw me. I couldn't even think of any lies to tell if they did.

CHAPTER 14

My mother stood outside the store, working a broom vigorously across the porch, her eyebrows drawn together as if she was worried or perplexed. She saw me on the sidewalk walking toward her, and something in my manner must have alerted her—she ceased sweeping.

"What is it, Kit?" she asked. "Where's Pop?"

"I don't know," my voice said, dully and automatically repeating Pop's words. "He said to tell you he'll be coming home late."

I entered the store with my mother following. As a toddler, I used to sit underneath one of the tables, squeezing in between extra barrels of nails or crackers. From there I could watch the front door or look out the window and pretend I was invisible. I pushed aside the barrels and squeezed in again, to sit and watch and wait for Pop to come home.

My mother stared at me without saying a word. She turned around, put the closed sign on the door, and locked it. "Clara Grace," she called, her voice sounding wobbly. "Get your prayer beads; something's wrong with Pope. We need to pray for him."

Any other woman would have insisted on more information, but Clara Grace joined my mother at the back table, no questions asked. They turned the chairs around and knelt with their elbows resting on the seats, Clara Grace quietly fingering her beads. I didn't move again from my spot, keeping my eyes to the front, but later, I could hear my mother's soft sobs and muted entreaties, begging for protection for my father.

People came, rattled the door, saw the sign, and left. Dusk fell, and still Pop did not come back. My mother lit three lanterns, one at the back of the store, one in the front, and the third she took outside, hanging it under the porch rafters so Pop could see the steps.

Asa came by and knocked on the door my mother had left unlocked. He opened it, sticking his head and shoulder inside the room. "Miss Dolly, is everything all right?" he asked.

She went to the door. "No, Pope is in trouble, and we are praying for him."

In the pale light, I saw Asa tense. "What is it?" he demanded.

"I don't know," she said. "He sent Kit home and told him to say that he would be late." Her voice caught in her throat. "I just know he's in trouble."

Asa glanced at me, but he, too, recognized the signs of shock on my face. "Would you like for me to pray with you, Miss Dolly?" he asked, turning to her.

"Yes, please," she said, stepping aside so he could come in. I expected Clara Grace to raise a howl, but she said nothing when Asa knelt beside them. I could only hope she was still praying for Pop and hadn't decided to pray that Asa would turn away from using grape juice in the Eucharist instead of wine.

I felt guilty I was unable to join them. I tried to pray, but my mind couldn't form the words. All I could do was sit, watch, and wait.

It was some time later I heard my mother say with relief, "It's okay now; he's all right. I can't explain it; I just know it."

"Are you sure, Miss Dolly?" Asa asked.

"Yes. You can leave now, Asa. Thank you so much for coming. Clara Grace, will you put water on the stove to heat? Pope will probably need to soak in the tub when he gets here." My mother was capable of remaining composed and dignified in public during calamity, and she disliked emotional exhibitionism, but in private it was not unusual for her to go to pieces, screaming and crying like she did when our dog Blackie died. But this evening, after hours of fitful sobbing, she was now calm and full of assurance.

Asa reluctantly left, and my mother, after following him to the door, bent down at the table I was under. "Kit, you go to bed now," she said. "Pop is coming home, and everything will be fine."

"Yes, ma'am," I said. Her serenity was so catching, I did feel better. However, once I went to my room, I closed the door and stood waiting for a minute or two, and then snuck back into the store, hiding near the shelves on the far wall close to the door.

It was some time later Pop limped in, filthy and smelling of smoke. My mother ran to him and hugged him. "Pope, we've been so worried."

"I'm all right now, Dolly, don't fuss," he said, taking deep breaths. He leaned on her, his legs weak and about to give way. "Where is Kit?"

"I sent him to bed," she said. "Come with me. I'll clean you up and put you to bed, too."

"In a minute. Let me catch my breath." He stood breathing heavily, his arm around her shoulders as she supported him. "It was awful, Dolly," he said. "You know that old farm Julius owns where Kit and Whitey like to pick wild grapes? Someone had put Indian hunting traps out there."

"Indian traps?!" she exclaimed in surprise.

"Yes, except this time they were traps for humans, not animals," he said. "I've been out there burning and covering up every bit of the evidence."

"Oh, Pope!"

"If the people of Muskrat Hill had seen them, they would have hanged Asa on the spot."

"Asa would know all about those kinds of traps," my mother gasped.

"Yes, but so would anybody who's ever sat in a saloon listening to ancient Texas Rangers jabbering about the old days. But that wouldn't have stopped people from blaming Asa."

My mother shook her head, and grasping Pop tighter, she kissed him, saying, "Don't talk anymore; you're exhausted. Let's get you cleaned up and put to bed."

They began to walk slowly toward the back. "Dolly," Pop said.

"Yes?"

"I shit in my pants."

"I know," she replied as she supported him. "I can smell it."

"Don't let Kit know," Pop said.

"Know what? That you saved Asa's life today?"

"Dolly, Kit . . . , Kit . . . ," Pop began, but he couldn't finish. Instead, he kissed her, saying, "He's a good boy, Dolly."

"Yes," my mother's voice floated back to me as they reached the rear of the store. "He has a good father."

On the porch, the lantern flickered out, and through the window, I saw a brief shadow in the moonlight before it moved away. I couldn't see the face, but I knew the tall, broad shouldered outline was Asa, waiting to see that Pop had made it home.

Pop wanted to tell my mother everything that happened, but he didn't and might not ever be able to bring himself to burden her with how close he and I had come to a nightmarish death. He couldn't get out of bed the next day, and my mother wouldn't have allowed it even if he had tried. She refused to leave him for long, and it was Clara Grace who went to the slaughterhouse and did any other outside errands that needed to be done in addition to running the store with only occasional help from my mother and me.

The mayor came in and demanded to know what Pop had found out.

"You can't see him," Clara Grace informed him. She was just as cool to him as she was to everyone else. "He's feeling liverish, and Dolly wants him to stay in bed."

The mayor balked, but everyone in Muskrat Hill knew that feeling "liverish" covered a broad spectrum of ailments, the main one being that a person just felt bad in general. "I've got to meet Melvin anyway," the mayor said, clearly put out. "I'll come by tomorrow."

My mother did allow Asa to visit Pop that afternoon. Pop sat up in bed and talked to Asa in a quiet voice. He had sent me from the room, but I couldn't bring myself to go far. I sat on the floor outside his bedroom with my back against the wall and listened.

"Someone is toying with us, Asa. We could have had a bullet put through our heads at any time when we've been on the trail. This was meant for me, but if something had happened to me or Kit out there, you would have caught the blame."

"You should have had Kit come get me, Pop," Asa scolded. "I could have helped you."

"No," Pop said. "I couldn't have you anywhere near there. If it ever got out, the first thing someone would have said would have been that they had seen you out there, never mind the time frame."

Asa agreed with Pop that there was no need to alert the whole community since it seemed a vendetta against the two of them. "This town is already sitting on a tinder keg," Pop said. They both thought, however, that the children in and around Muskrat Hill should be warned to stay out of abandoned buildings and caves, and even better, to not go anywhere alone.

"I hope one day," Pop told me privately after Asa had gone, "that I can make up for the injustice and disrespect I've shown you and Smokey, but right now this is how it has to be."

What if someone hadn't pushed that dead tree into the road? What if Gastor hadn't kicked Asa's wrist, forcing me to learn how to use an animal to move something? Or worse, what if Mr. Petty had put Gastor on the buggy instead of Smokey? I couldn't bear thinking about it, and I threw myself on Pop and hugged him tightly.

Whitey came by, and it was hard for me not to confide everything, especially since he was still miffed I had kept him from retrieving the knife.

"Don't you understand, Whitey?" I kept saying. "A bad man put it there to hurt us." I couldn't tell Whitey the whole truth. Pop had too deeply impressed upon me how any little thing could send a crowd into hysterics and leave them ready to throw away all common sense and decency. No one person in Muskrat Hill would harm Asa, but a group of people might tear him to pieces, and one word from me to Whitey could set that in motion, Pop had warned.

That evening at dusk as Clara Grace was putting the closed sign on the door, Melvin pulled his wagon up to the store with his housekeeper next to him on the seat.

"I need to see Pope immediately," Melvin demanded.

"He isn't feeling well; you can't see him," Clara Grace said.

"I know that, but this is important. You get him out here at once," Melvin said. "Someone tried to attack my housekeeper just now." But while Melvin argued, Clara Grace remained firm. "Then get Dolly out here this instant," Melvin yelled.

Clara Grace yielded to this. I hung around the front door while Clara Grace went for my mother, wondering why anyone would want to attack Melvin's middle-aged housekeeper. In the darkening light, I could just barely see her in the wagon, cowering in fear.

My mother came to the door. "What is it, Mr. Foster?

Captain Robertson is unwell."

"I must speak with Pope, Dolly," Melvin said. "My house-keeper was attacked this evening."

My mother paused, not knowing what to do. She gave a sympathetic glance at Melvin's housekeeper, who seemed to shrink even more in shyness and terror into a handkerchief. A look crossed my mother's face as if something perplexed her slightly. She gave a slight movement of her head as if to shake off a thought and turned back to Melvin.

"I think you should let Marshal Asa handle this, Mr. Foster," she said.

Melvin huffed. "Dolly, you know very well that Asa can manage the everyday duties of a town marshal, but when something out of the ordinary comes along, he is too inexperienced to deal with it. I want to talk to Pope."

She gave a sigh. "I'll tell Pope you are here," she said. "Please ask Miss . . . I don't know your housekeeper's name."

Melvin stared at her, and for a moment, I thought he wasn't going to answer. "It's Luci," he said. "Her name is Luci, but she's afraid and doesn't want to leave the wagon."

"All right," my mother said. "I'll tell him. Kit, you come with me. Pop may need you for something."

I dutifully followed her into the store and their bedroom, having no desire to stand outside with Melvin and his house-keeper anyway. The night was warm, and Pop lay on the bed in his long johns, looking old and worn out. My mother hesitated, and Pop said, "What is it, Dolly?"

"It's Melvin Foster," she said. "He said someone attacked his housekeeper this evening, and he demands to speak to you. She's all right; she's in the wagon waiting with him."

Pope heaved a sigh and said, "Shit." He rarely cursed in front of my mother. He thought for a moment. "I can't interview her anyway; she doesn't speak English. Kit, go fetch Asa to talk to her. Before she leaves, get Asa to translate what she said and come tell me. If I have any more questions, you can relay them."

"Yes, sir, Pop," I said, and ran out of the bedroom. I went outside and stopped short in front of Melvin. "Pop said he can't understand her anyway, Mr. Foster. He said to get Asa to translate, and then I'm supposed to tell him."

Melvin fumed, but had to agree. I ran across the street and down to the jail, pounding on the door. Asa's lantern in the back was lit, and in a minute, he came to the door. I told him what happened and Pop's instructions.

Asa looked up the street. "All right, let me get my boots on."

He went to the back, found his boots, and a minute later rejoined me at the door. "Pop didn't say anything else?" Asa asked as we walked back to the store.

"No, sir," I said, looking at Melvin as he waited impatiently by the wagon.

When Asa and I reached the wagon, he looked up at the woman and spoke kindly to her in halting German. When he said, "*Ich bin* Marshal Jenkins," I knew he was reminding her who he was, but that was all I understood. As she made her replies to his questions in low guttural syllables, Asa nodded his head sympathetically. He took his time and didn't hurry, but even so, the interview did not last long.

Turning to me, he said, "Tell Pop she said a man came up behind her when she was coming out of the barn at sundown. He grabbed her, putting his hand over her mouth. She was able to bite his hand, causing him to lose his grip, and she ran into the house as fast as she could. When she told Melvin, they looked for him, but he was gone."

"Yes, sir," I said, and ran back into the store.

When I repeated what Asa had said, Pop shut his eyes. After a pause, he opened them and began his instructions. "Tell Asa to ask her if she drew blood when she bit him. She should have tasted blood if she had. Was his hand white, black, or brown? Ask her what he smelled like. Did he smell of dirt like a farmer? Did he smell of horses like a rancher? Did he smell like a white man or a black man? Was he wearing long sleeves? What color were the sleeves? Was it a poor man's shirt or a fancy shirt? Could she tell how tall he was? Was he taller than she was? Did she see his boots?" He paused for a breath. "Do you think you can remember all that, Kit?"

"Yes, sir, Pop," I said and went outside to pass the questions on to Asa.

This time the questions and answers took longer. At one point, she put the handkerchief to her eyes again and rocking back and forth cried something that sounded like, *"nix, nix."*

"That's enough, Jenkins," Melvin said, getting into the wagon. He took the reins and looking down at Asa said, "You and Pope better get your thumbs out of your asses and solve this. Pope is too old to threaten, but I can write the governor and demand you be fired and kept from holding any public office whatsoever, including preaching. If you're wise, you'll look right here in this town for the killer—beginning with those two newcomers down the street."

Asa's face didn't show what he felt as he watched the wagon roll away into the night. He looked down at me, patted my shoulder, and said, "I'll go in with you to talk to Pop if he's up to it."

Pop lay propped up with several feather pillows. Asa drew a slat-backed chair nearer the bed and relayed the woman's story. She wasn't sure if she drew blood or not. It happened so fast, she didn't have time to look at his hand or think of what he smelled like. She thought he was wearing long sleeves, but couldn't tell anything about the fabric. He was taller than she was—she would guess about the height of Julius, Melvin's brother. She hadn't noticed his boots.

"Pop," Asa said at the end of his story. He paused before continuing. "You know I don't know much about women, but I couldn't help feeling she was exaggerating about what happened."

Pop lay silent for a moment. "How well do you know this minister she is supposed to have stayed with in Sulfur City before coming here?"

Asa shrugged. "Just to speak to."

"Regardless, you'll have to go by Melvin's place in the morning and look for tracks. I'd like for you to ride on to Sulfur City and ask that preacher about this woman. I don't know what else to do," Pop said in frustration.

"I'll ride to Sulfur City in the morning," Asa agreed. "Maybe I can find out something."

Pop got up the next day while Asa was gone, but my mother allowed him to do very little. The following morning, he dressed and sat at the table in the back of the store. The mayor came in, still claiming the knife incident had been the figment of two boys' overactive imaginations and the pig with Pop's name on it was just somebody's idea of a joke. He was certain Melvin's housekeeper saw a shadow and blew the whole thing up into an exciting attack to gain Melvin's sympathy.

"Not that I really believe there is an ounce of pity in the man," he said under his breath.

"Julius," Pop said. "The boys were telling the truth about the knife. Get that into your head. As far as Melvin's housekeeper goes, I don't know. Something evidently scared the woman."

Pop's insistence that I had been telling the truth meant more to me than anything else. Nonetheless, it humiliated me that I had blubbered like a baby that day at the shack, and I was too ashamed to confess my feelings of cowardice to Pop.

CHAPTER 15

Asa entered the store immediately after the mayor left, almost as if he had been waiting for him to leave.

"Let's sit on the back porch," Pop told Asa. "Kit, there ought to be some coffee left in the pot, bring Asa and me a cup, please, sir."

"Yes, sir, Pop," I said, pleased because I knew if I brought the coffee cups, I would be able to hang around and hear Asa's news.

It happened just as I thought. We had a rocker and settee on the back porch. Pop sat in the wooden rocker while Asa sat on the wicker settee with his legs stretched out. After handing them their cups, I went back to the doorway, sat on the sill, and tried to look nonchalant while I listened with both ears wide open.

"First of all," Asa began. "The sheriff there said as far as he knows, there are no missing prostitutes in the area."

"So, all the soiled doves are accounted for," Pop said.

"Yes, according to him," Asa said. He took a deep breath, hesitating.

"Well, you didn't find any viable tracks or clues at Melvin's," Pop said, "and nobody is missing any wag-tails, so what about the preacher? Did you find him?"

Asa nodded. "The preacher and his wife are an old couple, Pop, and they don't see or hear well. They've been trying to raise a granddaughter and finding it difficult. He didn't want to

161

talk about Melvin's housekeeper at first. It was only after I explained what has been happening in Muskrat Hill and impressed upon him how vital any scrap of information could be that he agreed to tell me everything."

"Yes," Pop said, nodding his head in encouragement.

"The beginning was like the mayor said. She had what appeared to be a genuine letter of introduction from the preacher of a big church in Houston. The letter said she was a widow who wanted to get out of town because she was having difficulties with her husband's children by his first marriage. Everything seemed legitimate and aboveboard. And at first, everything was all right. She was a poor housekeeper, and there was something about her he disliked, but he didn't hold that against her. She was just there until they could find suitable employment for her elsewhere. Then he began to suspect that she was leaving the house at night."

Asa let out a long breath and looked up. "I had to drag this next part out of him." He stopped to take a swallow of coffee, wiping his mouth with the blue bandanna he pulled from his pocket. "This woman, she took a special interest in the preacher's granddaughter. The girl is fifteen, and I saw her. She's quite a little beauty. The housekeeper was very friendly to the girl, very accommodating. She began by helping her dress, combing her hair, just innocent things."

Asa stopped and looked away. Pop watched him and waited patiently.

"She began to want to help the girl with her bath," Asa continued. "Getting the water for her, scrubbing her back. The minister began to feel uncomfortable about the situation. One night, he asked his wife to look in on them. When she walked in, she found the housekeeper apparently fondling the girl's breast with a washrag, both of them flushed and breathing heavily. The preacher and his wife intended on asking her to leave the next day, but she was gone, sending word she had taken a job with Melvin."

Pop let out a long slow breath. "Jesus," he said.

"You see the pattern, don't you, Pop?" Asa asked.

"Oh, yes," Pop said. "A prostitute, because I believe Horace was right about that regardless of whether one is missing or not, a child molester, and now a hen who thinks she's a rooster living with a rooster who thinks he's a hen." Pop looked away, staring at nothing in particular and concentrating.

"Do you think that's it, Pop?" Asa asked. "Some kind of religious maniac bent on vengeance killing?"

"I cannot see any other connection between these victims," Pop muttered, looking dissatisfied. "One pattern is there, but the other pattern isn't. This attack on Melvin's housekeeper appears to be just an impulsive botched attempt. Someone watched Oscar's comings and goings for some time, I think, before striking. The knife hanging from the string was thought out with patience."

Pop turned back to Asa. "And you got the feeling when you were talking to the housekeeper that she was exaggerating?"

"Yes, Pop," Asa said. "At the time, but it was just a feeling, not a sure thing."

Pop cursed softly, shaking his head. He looked up and spied me. "Kit, take these cups and ask your mother to brew a fresh pot of coffee, please, sir."

"Yes, sir, Pop," I said, gathering the cups. As I walked into the house, I heard Pop tell Asa, "Did you notice how she obliquely tried to throw suspicion on Julius?"

After Asa left, Pop spent almost all the rest of the day sitting on the back porch, looking off in the distance, resting and thinking. Ephraim Hutchins arrived at suppertime, so my mother felt obliged to invite him to eat with us, although she and I both realized Pop didn't want his company. Most of the time, Pop and

Mr. Hutchins talked business, but when the conversation lagged, my mother would ask questions she probably already knew the answers to. After we finished eating, Pop excused himself and went back to the porch, exchanging the rocker for the settee, while I helped my mother with the dishes and wished I had a sister.

"Kit," she said when we finished, "don't bother or tease Clara Grace now. You come out on the porch with me for a little while."

"Yes, ma'am," I said, having no desire to devil Clara Grace and her beau anyway, and even less desire to eavesdrop on a conversation about theology.

Pop made room for my mother on the settee while I sat on the edge of the porch. The moon was waxing and the cicadas were in full orchestra. It seemed ages since I had heard Pop play his guitar.

"Where's Whitey?" my mother asked. "I've barely seen him in the last few days. Kit, you've just been hanging around the house. Maybe you should find Whitey tomorrow and play with the other boys."

"Leave him be, Dolly," my father said.

It was so unlike Pop to tell her something like that, she stared at him. But she gave a little nod of her head and didn't say anything else.

"Kit," Pop said. "Go on to bed, son."

I got up obediently and kissed my mother's cheek, then walked around to Pop, kissing his cheek, too. Impulsively, I grabbed him and hugged him. He patted my arm, and said, "Run along to bed now. Tomorrow starts a new day soon enough."

Nodding, I walked back into the house. I had joined Pop in a conspiracy to protect my tenderhearted mother from emotional overload.

Usually, tired from running and playing, I would fall into bed and immediately into sleep. That night, my sweaty arms and legs stuck to the sheets. I couldn't get up and get a glass of water naked because of Clara Grace, so I reached for my pants and put them on. I could hear the murmuring of my parents on the back porch, although Ephraim Hutchins must have either run out of steam or been told by Clara Grace it was time to skedaddle. After getting the water, I walked to the back door and lay down on the cool floor, half in the kitchen and half on the porch.

"People are always getting on and off the train," Pop mused. "But the stationmaster swears he hasn't seen anyone like the woman we found." He paused for a moment. "Maydell hasn't been in?" he asked.

"No, I think she's avoiding me," my mother said. "It's kind of hurt my feelings."

Although my mother had a myriad of casual friends in Muskrat Hill, Maydell was one of the few who sought her out to speak in private. A snub from her would be that much more painful.

"Don't let it bother you," Pop responded. "She's feeling guilty for slipping around to see this man. You still don't have any indication of who it is?"

"No," my mother said. "And that's odd for Muskrat Hill. Usually somebody knows something if it goes on for very long."

Pop sighed and nodded. "True. It may not be important, but it's just one more piece in this puzzle that doesn't make sense."

He paused for a minute before continuing. "Scut Tabor's father likes to creep through every cracked doorway any woman is foolish enough to let him enter, but I can't see even Maydell stooping that low for him. Bruno? Bruno is so guarded; he would be humiliated if anyone laughed at him for courting an old maid." Pop changed directions. "And Oscar? The only people who would have anything against him would be the Tabors, and I'd swear they don't have a clue what their little gal was up to. You haven't heard anything else about Oscar, have you?"

"No, Pope," my mother said. "And I only saw Oscar when he came in the store to play his mandolin. You saw him every day."

"I know, Dolly, I'm just grasping at straws."

They were silent for some time. I was about to fall asleep when my mother asked a question that made my ears tingle because her voice was filled with fear.

"Where is he, Pope?"

"He's on a prison farm near Houston," he said. "Dolly, go in the house and get my shotgun."

I scooted out of the way and into a corner so my mother wouldn't see me. While she went for the gun, I peered outside, but I couldn't see anything. Pop didn't notice me because he was staring intently at the bushes beyond the outhouse. I heard my mother returning with the shotgun, and I scrambled to hide again.

She took it to Pop, and he told her to go back in the house. She did, but stood halfway inside the doorway peering out, just as I had done. I heard the "cha-chang" sound of Pop pulling back the pump. I looked from behind my mother's skirt and saw the bushes move.

"Don't shoot, Captain Robertson! Don't shoot!" A young man came out from the bushes holding up his hands. It was the teenager who had sassed Pop the day we found the woman's body.

"What the hell are you doing out there in my backyard?" Pop demanded.

"I . . . I . . . I'm with a friend," he stuttered.

Pop put the gun down. "Well, take her home, consarn it. There's a killer on the loose and you darn fool kids are out

166

there rolling around like this is some kind of brush arbor prayer meeting. Get on out of here."

"Yes, sir, Captain Robertson, yes, sir," he said and dived back into the bushes for his sweetheart. In a minute, two figures emerged and crept away.

"What was that all about, Pope?" my mother asked, rejoining him on the porch.

"Just two young idiots out there eating before they said grace," Pop said. Meanwhile, I slid back into my cool spot on the doorway.

"Yes, but who were they?" my mother asked, gazing curiously at their backs.

"I'm not going to get involved in the female grapevine, Dolly," Pop said. "Nine months from now, you'll figure it out."

She laughed at him. "Okay, Pope, be that way."

"I guess I know who my next store clerk will be," Pop said. "In a couple of months, he'll be in here looking for a job."

"If it's who I suspect it is, he's done everything he can to get your attention, hasn't he?" she said.

Pop shrugged. "Perhaps."

"Pope," she asked, continuing in a playful vein. "If Maydell has a baby, can we adopt it?"

"Hell, no," he answered. "It's unfair enough on Kit to have parents as old as Methuselah; I'm not going to do that to another child."

"Well, okay, Pope," my mother said, still teasing him. "You're as old as Methuselah; I'm only as old as Mrs. Methuselah."

"You are a sassy wench," he said, grabbing her chin.

They kissed, and this time, I really did fall asleep.

The next morning, trouble started with a trickle and ended with a wave that threatened to sweep the whole town over the edge. "What's this about someone trying to lure Whitey and Kit into a shack and Melvin's housekeeper being attacked?" people would enter the store and ask. In almost every case, they would add, "I heard it from Melvin Foster just now."

Even though only half of them bought anything, murder and mayhem still caused a brisk business. My mother pleaded with Pop not to put in a full day's work, and he still felt tired enough to acquiesce, but he stayed around to hear some of the discussions. People would talk and leave, and then come back. By the afternoon, the store bulged with panic-stricken men and women, while Pop sat wearily on a stool trying to answer their questions and reassure them.

A few bolder ones began talking about calling on the governor and insisting on more law enforcement. Pop had already warned them of the improbability of that, but it was the mayor who put the final kibosh on the idea.

"What are we going to tell them?" the mayor said. "That we've had two grisly murders probably committed by tramps passing through? That two little boys with overactive imaginations saw something shiny and thought someone was out to get them? That a hysterical German housekeeper thinks a man tried to grab her? It's ridiculous to even think they'd come to Muskrat Hill for that. Just be thankful all the reporters are flocked to that political scandal going on in Dallas, or we'd be overrun with journalists who would make us look like fools."

It disgusted me to be referred to as an overimaginative little boy, especially when I wanted to shout what Pop had gone through, but I kept quiet. Horace Dubois slipped in and unobtrusively made his way closer to Pop. He listened, trying to remain inconspicuous while other voices around him continued to rant—the mayor had only partially pacified the crowd.

"What are we going to do?" one woman wailed. "First some poor girl, then Oscar. Now women and children. What are we going to do?!"

"I'm telling you," the mayor said, raising his voice. "We've have two murders by tramps passing through. It has nothing to do with us! The other is just overreacting to what amounts to nothing!"

Netta Crenshaw's high voice chirruped above the others. Pointing a shaking finger at Horace, she shrieked, "This happened when he and that Bruno moved here! It all started then!"

Horace's naturally pale face went even whiter. He stood stone still and did not try to defend himself. Before Pop could intervene, more yells began.

"That's right! That's right! We don't know who you are!"

Pop got up. "Stop it! Stop it right now!" he hollered over the other voices. They quieted enough to listen to him, and he went on. "I have a friend in San Antonio who has written me a description of Horace and a glowing recommendation. There weren't any murders in San Antonio while he was there, so shut up! We can't condemn a man just because he happens to move in at the wrong time."

"What about Bruno?" someone yelled. "He could be in cahoots with Bruno!"

The voices of the crowd rose to a crescendo despite the efforts of Pop and the mayor to get them to stop. The people seemed to press in tighter toward Horace, and while he never twitched so much as a muscle, his face blanched even further as he stared at a terrified mob on the edge of igniting.

"It's them! It's them!" one woman began crying hysterically. "I know it's them!"

The door flew open, and a man came in. Every voice went mute, while every eye stared at the stranger who entered.

CHAPTER 16

Well-fed, of medium height, the man who entered our midst during a crescendo of fear wore a quality-made suit and a new derby hat. He looked so ordinary and average, the emotions that had been pitched to a fever seemed to pause in midair.

"Yes?" Pop said, forcing his voice to sound normal and calm. "May I help you? I'm Pope Robertson; I own this store."

The man looked around, mild disgust showing on his face. "I work for the Pinkerton Agency," he said in an abrupt tone. "We're looking for a man that we have information may be working as an undertaker in one of these towns."

No one said a word; I don't think anyone even breathed. "Who is this man?" Pop asked.

"Henri Deschamps. He comes from a wealthy old Southern family—his pappy and grandpappy were big Civil War heroes in South Carolina."

"Why are you looking for him?" Pop asked.

The man looked at the crowd, disdain on his face. Clearly, he was not impressed with Muskrat Hill. He turned back to Pop. "He killed a man in a duel."

"I didn't think South Carolinians were so particular about duels," Pop said.

"He shot a senator's son," the agent grudgingly added.

"Well, what for?" Pop asked, slightly deepening his Texas accent. I didn't know if he did it on purpose or not. "A man doesn't challenge another man to a duel without a reason."

The Pinkerton man looked around the room. "I can't say in mixed company."

Pop looked at the crowd. "Ladies?" he asked.

The women of Muskrat Hill dutifully put their hands over their ears and pretended they were unable to hear.

Pop nodded his thanks. He turned to the agent and said, "Now, what was this duel about?"

The man screwed up his face in aggravation. "He said the senator's son assaulted and raped his fourteen-year-old deaf-mute sister," he said shortly. "Look mister, I don't judge them; I just search for them."

Pop motioned for the women to take their hands down, which they promptly did. He turned back to the Pinkerton agent. "How are we supposed to know if he's here?" Pop asked innocently. "What does he look like?"

I didn't dare sneak a direct glance at Horace, but by looking at Pop's left ear, I could see him in the corner of my vision, standing like a tall tombstone, his eyes wide, his face white.

"He's tall, thin, dark-haired, and can shoot the eye out of a man at a hundred paces," the agent said. "Look, people, I've got the train waiting on me. Now do you have somebody answering that description here or not?"

"No," Pop said, his face so guileless one might expect to see a halo around it. "Doesn't sound like anyone we know. Asa," he asked, "does that sound like anybody around here?"

"No, Pop," Asa answered just as blandly. "Don't have anybody answering that description in these parts."

Several people shook their heads in just as much virtue as Pop and Asa.

The Pinkerton man gave a disgusted sigh, casting his eyes around the room once more. I couldn't understand why he failed to see Horace until I perceived that my mother had placed herself and Clara Grace in front of him. No man alive would notice Horace with Clara Grace directly in view. The agent stopped scanning the room when he saw Harmonica John standing in the rear. "What about you, jigaboo?" he asked. "You seen any so-called Southern gentleman like that hanging around?"

John shook his head. "Naw, suh," he answered, making himself look and sound like a slave from the 1840s. "I sure nuff hadn't."

The train whistle blew. Pop turned to Asa. "Asa, didn't you once tell me you thought of working for the Pinkerton Agency? Why don't you escort Mr. er, the agent, to the train station and discuss it with him on the way?"

"That's a good idea, Pop," Asa said. He unconcernedly headed for the door, following the Pinkerton man out.

No one spoke. They stood waiting expectantly until they heard the sound of the train leaving town. It was only then they began to file out one by one. "I expect the mayor is right," one woman told another. "It probably was strangers passing through," another man added. When at last everyone but the mayor and Horace had gone, Pop turned to Horace.

"It is your sister who is a deaf-mute, not your parents, isn't it?" he asked kindly. Horace nodded miserably, and Pop patted him on the back.

"Horace, go home. It's not over, though," Pop said. "I don't want you and Bruno stepping foot outside your house at night. Someone may take a notion to waylay you yet."

Horace could barely speak. "I have to tend to my horses."

"Then sleep in the barn," Pop told him. "You'll all be safer that way."

Horace paused before leaving. "Pop . . ."

"Horace," Pop interrupted. "I would not let my son associate with you if I believed you had committed these heinous crimes. Now go home."

He nodded and left. As soon as he shut the door behind him,

Pop turned to the mayor. "Julius," he said in anger. "Melvin and I are both too old to get into a fistfight, but you tell him if he doesn't stop stirring up trouble, I'm putting him and his housekeeper on a train for a mandatory three-month vacation from this town."

"Pope," the mayor said, sounding spent of emotion and energy. "If I told that to Melvin, he would just do it that much more to spite me. It's best to leave him alone. He'll go on to something else."

I looked at Whitey. "Come on, Whitey, let's go outside."

"Kit," my mother called. "You and Whitey leave Mr. Dubois alone for today. He's had a shock. You can see him tomorrow."

"Yes, ma'am," we answered and left the store.

The town was silent. It was as if all its energy had been depleted to almost zero. We went in the livery stable to talk to Mr. Petty and pet Smokey and Gastor, but even Mr. Petty, who could talk the ears off of corn, was uncharacteristically taciturn.

Whitey was in one of his moods where he didn't want to go home, so he spent the night with us again. Asa came by in time for supper, but Clara Grace barely said two words to him. Yet I caught her looking in our small kitchen mirror and patting her dark hair in place. She whirled when she saw me and thrust a dish in my hand, ordering me to put it on the table.

"I want to interview Melvin's housekeeper again tomorrow while he is at work," Pop said when we finished eating.

"I think that's a good idea," Asa told Pop while his eyes watched Clara Grace's backside as she left the room.

Melvin's housekeeper wasn't to be found the next morning when we arrived. "Is the door locked?" Pop asked Asa as they stood on the front porch.

Asa tried the doorknob. "Yes," he said. He peered into the window. "I can't see anything. I'll check the back."

He returned shaking his head. "She's not here."

Pop gave a sigh of disgust. "A wasted trip," he said, and turned to go down the steps.

"At least it's not that far from town," Asa commiserated.

When we returned home, Pop wasn't feeling well, and my mother insisted he rest on the bed. He nodded, but before he did, he told Whitey and me to check on Horace and Bruno.

"Yes, sir, Pop," I said. "Anything else?"

"No," he said, sounding tired and weary. "Just go about your business, keep your eyes and ears open, and stay out of trouble. Do whatever your mother tells you."

For the next two days, Muskrat Hill remained unusually quiet. Horace and Bruno had taken up residence in the barn, but I don't think they cared much. The barn was better than a prison, and Horace never minded the smell of horseshit anyway. Whitey went home for a night, but returned to Muskrat Hill the next morning. He hardly said three words to me or anyone else all morning, but by afternoon, he was more of his natural self. That evening we reported back to Pop.

He was feeling better and sitting at the table in the store. I slid into a seat on one side of him while Whitey sat on his other side. Usually Whitey always sat by me, but he seemed to want to sit by Pop and neither one of us said anything about it.

"Mr. Petty said Mr. Melvin hasn't been in town. He said he must have heard how mad you were at him for stirring up trouble," I said.

"I don't think how I feel would ever influence Melvin one way or another," Pop grunted. "What else is going on?"

"Mrs. Crenshaw is furious because somebody killed one of her cats and gutted it," I continued. "She went to Asa about it. He said somebody probably wanted the catgut for something, but he would put the word out to leave her cats alone."

"She asked us to bury it," Whitey said. "We pretended we were undertakers. Kit was Mr. Bruno and dug the grave, and I was Mr. Horace and put the cat in a box."

Pop gave a little smile. He grew serious and asked, "Was the cat tortured first?"

"No, just slit and gutted," I said.

"I bet it was Scut Tabor," Whitey said. "He's been talking about making a slingshot."

"I'm not going to ask him," I said.

"Why?" Whitey asked. "He's been a lot nicer to you since you whaled the tar out of him."

"I might not get so lucky next time," I said, and Pop laughed.

"He told me he wished his pa was more like yours," Whitey blurted. He looked up at Pop, but didn't say anything. I wondered if he wished his father was more like mine, too. I realized he would never say so.

"The mayor's wife, Mrs. Foster, got mad at Mrs. Crenshaw and accused her of coming into her house and messing with her stuff," I said, continuing my narrative.

"What stuff?" Pop asked instantly.

"She wouldn't say. But Mrs. Crenshaw got real huffy with her and said she did no such thing."

My mother came in and warned us that supper would be ready in thirty minutes. "I want those hands clean, boys," she said.

We nodded, but before we went to the kitchen to wash our hands, we told Pop about Horace and Bruno.

"Mr. Horace let us race Nighthawk, Nero, and Ace today," I said. "I know Ace is supposed to be the finest horse, Mr. Petty said so, but he's no faster than Nighthawk and Nero."

"It takes more to being a fine horse than just speed, Kit," Pop said.

This time, Ephraim Hutchins waited until we finished with supper to drop in on us, much to Pop's relief. My mother and I expected Pop to be aggravated at the intrusion, but he asked to be excused politely, explaining that he was tired and wanted to go to bed early. Whitey and I took turns reading *King Solomon's Mines* aloud in my room, and then we, too, went to bed early.

The next morning, I suggested we go to the livery stable to pet Gastor and Smokey.

Whitey nodded in agreement, and we left. My idea didn't turn out to be so good. Mr. Petty was in an even fouler mood than usual, throwing tools against the livery wall and pitching horseshoes out of his way with such ferocity, it was scaring even the gentlest nags.

"Gosh darn fickle women," he grumbled, "causing a man nothing but a muck load full of trouble and misery."

"Let's get out of here," I whispered to Whitey.

Once outside, Whitey said, "What's wrong with him?"

"It's because Ephraim Hutchins came courting Clara Grace again last night," I explained as we walked slowly down the street, kicking at pebbles with our bare toes.

"He's in the Klan," Whitey said.

I stopped. "In the Klan? How do you know?"

Whitey flushed. "I just know."

I started to say, "Pop don't like the Klan," but I stopped. If Whitey's father was a member . . .

"They pulled old E-Poo Allsup out of the Baptist Church one Sunday and tarred and feathered him for beating his wife and kids," I ventured. "Marshal Asa said they better not try that on the Methodists, wife beating or not."

"Yeah," Whitey said. "I think Mr. Hutchins was one of them."

"Whitey," I blurted out. "How do you know this stuff?"

But Whitey had spied a group of boys loitering by the slaughter pens. "Let's go down there," he said in a loud voice and began walking away.

I took the hint and shut my trap. Scut saw me, and looked at me asquint, trying to act tough. I nodded to show him I hadn't forgotten my promise and looked away. Did everyone in Muskrat Hill have a secret, I wondered? In a little while, I left and moseyed back to the store. Just then, I couldn't stand being away from Pop for too long.

As I walked up the sidewalk to the store, I saw my mother coming out. At the same time, Miss Maydell came out of the millinery shop where she sometimes worked. I guessed she had been helping out, because her hands were empty. My mother spotted her and called, "Maydell! Maydell!" and waved. Maydell half turned as if to escape, but my mother hurried toward her just as I came closer.

"I haven't seen you in a while, Maydell," my mother said, catching up with her.

"I've been busy," she responded, looking uncomfortable and a little angry. When my mother did not answer right away, Maydell blurted, "I know you disapprove of me, Dolly."

"That's not true," my mother said gently. "I just want what's best for you."

However, Maydell appeared to be trying hard to work herself into a snit and didn't want to be gentled out of it. "What's best for me?" she repeated sharply. "Why can't I have what other women have? What's so wrong with me reaching for that? Why can't I have what you and Pope have, Dolly? Do you know how many women in Muskrat Hill would love to see you in the grave so they could have a chance at Pope?"

"Maydell . . ." my mother began helplessly.

Maydell shook off the hand my mother had placed on her arm. "You just don't understand what it's like, Dolly!" she cried, and walked briskly away.

"Oh, yes, I do," my mother said softly, looking at Maydell's back. "I understand perfectly."

She noticed me and said, "Kit, come in and eat some dinner. Where's Whitey?"

"He's still down the street with the other boys."

She put her arm around my shoulder and walked to the store with me. "I'll put something back for him in case he wants it later," she said.

Pop, sitting at the back table, looked up and made a show of looking around me. "Where's your shadow?"

"He's hanging around somewhere, Pop," I answered. "Mama said she'd save him something to eat."

Pop nodded and, looking at my mother, said, "Dolly, I am correct in assuming the boy is not an orphan, right?"

"Pope," she said in her "behave yourself" voice.

Whitey, however, decided he better go home, and late in the day, just about closing time, I walked by myself to the back of the store where Pop sat at the table tying fishing lures. Asa stood nearby, one knee bent and his bootheel propped on a shelf behind him.

"Why haven't we heard from that warden?" Pop was saying. "How long does it take to check on somebody working on a prison farm?"

"I don't know, Pop," Asa replied. "I'll wire him again tomorrow if you want me to."

I reached Pop's chair and leaning on the arm, watched him tie lures. His fingers were giving him trouble. "Tie this knot for me like I taught you, will you, Kit," he said.

While I tied the knot, Asa stood upright and said, "I guess I best be leaving," but he didn't go. He stood resting his weight on one foot, then the other, staring around the store. Pop peered up at him.

"Would you like to stay for supper, Asa?" he asked.

Asa flushed. "I'm not sure Miss Clara Grace would want me to," he said.

Pop scowled. "The last time I looked, my name was on the

deed to this property, Asa. Now do you want to stay for supper or not?"

Asa nodded. "Sure."

I knew I shouldn't interrupt, but I was about to bust wanting to know. "Who's working on a prison farm, Pop?" I asked.

"We'll talk about it some other time," he said. "Dolly!" he turned and hollered toward the back. "Put out an extra plate; Asa is staying for supper."

"That's good," my mother called back. "Clara Grace is fixing supper tonight, and we've got plenty."

"Ah, jeez!" Pop moaned, furrowing his brows as if in pain. "Last time she cooked, I had dysentery for two days."

CHAPTER 17

Clara Grace did not say much at supper. I thought she was acting kind of nervous until we assured her supper tasted fine. It
wasn't fine, but it was better than her previous attempt. My
mother made every effort to keep the conversation away from
the nightmare looming over our heads and appeared relieved
when Pop and Asa started talking politics. When that discussion
lulled, I yearned to show off my newfound knowledge.

"Ephraim is in the Klan," I said. "Whitey told me, but he
wouldn't tell me how he knew."

"The Klan!" Asa said, while my father stared in shock. My
mother, however, said, "Mr. Hutchins, Kit. Address him as Mr.
Hutchins."

"Well, Mr. Hutchins is," I said. "He was with those men who
dragged that man out of the Baptist Church and tarred and
feathered him. Whitey said so."

"I never thought of that," Pop muttered. "I've been looking
for one killer. What if it is a group of men? What if it's some
kind of even more radical faction within the Klan?"

Asa drew himself up and with a stiff back, turned to Clara
Grace. "Miss Clara, as this town's marshal, I insist that you
refrain from going alone with a man on a buggy ride or
anywhere else until this is cleared up."

Clara Grace, shocked over my revelation, rallied herself
enough that she was about to protest she would do as she
pleased when my mother interjected. "He's right, Clara Grace,

dear. We shouldn't let ourselves be overly influenced by gossip, but I think he's right."

Pop acted like he never heard the exchange. "This puts a new light on everything," he said.

"Pope," my mother implored. "Please don't ruin your digestion thinking about this right now. Put it out of your mind for the time being."

He looked at her and said, "Yes, yes. You're right. Pass the cabbage, please."

But I knew he was thinking about it, even though he pretended along with everyone else that there wasn't an elephant in the room.

When supper ended, my mother made to rise to clear the table, but Pop grabbed her hand and gave it a light tug. She remained seated, and turning to Clara Grace, said, "I'm all-in, Clara Grace. Would you mind doing the dishes?"

"Not at all," Clara Grace said and rose.

Asa jumped to his feet. "If I may be allowed to assist you, Miss Clara Grace?"

She gave a short nod but eyed my mother suspiciously. However, my mother kept her face bland and innocent. She and Pop sat at the table while Clara Grace and Asa cleared the dishes and took them into the kitchen.

"Pope?" my mother said.

He shook his head, and she remained quiet. When Asa came out of the kitchen some time later, Pop apologized. "I think I'd like to study on this awhile, Asa. We can talk about it in the morning."

Asa agreed and after he left, Clara Grace went to bed, and my mother began extinguishing the lanterns. Pop remained seated.

"Kit, fetch my cane for me, please, sir," Pop instructed, and I obeyed, bringing it back to the table.

"What is it, Pope?" my mother asked.

"When you get the lights out, Kit and I are going across the street to talk to Tull Petty."

"Don't you want a lantern, Pope? It's cloudy tonight and black as pitch."

"No," he replied. "I don't want anyone seeing us and taking a notion to eavesdrop."

"All right," she said. "I'll wait up for you in the back." She kissed both of us and left us sitting in darkness.

When our eyes had accustomed to the night, Pop rose. "Take my hand, Kit, and be as quiet as you can."

I did, and he used the cane in his other hand. "I hate this thing," he said, "but that's all I need now, is to trip and fall in the middle of the street."

We made our way out of the store and crossed the street. The livery stable was in darkness; the horses sensed us, but recognizing our smell, they made no ruckus. Pop went around the back and tapped on Mr. Petty's window with his cane. From inside came the sound of feet falling and mild cursing. "Open up, Tull," Pop whispered. "It's me, Pope."

The door to the back opened, and we went inside. Mr. Petty shut the door behind us before fumbling for the lantern and a match. I heard the striking of the match and saw the flame wobble in his fingers, the smell of sulfur wafting across my nostrils. In the dim light, I was able to look around his minute sleeping quarters; the starkness of it surprised and depressed me. He had a narrow bed, a table, and a chair. He motioned for Pop to take the chair, while he pulled up a short barrel to sit on across the table. I sat on the floor behind Pop with my back against the wall.

"I been expecting you, Pope," Mr. Petty said.

"Did you know her, Tull?" Pop asked, discarding the preliminaries. "Did you kill her?"

"No," Mr. Petty said with a heavy sigh. "I didn't know her, and I didn't kill her."

"I was relieved that she was much too young to be Gypsy."

Mr. Petty looked away. "I haven't seen Gypsy since the day I caught her in bed with that tinhorn Frenchman." He looked back at Pop. "I killed him, and I wanted to kill her, but I stopped just shy of it."

"You beat her so badly her own mother would have hardly recognized her, Tull," Pop said. "I hated to take you in, though. She was no good, Tull. Not ever."

To my shock, Mr. Petty lowered his head and began to cry. "I loved her, Pope," he said through his tears. "I loved her, though."

"I know you did, Tull," Pop said. He said nothing else, but allowed Mr. Petty to sob without interference.

"She was ashamed of me," he said through his tears. "She never would even let me take her into San Antonio to meet her folks. I don't think she even give me her right name, but I didn't care. I loved her anyway. I spent two years in jail for it, Pope. But I never forgot her, never."

"I know," Pop said. "I felt bad about that. But the judge thought he had to do it. He was afraid you'd go on a rampage and kill every man she'd been sleeping with. He did it for your own good, Tull, hoping two years in the pen would cool you off."

Mr. Petty snuffled and tried to stop his tears. "I thought he did it because I was a Catholic Mick."

"No, that's not why," Pop said.

"Pope," Mr. Petty beseeched. "Tell me the truth. Did you lay with her?"

"No," Pop said with a slight shake of his head. "I didn't."

I wasn't too sure what they were talking about, but I knew Pop wasn't fibbing, and so did Mr. Petty.

"What about Julius?" Mr. Petty asked.

"I don't know," Pop said, "And I wouldn't tell you if I did."

Mr. Petty nodded. "Fair enough." He couldn't seem to stop his sporadic weeping. Pop sat patiently, waiting for him to cry it out.

"I've never told anyone, Tull," he said. "Not even Dolly knows about it. And I don't think Julius was ever close to San Antonio during that time.

"Not long after I came to Muskrat Hill, Julius and I discussed how badly we needed a well-run livery. I suggested you as the best man for the job, and he fell right into agreement with it."

"Dolly doesn't know?" Mr. Petty asked.

"No, she doesn't."

"Nor Clara Grace?"

"No," Pop replied. "And I'm not going to tell her either. If you ever feel it propitious to propose to her, you're going to tell her yourself."

Mr. Petty lowered his head. He took a handkerchief out of his pocket and blew in it loudly. He looked up at Pop. "You've got a good woman, Pope," he said. "Do you know how many men would kill you if they thought they would have a chance with her?"

My eyes widened. I had heard Miss Maydell say the same thing earlier that day about Pop.

"Yes, I do," Pop said.

The old Mr. Petty began to resurface. "If you knew the whores in this town, all the slipping around I've seen. Poor little kids look like the neighbor instead of their own pa."

"And Oscar?"

Mr. Petty paused. "It was that little Tabor girl, wasn't it?"

"If you saw her, why didn't you tell me?" Pop asked.

"Because I can't see as good as I used to, Pope, blast it to hell," Mr. Petty said. "I couldn't say anything because I couldn't be sure. I just saw something fuzzy that looked like a little girl in a dress slipping in there of a mornings. I didn't see nothing that morning because something had upset the horses, and I was on the other side of the lot trying to calm them.

"Then the other day, I knew she had stayed in the store a long time in the back, and she come out with a jacket, so I put two and two together and figured you'd been questioning her."

"Do you think the Tabors know what was going on?"

"No," Mr. Petty snorted. "They're too busy throwing things at one another, fighting. They ain't got time to look after their children or do a decent day's work. If somebody was to tell them, they'd probably raise Cain and call it all a lie."

Pop nodded. "What about Maydell?" he asked. "Who's she been seeing?"

"I don't know. I know she's been pirooting around. You can always tell when a woman starts that business," Mr. Petty replied in disgust. Whether in disgust with all women in general or just because Maydell wasn't pirooting with him, I didn't know. "But somebody is being darn careful not to let it get out," he added.

"She won't tell Dolly who he is," Pop said. Mr. Petty remained silent, and Pop continued. "Tell me what you think of Horace and Bruno."

"Bruno is a jailbird," Mr. Petty said. "You know that as well as I do, Pope."

"He told Kit he just got out of prison for killing a man years ago," Pop said.

"Yeah, well," Mr. Petty said. "Bruno is the kind of man who wouldn't mind killing somebody if he thought they needed it, but I can't see him making a big to-do over it. He'd just knock them in the head and go on."

Pop nodded. "I know, but I worry about Kit and Whitey being over there so much."

"Let me tell you something, Pope," Mr. Petty said. "I went over there one day to watch those boys racing, and I stood back some so they wouldn't notice me. Bruno never takes his eyes off those boys. If they take a tumble, he's right there to make sure they're okay."

"Yes," Pop agreed. "I hate to be suspicious of any man who is kind to my son, but this case has me suspecting everybody of everything."

"Naw," Mr. Petty assured him. "You ain't got anything to worry about there. Kit told me Horace is in love with some good-for-nothing heinie shaker back East, and he ain't got the inclination to court Clara Grace, but that don't stop him and Bruno from positioning theirselves in the alley so when she walks by of a mornings to go to the slaughterhouse, they can watch her twitch her bustle."

Pop laughed. "Well, that's a relief," he said. "What do you think about Horace?"

"Pope, he's a mortician," Mr. Petty said. "Anybody that don't mind fooling with dead people ain't like us. But other than that, he knows good horseflesh, and I suppose he's an all right fellow even if he does have some French blood in him."

Pop nodded, and taking a deep breath, went on. "I've got to ask you about the Klan."

"I don't know nothing about that shit," Mr. Petty said emphatically.

"Yes, you do," Pop said. "You know more gossip than Melvin Foster."

"Humph," Mr. Petty said. "Melvin just likes to pretend he knows everything. Melvin don't know whether to scratch his watch or wind his ass."

"Tull," Pop persisted. "Whitey told Kit that Ephraim Hutchins is in the Klan."

"I have heard that," Mr. Petty conceded. "Most of that worthless scutter comes out of the Cedar Bend community, closer to where Whitey's parents live."

"We've already figured that Whitey's father is probably in it," Pop said, "but the boy didn't tell us."

"He wouldn't. His pa would torture him in ways you don't even know about. Whitey's probably sweating blood right now because he blabbed to Kit about Ephraim. Whitey's old man is the one who should have been taken out and tarred and feathered."

"I hardly know Whitey's parents," Pop said.

"They do most of their trading at Cedar Bend," Mr. Petty said. "Whitey's mother is the one who encourages him to come over here and play with Kit. She's sickly, and she is hoping that if something happens to her, you and Dolly will take Whitey in."

"Things are as bad as that for the boy?" Pop asked.

"Worse," Mr. Petty said. "But for now, the old lady needs him around at least part of the time.

"Look, Pope. I appreciate you and Julius setting me up here and letting me pay you out. But if word gets around I said anything to you about who rides with the Klan, my barns, my stables, my wagon yard are poof! Up in smoke."

Pop gave him a steely look. "Maybe you think a whore and Oscar got what they deserved, Tull," he said. "But a trap was set that almost had Kit and Whitey as the victims. Tell me if you know something else. Now, on the nights when the Klan rides, does Julius take his horse out?"

Mr. Petty snorted. "No, he hasn't got guts enough to ride with the Klan, and he wouldn't take a horse that distinctive out if he did. Most of them ride dark horses. Sometimes they'll paint a white sock on one to disguise it, or cover a white star or a sock with stove black. But they don't take nothing out that could identify them.

"You're letting yourself be influenced by Melvin's wild talk," Mr. Petty continued. "Melvin has hated Julius almost from day one, and when their pa left all that land to Julius, that's when Melvin really went loco."

"I know, but Julius is holding something back from me, and I don't know what it is," Pop said. "What about this Tabor, does he ride with them?"

Mr. Petty pooh-poohed that idea right away. "They wouldn't let the likes of him ride with them to a privy painting party."

Pop pounded a fist on the table in frustration. "I don't know if it's one person causing all this misery or a group of nuts out there deciding who's sinful and who's not."

"I don't think it's the Klan, Pope," Mr. Petty said. "The Klan never did much here on account of you. They know you let Harmonica John trade in your store and play music. They know they'd have to answer to you. And after that tarring and feathering incident, you and Asa made it pretty darn plain they better not pull that trash in the Methodist church.

"And I hate to admit it, but that dunce-head Ephraim Hutchins isn't going to do anything to sour his chances with Clara Grace."

Pop rose. "Thank you for being honest with me, Tull," he said.

"Pope, I knowed you since I was old enough to feel the itch and too young to know to scratch it. You'll figure this out and put a stop to it," Mr. Petty said, rising.

"Well, thank you. Kit," Pop said turning to me, but I was already up off the floor and by his side.

Mr. Petty walked in front to open the door, but he paused with his hand on the knob. "She was a pretty *fraulein*, wasn't she, Pope?" he said wistfully. "Such tits! I love a woman with big tits."

"Yes, she was, Tull." Pop nodded. "She was pretty at that."

He opened the door, and as I passed by him, Mr. Petty gave the top of my head a surprising rub. Pop and I went out into the night, hand in hand as before. As soon as we walked into the store and shut the door behind us, I asked, "Pop, Mr. Petty is a brave man, isn't he? He's not a coward?"

"Yes," Pop replied, hanging up the cane and taking off his jacket. "I'd say Tull Petty is one of the bravest men I know. The only thing he is afraid of is losing at love."

"But he cried, Pop," I said as we walked to the back.

Pop halted and looked down at me. "Kit, that doesn't mean anything. I've seen men in combat killing the enemy right and left, behaving as heroically as a man can do in those circumstances and still have tears streaming down their faces. All that matters is if a man runs from himself and his friends, or if he stays and faces trouble."

I nodded, and Pop hugged me. I looked up into his face. "You're facing trouble right now, aren't you, Pop?"

"I sure as hell am, boy," Pop said. "Now let's go to bed."

As we began walking to the back of the store again, I whispered, "Pop."

"What?" he whispered back.

"Clara Grace doesn't have big tits."

"Kit," Pop said conspiratorially. "I imagine Clara Grace's tits would suit Tull Petty right down to the ground just the way they are."

The next day, Mr. Petty was back to being a grouchy old man, and I was back to being a pesky little kid. But Mr. Petty told the mayor if he didn't stop saying Whitey and I were making up that business about the knife, he was going to hit him between the eyes with a singletree, and I told Clara Grace I thought she ought to be nicer to Mr. Petty.

CHAPTER 18

Whitey didn't show up, so I had to visit Horace and Bruno by myself. I petted Ace, happy to see that he was his old self again.

"Did you ride?" Pop asked at supper. He looked around the empty table and gave a sigh of pleasure. Clara Grace said she wasn't feeling well and had stayed in her room. Our house was happily free from lovesick suitors for one night.

"No, sir," I answered, trying to remember not to talk with my mouth full. I swallowed and said, "Mr. Bruno wasn't there when I got there; he'd gone to the train station to fetch the mail. When he came back, he had a letter in his hand, and he told me he thought I'd better go on home."

"A letter?" my mother asked as she poured Pop another glass of water. "I wonder if it was from his sister or his sweetheart?"

"I don't know," I said. "I just know Mr. Horace got all excited when he saw the letter."

"Maybe Melvin will tell us tomorrow," Pop said dryly.

That night, Pop picked up his guitar and began strumming for the first time in a long while. First one and then another drifted in until we had a small knot of people who said almost nothing, but expressed all their fears and emotions into the music they played. Clara Grace didn't go to the back or wander around restlessly. Instead, she spent almost the entire evening sitting beside my mother as they both listened. Asa came in, but lounged across the room with the other men and carefully avoided looking directly at Clara Grace. Tull Petty usually went to bed with the chickens, but that night he came, taking a spot some distance from Asa, but he wasn't quite as successful at keeping his eyes off Clara Grace. Toward the end of the evening, Clara Grace surprised my parents when she quietly asked if someone could play "Ava Maria." Pop said he thought he could, and when she replied, "Thank you, Captain," I thought both of my parents showed unusual control by not falling out of their chairs. Clara Grace couldn't bring herself to call him "Pope," but I figured it was just a matter of time before she began calling him "Pop" like everybody else.

"She didn't call me Edmund," Pop whispered to my mother later that evening as they locked the store.

"She hasn't called you Edmund since that night we were so worried about you, and I asked her to pray."

"If I'd known that's all it took," Pop said, "I would have asked her to pray for me a long time ago."

The next morning, even before we finished breakfast, Ephraim Hutchins arrived with a wagonload of supplies, having decided to deliver Pop's order personally. Asa saw the wagon and ambled over. Pop had Mr. Hutchins drive his wagon to the west side next to the storeroom. After Pop checked it in and instructed Mr. Hutchins's hired help where to unload it, he gestured to a large post oak nearby.

"Could I talk with you a minute over yonder, Ephraim?" he asked. He looked at me and said, "Kit, fetch us a couple of chairs off the storeroom wall, would you, son."

"Is this about Miss Clara Grace?" Mr. Hutchins asked. "I've been trying to draw her slowly away from that Scarlet Woman, Pope."

Pop took him by the arm. "Good luck with that," he said, and began to guide him to the shade tree.

Asa went with me into the darkened storeroom, pulling an old slat-back chair off the wall and handing it to me. He took another, and we went to where Pop stood talking to Mr. Hutchins, who now wore a frown of unhappiness and belligerence. I placed a chair close to the tree trunk for Pop and went around to the other side, plopping down at its base where I would be partially hidden. I picked up a little stick to play with while Asa gave the other chair to Mr. Hutchins and leaned against the tree. Pop sat down and crossed his legs, while Mr. Hutchins sat down slowly, stiff with legs spread, as if he might jump up and run away any second.

"Pope, I only rode with them that one time," Mr. Hutchins was saying. "If you had seen what we had witnessed! That poor woman was repeatedly abused by the hand of a fiend. I know the Bible intones fathers to be diligent in disciplining their children, but he was not whipping them for their own good; he was beating them nearly to death for his own sinful pleasure.

"We had a right and moral obligation to the community to put a stop to it," he thundered self-righteously.

"Ephraim," Pop said sternly. "I know you had the woman's best interests at heart, but did it ever occur to you that you were riding with men who were probably doing the same things to their own families? That man most likely owed one of those men money or had some other grudge against him, and I can almost guarantee you that one or two men within that group got everybody else stirred up for reasons of their own. And you fell right into the trap, and your good name was used to lend respectability to it."

Mr. Hutchins didn't answer, and I peeked around the tree. His face showed the storm raging within him. He didn't want to believe Pop, but knew what Pop was saying might be true.

"I don't care if Clara Grace is a Catholic," Pop said. "People can search for God any way they choose, and as long as they don't interfere with my search, I don't care. Right now, I don't even care about the Klan as long as they are not causing trouble in Muskrat Hill. But we have got to catch a murderer or murderers. Now, Ephraim, tell me the truth, do you think the Klan had anything to do with these murders?"

"I did not know the dead woman," Ephraim said through tight lips. "As far as I know, Oscar Sorenson was a good practicing Protestant with no cause to incite hatred against him."

"The woman was probably a prostitute, and Oscar had a secret sin that I will not reveal," Pop said. "Was there any person or persons in your short dealings with the Klan who you thought might be unbalanced enough to kill in such a brutal way, thinking they were ridding the world of sin?"

Mr. Hutchins again did not answer right away. He sat with nostrils flared, either in anger or fear, I could not tell.

"You are thinking I did this, aren't you, Pope? Because of what happened to my wife," he said.

Pop didn't say anything. Rotating his head back and forth between Pop and Asa, Mr. Hutchins said, "I did not kill her. She was an unhappy, unbalanced woman. There was insanity in her family that I overlooked when I married her, thinking surely it would not happen to her. It did, and she killed herself."

"I know all those things," Pop said quietly. "And I was not thinking of your wife. But I do need an answer. Don't you see how important it is, Ephraim?"

Mr. Hutchins closed his eyes, and it really did appear as if he was thinking mightily about it. His lips moved silently for a moment. Opening his lids, he looked straight at Pop.

"I realize now you are probably right about them using me, Pope," he said. "But I can think of no man or men who would go to those lengths."

Pop let out a long sigh. "Thank you, Ephraim," he said. He and Asa were no closer to an answer than before.

"Pope," Mr. Hutchins asked rather timorously. "Does Miss Clara Grace know about this?"

"About you riding with the Klan?" Pop asked. "Unfortunately, yes. I would advise you to tell her what you told me. If you want to explain about your wife, that's your business."

Mr. Hutchins stood up. He straightened himself so that he resembled a stiff soldier. "Pope, Asa, since you have asked me about these murders, and I have assured you I had nothing to do with them, I will tell you what I really think."

"What is that, Ephraim?" Pop asked tiredly.

Mr. Hutchins looked from him to Asa and back again. "God Almighty has allowed Satan to unleash his hand in Muskrat Hill as an indictment against the music you play in your store, Pope. It is a direct punishment against the sinful revelry of this community."

Pop looked up at Mr. Hutchins. "Tell Clara Grace that, too," he said.

Mr. Hutchins turned on his heels and headed for the front of the store. Pop rubbed his forehead with his fingers. "I think I just lost my best supplier," he said.

"No, you didn't," Asa said. "He'll be back to talk more about his religious beliefs. You'll never shake him."

"You're probably right at that," Pop said.

"Pop," Asa said. "I just remembered something."

"What?"

"Nieman is the German word for 'no man.' That's probably not Bruno's real last name."

Pop let out a long breath. "I didn't think it was," he said. "Kit, go find Whitey and see if he wants to go squirrel hunting or something with you for a while. And don't put any more burrs on Mr. Hutchins's wagon seat to see how high he jumps when he sits on it like you did the other time he was here. He deserves it, but don't do it."

But I didn't feel like deviling Mr. Hutchins. I went in search of Whitey, wondering why I liked Mr. Petty, who had almost killed a woman, and disliked Mr. Hutchins, who had wanted to save one. It didn't make sense.

I spied Whitey just as he strolled into town. I began walking toward him, but as I passed the undertaker's parlor, Bruno appeared in front of me. I stopped short.

"What is it, Bruno?" I asked, because he looked upset.

He signed for me to go back and get Pop right away. I nodded and hollered at Whitey. "Whitey! Come on!" I waved my arm to him before speeding back to the store. I burst through the door as Asa and Pop looked up in surprise. Whitey busted in right after me.

"Pop!" I said. "Mr. Bruno said for you to come to the undertaker's parlor right now. I think something's wrong, Pop."

He rose immediately. "You better come with me, Asa," he said. He began to holler "Dolly!" but turned and saw her.

"I'm right here," she said, her forehead creased in worry. "I hope it's nothing bad."

"We'll see," Pop said, reaching for his hat.

Bruno waited for us in the alley. He didn't seem to mind that Pop had brought an entourage. He began to sign to Pop, so fast that Pop had to ask him to slow down. Pop translated while Bruno signed.

Horace's letter of the day before was from the girl he loved, informing him she was marrying another man. Her parents had convinced her she wouldn't be happy married to an undertaker, and their children might be born with the same affliction Horace's sister had.

"They probably just didn't want her to move to Texas," Pop muttered.

She had decided to marry a cousin instead.

"That makes no sense if they are worried about hereditary problems," Asa said.

Bruno grew agitated and signed "Stop." Pop and Asa nodded

and Bruno continued.

Horace had started drinking the day before and had been drinking steadily since then. Bruno was afraid he would kill himself. He had a gun that Bruno was unable to get away from him. Could Pop please do something?

Pop nodded, thinking hard for a moment. He looked down at Whitey and me. "Whatever I say, you boys go along with it. Got it?"

"Yes, sir," we agreed.

"Where is he?" Pop asked.

Bruno pointed to the barn and led the way, pausing to let us go in first. Pop stopped at the stables and called, "Horace, it's me, Pop."

We heard a thud that sounded like a chair falling behind a door at the back of the barn and the echo of boots walking unsteadily. Horace opened the door, his face unshaven and his clothes disheveled. "I am afraid I am unable to entertain callers at the moment," he mumbled and turned to go back.

"Wait, Horace," Pop said. "Today is Kit's birthday. We want to organize a little horse race down by the river for him this afternoon. He wants that more than anything else for his birthday." Pop shoved my back, and I jumped.

"That's right, Mr. Horace. Please let me have a horse race with Nero and Nighthawk for my birthday," I pleaded.

Horace looked at me unsteadily, rocking back and forth. "A horse race?" he slurred.

"Yes," Pop said. "Please, sir."

Horace stood there contemplating me, trying to focus his eyes. "I fear I am intoxicated."

"That's all right. We'll get you sobered up," Pop said.

Horace stood there blinking and staring. I was afraid he was going to refuse. He turned and stumbled back into the room, but came out again carrying his coat and hat. "Bruno," he said, trying to measure his words correctly. "Would you make some coffee, please?"

It started out small, like so many things in Muskrat Hill did, and exploded into an extravaganza of people wild with emotions. We left Bruno to sober Horace up and help him get cleaned and dressed. At the store, my mother clasped her hands together in delight at the news. "A race for Kit? Can we close the store and make it a picnic? Please, Pope? Please?"

"A horse race?!" Clara Grace exclaimed. "I'm not going to any horse race."

"It's just for children, Clara Grace," my mother explained.

"I'm not going," Clara Grace said. "They'll be gambling there, and I am not going to contribute to the downfall of Muskrat Hill society."

"Oh, Clara Grace," my mother fretted. "There won't be any serious gambling. Not the kind where if they don't pay up they get their legs broken."

Clara Grace crossed her arms, looking pig-headed. "I'm not going, Dolly," she said.

"Then I can't go either," my mother cried. "I can't leave you here alone all afternoon."

Clara Grace said nothing; my mother looked down. She said with her voice catching in tears as she dabbed at her eyes, "I won't get to see Kit race."

"Oh, all right!" Clara Grace burst out. "I'll go. As long as you promise it will not turn into a drunken revelry with men betting money that will cause their children to go hungry should they lose it to some sharpie."

"I promise," my mother said excitedly. "Let's make it a picnic, Pope. Yes?"

"Yes, yes, yes," my father said. "Great Scott! Does everything have to be so dramatic?"

Whitey and I ran to the livery to tell Mr. Petty, but it wasn't necessary. Somehow, he already knew, and five men were talking about running their horses in our race. Pop came in behind us in time to hear Mr. Petty say, "I'm going to see if Horace will let me run Ace. Thunderation! What a horse!" He caught sight of Pop and started yelling. "Pope, don't you try to race Smokey. He's too old for that. You let him go so he can see, but don't you race him."

"Tull," Pop said in exasperation. "I have no intention of racing Smokey or any other horse. Kit and Whitey are racing, I'm not."

Asa stood beside Pop, a strange mood flooding his face, causing him to look more like Chief Asa than Marshal Asa. "If these men are racing their horses," he said. "I'm going to race my bay."

"Well, tarnation!" Tull Petty roared, throwing down a towel. "That just tears it. That gelding can outrun anything around here."

"Tull!" Pop exclaimed. "You've never even seen Asa's horse in a race."

"I know race flesh when I see it," Mr. Petty bellowed.

The mayor came in and joined us. "My palomino. Tull, do you think my palomino has a chance?"

"No!" Mr. Petty hollered. "Besides, who's going to stand at the finish line and judge the race? That's your job."

"I have a business to run," Pop said. He turned to Whitey and me. "See if Horace needs you to do anything and then come back home. I want you boys to rest before the race. I don't want the water dripping out of your kettle before the fire warms up."

"Yes, sir, Pop," I said and Whitey nodded.

"I'm going with them," Mr. Petty said. "I've got to ask Horace if I can race Ace before somebody else does."

When we left, the mayor was wringing his hands in a dither,

knowing he should judge the race, but dying to run his palomino.

Horace didn't need or want us. He wanted to prepare his babies by himself. The man who had been so inebriated he could hardly walk thirty minutes earlier now worked on his horses like an evangelist building up his congregation for the big altar call. When we left, Mr. Petty was jabbering in his ear, telling him how hurt Ace would be if he didn't get to run.

Before we made it back to the store, Scut Tabor caught up with us. "Do you think the mayor would let me race his palomino? I've been sitting in the trees peeking in on you and Whitey. Every time Horace tells you something, I go home and try it on our old mare. I know I can do it."

"You can ask him," I said, a little bewildered to know we were being spied upon.

"No, you ask him for me. Whitey, you ask him; he likes you for some reason."

"Me?" Whitey said.

"Yes, ask him," Scut urged.

We went back to the livery, and in a quivering voice, Whitey repeated Scut's request to the mayor.

"No!" he exploded. "I'm not going to let that boy on my horse." He paused in a quandary. "But I want to see my palomino in that race! But no! Yes! No! Tell him maybe."

We went back and told Scut he had a chance. It was up to him to be on hand to take it.

In the back of the store, my mother had become a whirlwind in the kitchen. She was throwing blankets, plates, napkins, and everything else she could think of in one corner, while running to the stove and tossing food on it in the other. Clara Grace avoided the fallout by announcing she would work in the store until time to go. Pop herded us to the back porch and told us to lie down, while he lay on a cot next to the wall.

My mother ran to the back door. "Pope, can Mr. Petty hitch

Gastor to our old wagon? I'll never be able to get all this stuff in the buggy."

"I already told him, Dolly," Pop said. "Go back in the house and try to pace yourself so you don't fall to pieces before we get there."

"Yes, Pope," she said breathlessly, and ran back into the kitchen. Pop just shook his head.

Men kept coming around to the back of the house to talk to Pop about the race, but he refused to get up and wouldn't let us either. We looked like a bunch of lazy hillbillies, but Pop didn't care. When we weren't being interrupted, we went over the things Horace had told us about racing. Pop added to our store of knowledge, and I learned something else about him that day. Evidently, he had raced more than just a few times himself.

When the time came to leave, Mr. Petty had two of his men bring the wagon around to the back of the store and load our things. Pop grumbled that he would have to pay them for the whole afternoon. They would have to unload everything at the river, pack it back up after the race, and unload it again once we returned home. My mother was so happy, she pretended not to hear him, but Clara Grace gave him a withering, "I have no pity on you" look. Whitey and I, excited beyond belief, acted just like my mother. The men drove the wagon around to the front while we tramped through the store, locking things up.

On the sidewalk, we were greeted with a knot of stern-faced citizens led by Netta Crenshaw and Louella Foster. "We are protesting this horse race, Pope," Netta said. As she went down the list of reasons why we were morally wrong and would bring ruin upon us all, Horace arrived riding Black Jack and leading Nero and Nighthawk. Next to him sat Tull Petty on Smokey and leading Ace. The mayor tried to hide behind them with his palomino. Asa let the widow wind down before speaking to her in a kind voice. "This race is planned for the enjoyment of our citizens, Miss Netta. I assure you we will not allow organized gambling."

Louella Foster caught sight of her husband lurking behind Mr. Petty. "Julius!" she barked. "You are certainly not riding in this race."

"Oh, no, dear," he said coming out of hiding and trying to put on a good front. "I have to go because I have to judge. They need a judge, and it is my duty," he said, his voice ringing in righteousness. "No, I'm going to sponsor one of our town's youngsters and let him ride." He looked around in a mild panic and found Scut Tabor, who had been dogging his heels all afternoon. "I'm going to allow this young man to participate," he said, making it sound like he was promoting Scut down the road to responsible citizenship by letting him ride his horse.

Louella gave Scut a look of disgust and shook her head. "Well, I'm not going. I will not be a part of this."

My mother pretended deafness with Louella as easily as she had done with my father earlier. Climbing into the wagon, she told Horace, "We'll have a picnic after the race," she said. "And there will be plenty for you and Mr. Bruno."

Horace glanced unhappily at the citizens' protest group, but turned back to my mother and said in his well-bred way, "Bruno prefers to stay here, madam, but I will be honored to picnic with you."

"What are we waiting for?" Mr. Petty bawled. "Let's go!"

I expected Louella Foster to give Mr. Petty the same glare of disgust she gave Scut, but the stare she gave him was full of some stony and hidden emotion I didn't understand. Regardless, she turned on her heels and stomped away as our wagon rolled out of town.

CHAPTER 19

When we arrived at the wide flat bottomland near the river, there were probably fifty men with horses loitering near the starting line. When my mother saw them, her mouth dropped open in shock. "Pope!" she cried, turning to him. "We can't let Kit ride with those men. He'll fall off and be killed!"

"Now, Dolly," my father said gently, patting her hand to calm her. "When Kit was born, we made a pack that we wouldn't baby him."

"You decided on that and made me agree!" my mother cried. Her eyes filled with tears, and she looked miserably at the group of men intent on racing. "He's our only child, Pope!" she said, turning back to my father.

"Dolly," Pop said, and the way he said it let her know his mind was made up.

"Oh, all right," she agreed. I let out a huge breath I hadn't realized I'd been holding. She leaned over and kissed me and then Whitey. "God be with you," she said. "I'm praying for your safety."

I hugged my mother and kissed her right there in front of everybody.

Pop had the men set up the blankets and chairs on a knoll in front of the finish line where they could see above the heads of the crowd. Horace had been standing there waiting, watching the men with their horses just as miserably as my mother had, but for a different reason.

202

"It is not seemly for a man in my profession to race," Horace murmured dolefully as Pop stood near him. Before Pop could reply, Asa rode up on his bay.

"Miss Dolly, Miss Clara Grace," he said, nodding his head in greeting.

We stared because he was almost unrecognizable. Hatless and shoeless, he had tied a twisted red bandanna around his forehead to catch the sweat. Gone were the suit, tie, and vest, replaced with an old cotton shirt and tattered pants. Like Whitey and me, he would be riding bareback.

"Good luck, Asa," my mother said gaily, while Clara Grace continued to gape in surprise. He gave us a happy wave and turned his horse to join the other men.

"He's a preacher, too, isn't he? Besides being a marshal?" Horace asked my father for confirmation, although Asa had invited him to church many times.

"Yes," Pop replied. "Look here, Horace. I don't know what the people in Charleston are like, but in Texas, if our undertaker wants to be in a horse race, we don't care."

Horace jerked his jacket off and removed his hat and tie. "Miss Dolly," he said. "May I ask you to mind my things until after the race?"

"Certainly," she replied graciously.

Whitey and I grinned. Black Jack was in the race!

Pop took us down to where the men were preparing to line up. It was a rowdy mixture of slick fast horses, slow nags, and stubborn mules. Men smiled, spit tobacco, joked, and cursed while the horses milled around us, many of them pawing the ground in nervousness. We were near Asa and Horace, who somehow managed to look somber and happy all at the same time. Harmonica John walked up leading one of his grandsons astride a swayback nag whose best days ended shortly after birth many years previously. The boy, however, was as excited and afraid as we were.

"Pop," John said, "I thought this was supposed to be a race for children."

"It was, John," Pop said. "But something happened along the way."

A man sitting on a stout workhorse turned to glare at John and his grandson. "This here race ain't for no jungle bunnies," he said. "Get on out of here, niglet!"

Horace whirled Black Jack so fast, it startled everybody. He gazed down at the man imperiously. "It is my understanding that this race is for anyone who cares to enter, sir," he said in an icy drawl.

As I watched Horace stare the man down, I realized then he was a killer. He would kill for what he perceived as an honorable reason in an honorable way, and he would do it with no compunction whatsoever.

The man, not wishing to die that day, backed off. "I guess I misunderstood," he mumbled and turned, riding away.

Horace did not look at John, and John did not look at Horace. They might never like one another, but they both knew how to act like gentlemen.

"Kit, Whitey, come here," Pop said. "Let me talk to you."

We obediently moved closer to Pop as he bent down to talk in a lower tone. "What is the most important thing to do in a horse race?" he asked.

"Stay on the horse," we repeated faithfully.

"That's right," he said. "Now some of these men get mighty excited and lose all their self-control in a race. They may try to kick you off your horse, so don't be taken off guard if someone takes a poke at you. Just hold on to that mane and keep going."

"Yes, sir, Pop," we nodded.

He described two men some distance away from us without looking directly at them. "They'll lose their heads in a race and do every underhanded thing they can think of, and then be sorry about it later. Steer clear of them if you can."

He rose and called to Asa and Horace. "Can we line the boys up on your right so they don't have to mingle with the grown men?"

They both agreed it was a good idea and began to try to get the children, boys with one girl included, to move to one side of the starting line. Pop gave us a leg up on our horses and patted our legs, smiling. He left us on our own and went back to where my mother waited, chewing on her handkerchief.

I saw the two Indian men we had visited a few weeks previously. How had they heard about the race and gotten to Muskrat Hill so fast? They caught Asa's eye and waved. "We are with you, brother!" they called with big grins. Asa returned their encouraging words with a wave and smile of his own.

I hadn't even noticed which horse I had gotten on until then. When I realized I was astride Nero, I smiled. Whitey and I loved both horses, but I favored Nero while he was partial to Nighthawk. Whitey was on my right; Mr. Petty was murmuring heartening words to Ace on my left. Horace sat upright, but casually, as if he was waiting for the horn to blow and someone to let out the hounds. Asa sat beside him on his big bay. Two men took bags of lime and sprinkled a starting line, placing another sprinkling a little over half a mile away to mark the finish.

The mayor walked up and down the line, shouting mostly useless instructions. "Settle that horse down! Get back, move back." Although Asa had been telling the truth about organized gambling, behind us, unorganized gambling flourished. Money kept passing from one hand to another as horses were stared at and heated arguments broke out over which one was better. Nero and Nighthawk were nervous being in such a rough crowd, and Whitey and I had a hard time keeping them under control.

Watching Mr. Petty murmuring sweet nothings into Ace's ear, I decided to do the same. As I stroked and talked softly to Nero, he calmed, and Whitey, seeing the luck I was having, did the same with Nighthawk.

There should have been a hard knot of fear in my stomach, but I was too young and naive to be anything but jumpy and scared. With all the men in the race, I figured I didn't have a chance so I didn't worry about winning. I just wanted to be able to stay on Nero and enjoy the thrill of the ride.

Horses and riders grew increasingly impatient for the race to begin. As tension grew, the crowd began to move to the finish line, leaving us feeling alone and as if in a vacuum. The mayor placed a chair in the most advantageous position to judge the horses coming across the white finish line. Men ready to challenge his decision if necessary gathered around him. Standing on the chair, the mayor looked at us, and then looked at a man standing midway and to one side, holding a pistol. The mayor raised his hand in the air.

I let my eyes find Pop in the crowd. He smiled and nodded to me. The mayor's hand went down; I heard the pistol fire and immediately urged Nero on as hard as I could.

Horses surged forward in a mass. Glancing beside me, I looked in horror as Whitey slid to one side of Nighthawk. Holding on to the mane, he managed to inch his way back up. On my other side, Tull Petty's eyes glazed in a rapture that excluded everything except himself and Ace. Horace and Asa were running neck and neck in front of us. I realized I didn't have to worry about anyone kicking me off my horse because there was no one else with us. It was Asa and Horace racing in front, and Mr. Petty, Whitey, and me leaving everyone else in the dust.

The horses' exhilaration outstripped ours as they raced with all their might. Horace had trained them so much as a team that Ace, Nero, and Nighthawk raced side by side, and I don't think it occurred to any of us to try to spur our horse to pass the other.

Pop told me later it was the most beautiful horse race he'd ever witnessed. Asa's bay would take the lead, and then Black Jack would take it away. At the finish line, they were so close, it was judged a tie. Nero, Nighthawk, and Ace came barreling in directly after Asa's bay and Black Jack, bringing in a three-way tie for second place.

Asa smiled happily; Horace sat astride Black Jack, clutched in the throes of silent ecstasy. By the way Mr. Petty carried on, you would have thought Ace had taken first place. As I looked happily and out of breath around me, I saw a few men cursing and abusing their horses for losing. Not wishing to be like them, I copied Mr. Petty again and praised Nero, knowing I had done nothing to win except to hold on. I didn't know how Scut and Harmonica John's grandson fared, but they were smiling the same as we were, thrilled to have participated. I kept trying to find Pop in the wildly exuberant crowd around us, but I couldn't see him. When he did arrive, I slid off Nero and hugged him with all my might.

"I stayed on, Pop," I said, looking up at him and grinning.

Pop hugged me again. "That you did, boy. That you did."

Asa, Mr. Petty, and Horace sat on our blankets and ate like ravenous wolves all of the food my mother had almost killed herself preparing. Looking blissfully at Whitey and the rest of the people surrounding us, she smiled at Pop and me with a face filled with joy. Clara Grace almost smiled several times, but caught herself before letting a rampant emotion like mild happiness overwhelm her.

Just before time to go back to Muskrat Hill, I found Horace to one side, alone, and thanked him again for letting me ride Nero. He looked down and gave me a gentle smile.

"It's not really your birthday, is it?" he asked.

"No, sir," I grinned. "But it feels like it."

Horace smiled again and looked abstractly at the people around us as they prepared to leave. "Your father is the only person keeping this town from self-destructing, Kit," he said, almost to himself. "He's the only one."

Although there were eventually many more races, the impromptu race that afternoon was to be talked about more than any other for years to come. Black Jack, Ace, Nero, and Nighthawk generated more money in stud fees than they ever did pulling a hearse. Generations later, people would still brag about owning a horse that came out of the "Dubois" line.

The Widow Crenshaw met Pop back at the store with both jaws flapping. "Pope, you must have that man arrested."

"What man, Netta?" Pop said, unable to get away from her.

"That Bruno person," she said. "Do you know what he did? He sat there in front of that mortician's parlor and never moved an inch. Just sat there giving everybody that walked by the evil eye."

"A man can't be arrested for sitting in a chair on the sidewalk, Netta," Pop began and stopped. "Did you say he sat in front and never moved?"

"Yes, are you getting deaf, Pope? Everybody says you are because you are having Horace Dubois teach you sign language."

"I'm not there yet, Netta," Pop murmured. He managed to get away from her, and taking Asa aside next to the storeroom, he repeated what she had said.

"In front?" Asa asked in surprise.

"Yes," Pop said. "He always stays in the back away from people, but with more than half the town gone, Netta said he sat in the front and refused to budge until we came back."

Asa scratched his ear with an abstracted air and removed his headband. "I don't know what to think, Pop."

Pop looked in the direction of the funeral parlor. "It was like he was guarding the town," he said. "I think Bruno knows more than he's telling."

CHAPTER 20

The next morning, Horace, flush with excitement, entered the store waving a letter. "It's from my sister," he said. "She and my mother are leaving to visit relatives in Mississippi. They want me to meet them there and bring them back to Muskrat Hill."

"Oh, that's wonderful!" my mother exclaimed. "Do you think they will stay?"

"I don't know," Horace said. "I've been writing them about Muskrat Hill, but it has still taken me by surprise that they are so anxious to come here." He paused before continuing. "We will be traveling under the name of Dubois."

"Of course," Pop said.

"There is one more thing," Horace said, hesitating again. "My sister is bringing her newborn with her. I think perhaps that's the real reason they are coming. My mother hinted that she and the baby girl might have a better chance in Muskrat Hill."

"Oh, yes," my mother said, smiling and nodding her head. "You mean the younger sister whose husband was killed in a tragic railroad accident? Such a sad thing for a handsome and wealthy young man to have his life cut so tragically short. I'm going to tell Netta Crenshaw and Louella Foster all about it later on today."

Horace looked at my mother as if she had taken leave of her senses. It took a moment for the realization of the protection she was offering his sister and her infant to sink in.

"What was that poor boy's name again?" my mother asked.

Horace sunk into thought, desperately trying to make up a name. "They named the baby Giselle after my Grandmother Thibodeaux," he offered.

"What a lovely name," my mother said. "Thibodeaux, yes, Charles Thibodeaux—that's what I'll tell Netta and Louella."

Horace and Pop walked out onto the porch together. "Miss Dolly is a remarkable woman," Horace said. "But everyone heard from the Pinkerton agent what happened to my sister and will know this fairytale husband was not real."

"Of course, they'll know it," Pop said. "But for the child's sake and their own desire for romance, they'll let themselves believe it. Dolly knows what a hard time Asa has had struggling with that, and she doesn't want to see a little girl go through it."

Horace stuck out his hand. "Thank you, Pop. Thank you for everything."

Pop nodded and shook his hand. "When are you leaving?"

"The first train out in the morning," Horace replied. "Bruno has agreed to look after my horses and conduct what business needs to be done. Marshal Asa said he would help him with the, uh, customer relations part."

"Horace," Pop said. "What is Bruno's real story? You must know more than you are telling us."

Horace looked at Pop for a minute before shaking his head. "I cannot betray a trust," he said. "You will have to take my word as a gentleman that Bruno's interests here are pure and noble."

Pop couldn't get any more out of him but didn't get mad about it. He cheerfully wished Horace a safe trip and went back into the store. Later he repeated it to Asa, saying with a short laugh, "But Horace has his own ideas about what is pure and noble. If Bruno told him he was here to avenge the murder of his crippled wife and kill the man who destroyed half of his face, Horace would see that as pure and noble."

I went outside for a while that afternoon, not really knowing what to do with myself. Whitey had gone home. I played ball with other friends, but unable to keep my mind on the game, decided to go back to the store. Unfortunately, the Widow Crenshaw caught me meandering down the street.

"Little boy, little boy," she stood on her porch and called in a high falsetto.

I looked around the street, but I was the only little boy in it. I turned back to her and took a step forward. "Yes, ma'am?" I said, afraid to come closer.

"I want you to go fetch your father here right this minute. No dawdling, now," she instructed. "It is imperative that I speak to Pope at once. Imperative."

I nodded my head. "Yes, ma'am, I'll tell him."

"Without delay," she said.

"Yes, ma'am," I said, nodding and backing up. I turned and ran toward the store. I slowed down when there was no longer any danger of her yelling at me.

I found Pop behind the counter.

"Pop, the Widow Crenshaw says she has to see you right now," I said.

"What now?" Pop moaned. He made a frown. "Did you tell her to only take one of those powders a day?" he asked.

"Yes, sir, Pop," I answered indignantly. "I told her twice."

Pop shook his head in annoyance and pulled his apron off. "Go back and tell her I'm at the marshal's office and to meet me there."

"But you're not at Marshal Asa's office, Pop," I said.

"Well, I will be in a minute, now scoot," he said. He turned around and called, "Dolly!"

"I know," my mother called back in resignation. "I'll be up front in a minute."

I knew Mrs. Crenshaw wouldn't like what I had to tell her, and she didn't, so I repeated the message as fast as decently possible and left the same way. I turned and ran back up the street, meeting Pop on his way to Asa's office.

"Pop, since you've got the lures already tied, can we go fishing today?" I pleaded. "I can catch some grasshoppers for bait, too."

"I promise you," Pop said as we crossed the street. "As soon as I've finished with this old bat, the first thing I'm going to do is head for the fishing hole to calm my nerves. But don't tell your mother I called the widow an old bat," he added.

"Okay, Pop," I said happily, jumping ahead to open the door of the marshal's office for him.

Asa's office had a desk against one wall, a door leading to the back where he slept, and a jail cell big enough to hold two people but usually sat empty. When I walked in, this time there were two occupants, both young men who looked to be in their early twenties and wearing rough homespun not too carefully stitched together. They stood at the front of the cells, faces to the bars and long, hairy arms dangling out.

"How long are you going to keep us here?" the shorter one yelled at Asa who sat watching them from his desk.

"As long as it takes," Asa replied, nodding to us. "Hello, Pop, Kit."

Pop glanced at the young men. "What are they in for?"

"They got mad at their uncle's mule and put him on top of the train station and left him," Asa said. "I had a devil of a time getting him off."

"We didn't hurt him," the tallest one said.

"Yeah," the other said, echoing his companion's thick country accent. "That mule's mean. He bit a hunk out of my shoulder."

With an air of virtue, his companion nodded his head vigorously in agreement.

"It's like this," Asa said. "Your uncle is walking around town with an ax handle threatening to beat the tar out of you. You're in here for your own protection. Besides, if I can teach you a lesson for mistreating a poor old mule, maybe I won't have to string you up later for killing somebody."

With a disgruntled pout, the short one said, "You're a fine one to talk. Everybody knows Indians would run a horse to death, then eat it."

Asa grimaced in aggravation. "There's no law that says just because my ancestors did something, I have to do it, too."

Pop laughed. "That's right," he said. "Just because I strung your old grand-pap up for horse thieving doesn't mean you have to keep the family tradition alive."

In response, the prisoners grumbled and looked mad because they could not come up with a snappy comeback.

The door opened, and Netta Crenshaw entered. She wore the same dark dress with fussy lace, but this time she had on a bonnet that looked as if it had been sat on numerous times, and she carried a dainty, slightly soiled handkerchief. Asa stood up.

"Miss Netta," he said, nodding a greeting.

"Netta," Pop said cordially.

She scowled and turned to Pop. "Pope, I wanted to speak to you alone." She gave Asa a pointed and significant look so overly exaggerated it would not have been lost on the lowest and stupidest dog.

"If it's important, Netta," Pop said patiently. "Asa needs to hear about it."

She drew herself up imperially. "I don't know that you would want Asa to hear what I have to say, Pope."

"Now, Netta, you just don't worry about that," Pop said.

Asa lifted his chair and moved in front of Pop. "Here, Miss Netta," he said. "You sit here, and I'll take a chair back there, and you won't even know I'm here."

Asa took a seat near the cell door. He patted his knee, motioning for me to move to the rear with him. I walked over and leaned against his side. The widow frowned at him and grudgingly sat down, facing Pop, with her back to Asa, me, and the cell.

"All right, Netta," Pop said. "What is it?"

She fidgeted, getting herself situated before looking at Pop. "Pope," she began once she thought the timing was right. "I know who committed these murders."

Pop's face mirrored our shock. "Uh, you do?" he asked.

"Yes," she replied.

"And who is the murderer, Netta," Pop asked.

She leaned forward. "It's Dolly."

Asa squeezed my arm, indicating I was to keep silent. His mouth creased in amusement, as if he was trying hard not to smile. The two cellmates looked surprised. They looked at one another and mouthed the word, "Dolly?"

Pop's face showed nothing. "Netta," he said. "Maybe you better start from the beginning. Why do you think Dolly is the murderer?"

"Because she came into my house."

"When did Dolly come in your house?" Pop asked.

"Last night," she replied. "After I went to bed. I couldn't sleep. I heard a noise, and I got up. And do you know what I saw?" she said, her fat chin quivering in triumph. "Dolly, standing by my desk, going through Wilford's papers."

Pop looked puzzled. "Going through Wilford's papers?" he said.

The country boys looked confused and mouthed the word "papers?" at one another.

"That's right," she said. "On dear Wilford's desk. All of his things are still stacked there, just like he left them."

"Okay, let's get this straight," Pop said. "It was dark. You heard a noise. You went to investigate. How did you know it was Dolly? Were you carrying a lamp?"

"No, Pope," she answered. "The moonlight was coming in through the windows. I think I know Dolly when I see her."

Pop glanced at Asa and then back to the widow. "Was her hair up or down?" he asked.

She looked at Pop as if he was stupid. "I don't know, Pope. She had on a veil."

"Then how do you know it was Dolly?" he demanded.

"Because when I called out 'who's there?' she tripped and ran. She ran with a limp, just like Dolly."

Pop exchanged glances with Asa. "You called out 'who is it?' The woman, I assume in a dress and veil, hit her foot on something and limped, where? Out the front door?"

"Pope, really," the widow said in exasperation. "For goodness sakes. The back door, of course. I have too much furniture in the parlor; no one can even get through there."

Pop shook his head in disgust. "Netta, Dolly was with me all last night," he said firmly. "I have witnesses."

Mrs. Crenshaw clasped her hands together and rocked back and forth in sympathy. "Pope, Pope. If you had just waited for me until Wilford died, Pope."

Pop twisted in his chair uncomfortably, while Asa smothered a grin.

The widow placed her hands over her heart. "I'll never forget that night in San Antonio, Pope."

Behind me, the country boys were eating up this drama. One of them made an O with his finger and thumb on one hand and pushed his other index finger through it several times, grinning salaciously. Pop covered his forehead in embarrassment.

"I know how highly you thought of Wilford, Pope," she said. "Your own captain in the Rangers. How hard it must have been for you to push aside your own desires and wants for his sake."

She clutched her bosom and tried to look noble. "The sacrifices one must make in the name of honor and duty."

Pop rose. He looked daggers at the prisoners and Asa, who were thoroughly enjoying the show. "Netta," he said. "I do not know who was in your house last night, but it was not Dolly. Now you go on home."

Asa, who was trying hard not to laugh, went to the widow and helped her to her feet. "I'll look into it, Miss Netta," he said. "Uh, you haven't been drinking any of that medicinal wine you make lately, have you?"

"Of course not," she snapped. She collected herself and taking a deep breath, addressed my father. "Mark my word, Pope. That wife of yours is nothing but a cold-blooded killer! She has hoodwinked you and the rest of Muskrat Hill."

With that, she sailed out the door. The prisoners looked at Pop in hopeful expectation. He growled at them and sat back down. Asa leaned against his desk and grinned. "Pop! Your boss's wife?"

"Believe me," Pop said. "I will regret those ten minutes until the day I die."

The tall prisoner looked at Pop, his eyes bright and cheeks flushed. "What was she like?" he asked.

"Shut up!" Pop roared.

"And you held Wilford in such high regard," Asa said, biting the tip of his tongue to keep from laughing. "Shame on you, Pop."

"No, I didn't!" Pop barked. "I hated that good-for-nothing bastard. He was so lazy, we had to tell him to move his feet so he didn't kill the grass. He built his whole reputation on the sweat of other men."

Asa shook his head and teased. "Pop, Pop."

"I said I was sorry, didn't I?" Pop growled. "I've paid for my sin, trying to avoid that crackpot for the past thirty years." He stood and shook his finger around the room. "And none of you breathe a word about this to Dolly."

Asa began to laugh. "Oh, Pop, she knows. She already knows."

Pop took the jail keys from the wall and tossed them to Asa. "I'm going fishing. Let these boys go, too. I'll have them back by nightfall."

Asa grinned and opened the cell door. The two young men came out and joined Pop. He opened the front door.

"Are you going to tell us some more San Antonio stories?" one of them asked hopefully.

"Not in front of my son, I'm not," Pop replied. He pushed them out the door but hung back. "Find Maydell and ask her what she was doing in Netta's house last night," he told Asa. "Sweet-talk her, and she might confide in you."

"Miss Maydell?" Asa said in surprise. "Sweet-talk? I've never sweet-talked a woman in my life."

"Well, it's about time you learned," Pop said, and herding me out the door, we left.

I walked outside. Whitey appeared by my side. I thought about the things Mr. Petty told us. I looked at him and smiled. "Want to go fishing with us, Whitey?"

We stopped by the livery stable to tell Mr. Petty that Pop wanted the buggy. While he was getting it ready, Pop, Whitey, and I walked across the street to inform my mother where we were going.

"Pope, Netta Crenshaw just left here, and she was acting so strange," my mother said as she followed Pop to the back where we kept our fishing equipment.

"Don't pay any attention to her, Dolly," Pop said as he opened a cabinet and grabbed the box containing his lures.

"Pope, has she been giving you that 'if only you had waited until Wilford died' stuff again?"

Pop whirled around. "How can we have any crime in this

town when the women in it know everything that goes on?" he complained bitterly. Holding his lure box, he stomped out of the store, but both my mother and I knew it secretly pleased him.

It turned into the best fishing trip we had ever been on. Those two young goobers who went with us could out-fish anyone I had ever seen and were patient and kind in sharing their knowledge. We were catching one fish after the other, so much so that soon it became less about fishing than it did about talking. Pop was in a good mood, and he told stories of the things he had done when he was a young man. Not like the Netta Crenshaw fiasco, but tales of adventure that boys of all ages love. It was another side of Pop I had never seen before. Even years later, when I would happen across those country boys, they would bring up Pop's stories and say, "Your old man was something else, you know that?"

CHAPTER 21

Asa met us at the livery stable when we returned. He took a mess of fish and his two prisoners back to the jail.

"Kit, you and Whitey bring the rest of the catch," Pop said. "I'm taking the rods in."

Pop departed, leaving us to show off the booty to Mr. Petty. He nodded and complimented us. "But what I really want to know is," Mr. Petty complained, "how come that foot-washing Baptist and that pontifying Injun eat at your place all the time, and I never get an invite?"

I turned red and started to stutter something. I looked to Whitey for support, but he was watching me with anxious eyes. I turned back to Mr. Petty, drew myself up, and did the manly thing.

"Mr. Petty, how would you like to have supper with us tonight?" I said. "We are having fried fish, and there will be plenty."

"Don't mind if I do," Mr. Petty said. "Got to get cleaned up first, though. A man ain't supposed to go to supper stinking like a shithouse in the summertime after a heavy rain you know."

Whitey and I nodded in agreement. "I reckon not," I said.

Whitey and I took the fish across the street to the store, arriving after the mayor and his stout wife. Melvin's wagon was in front, but his housekeeper wasn't in it. The three Fosters blocked the door, and we had a hard time squeezing through with all those fish, but we remembered our manners and said,

"Excuse me," quietly.

Louella Foster was anything but hushed. I noticed Pop had disappeared to the back and knew he was probably waiting for Melvin and Louella to leave before reappearing.

"I have relatives in Atlanta," Louella said. "I'll write and see if they know the Thibodeauxes. They sound like a fine family. Now, Dolly," she paused, taking a deep breath. "I have something else I have to talk to you about. Julius doesn't know it because I just heard about it."

Melvin's eyes lit up in puerile excitement. My mother, watching Mrs. Foster warily, said, "Oh really? What is it?"

"It's about Maydell. I have it on good authority that she has been seen out alone at night. Now, Dolly, you know what that means."

My mother opened her mouth, but before she could say anything, the mayor's wife had already interrupted. "Dolly, I know what you are going to say, but you know as well as I do what is going to happen. We might as well face the truth. Maydell is eventually going to be with child; now who is going to take care of it?"

My mother blushed and looked as if she wished she was anywhere but in the store. "I've already talked about it with Pope," she admitted. "We both feel we are too old to take on that responsibility."

"Well, somebody has to."

"We will," the mayor said, looking more at the nearby shelves than at the two women and his brother. "We can take the baby if it comes to that."

His wife's mouth dropped open. "Julius!" she said in shock. She tried to say more, but he stopped her.

"It is my duty as mayor of this town," he said with more pomposity than usual. "And I shall not shirk it."

"Julius!" Melvin twittered. "You have no business adopting a child. The mere thought of it is ridiculous."

The mayor refused to answer his brother, but merely pursed his lips together in obstinacy.

His wife stared at him for a long minute. "We'll talk about it when we get home," she snapped.

Feeling he had extracted all the juicy gossip he could for the day, Melvin left. As soon as he was gone, Louella began on my mother again.

"And another thing, Dolly," she said, setting her jaw unpleasantly. "Someone has been taking items from our house. Julius is missing a silk handkerchief, and I, er, I'm missing something . . . things, too."

"I'm sorry to hear that," my mother responded uncertainly. "Do you . . ."

"I've talked to our housekeeper and the woman who does our laundry," she butted in. "They both swear they know nothing about it."

"I'll tell Pope," my mother said with finality.

As soon as they left, Whitey and I showed her our fish and Pop reappeared.

"I caught the biggest one," Whitey said.

"You did!" my mother exclaimed.

"Come on, Whitey," I said. "Let's take these to the back, and I'll show you how to clean them just like Pop showed me."

"Maybe you should go with them, Pope," my mother suggested, "to keep them from cutting off a thumb. Oh, and by the way, Louella informed me that Julius is missing a silk handkerchief, and she is missing something too, although she was careful not to let me know what it is."

Pop nodded. "All right," he said, and as we three headed for the kitchen, I remembered something. "Oh, Mama, Mr. Petty is coming for supper."

Whitey nodded. "He'll be here as soon as he washes the stink off of him."

"Oh, Great Scott!" Pop groaned.

Although he kept us waiting, unlike Mr. Hutchins, Mr. Petty arrived looking much like he normally did. I don't think he owned any other clothes except what he wore every day. When he removed his hat, we could see a comb had been run through his dampened hair. There wasn't much left on top, but it was full on the sides and back, and his great handlebar mustache looked as if he taken a comb to it, too.

As soon as Pop asked the blessing, we commenced eating. At first, Mr. Petty appeared shy and uncomfortable eating in front of us. Soon, however, he was enjoying the fish so much, he began sucking the bones loudly to remove all the flesh, creating a huge pile on his plate. He crumbled cornbread on his beans, and with his head bent down almost to the plate and elbows splayed out on either side of it, he slurped happily with his spoon. He became so intent on eating, he did not notice Clara Grace's appalled glances.

"These are some mighty fine vittles, Miss Dolly, Miss Clara Grace," he slowed down long enough to say. "Miss Clara Grace, you'd make some man a splendiferous wife. If you're in the market to take a gamble, I'd sure like to throw my hat in the ring here and now."

"Thank you, Mr. Petty," my mother murmured with a smile. "I'm happy you are enjoying the food."

Anything but gratitude showed on Clara Grace's face. His proposal of marriage at the supper table in front of everyone infuriated her.

"Mr. Petty," she said through clenched teeth. "Let us get one thing straight right now. I would never dream of marrying a man whose table manners are on par with a donkey's, whose whole dinner conversation consists of 'slide me one of them there corn dodgers, would ya,' and who smells and looks like he's been sleeping in the same clothes next to a horse for three months." With eyes snapping, she spat one more parting shot. "And one who has a head as bald as a hen's egg."

The shocked silence that followed did not diminish the fire in Clara Grace's eyes. As her words sunk into poor Mr. Petty, his eyes blinked, and I feared he might cry. Incensed at Clara Grace's treatment of him and goaded by her lack of remorse, I blurted the first thing that came to my mind.

"Well, you don't have to worry, Clara Grace," I said. "Because he don't like women as flat-chested as you are anyway!"

"Kit!" my mother screeched, slapping both her cheeks in horror.

Clara Grace shot me a murderous look. She stared at my parents with her lower lip jutted out, silently demanding my punishment. Mr. Petty sat shaking his head, unable to speak. My mother stared at Pop. "Pope," she cried. "You'll have to do something."

Pop rose and took off his belt. He indicated for me to follow him. Whitey stared at us, wide-eyed and almost scared out of his wits. I reluctantly got up, and with head down, shuffled my feet behind Pop into the darkened storeroom where my punishment was usually meted out.

Pop motioned for me to stand in front of him. He took his belt, raised his arm, and whacked a stack of hundred-pound bags of flour to his left with it. I stared at him opened-mouthed. He gestured to me and urged in a whisper, "Come on, Kit."

I caught on and let out a yell. "Pop, that hurt!"

He smacked the flour bags again, and again I cried, "Stop, Pop! Stop!"

He must have whipped those bags at least five more times, me all the time yelling and pretending to cry after each one. He placed his hand on my shoulder and began to guide me back. "Make it look good, boy," he hissed.

As I approached the table, I alternately rubbed my eyes hard so they would look teary and my rear end so it would appear to be hurting. My mother sat sobbing quietly into a handkerchief. Mr. Petty sat like a stone, only his eyes moved back and forth around the table. Clara Grace, although refusing to be penitent, did appear a little upset.

When my mother saw me, she cried, "Kit!" She turned to Pop. "I didn't mean for you to spank him that hard, Pope!"

"Dolly, something had to be done. He's paid for what he said. Now just forget about it and go on."

But my mother continued to sniff, and Clara Grace continued to look put out. Mr. Petty opened his mouth, wanting to tell Clara Grace her bosom was fine with him, but unable to think of a way to say it, he closed it and just looked miserable.

Pop, fed up with all of us, slammed both fists on the table, jarring the dishes. "I am sick and tired of everybody," he shouted to staring, shocked faces. "We have a vicious, crazed killer on the loose, and all I have is a houseful of people who couldn't care less about it. Dolly, you live in a dream world where everything is sweet and fine. Clara Grace, you are the most self-ish, egotistical woman who ever drew a breath. Tull, it doesn't matter to you who gets carved up next—all you can think about night and day is women."

My mother hated to displease my father more than anything in the world. She reddened at his words and momentarily cringed. After Pop finished his rant, we sat in silence for several moments. My mother took a breath, straightened, and turned to him. "Pope, there is nothing we can do about these murders. We cannot live every moment of every day under a black cloud without cracking, so we don't." She turned to gaze at us before looking at Pop again. "I know it is not fair to you that the responsibility of catching a killer rests almost solely on your shoulders, but we are helpless, Pope. There is nothing we can do."

No one said anything at first. After a moment, Clara Grace spoke unexpectedly. "It is hard enough for me to feel like a parasite," she said, "without having to deal with your constant attempts to get rid of me through matrimony."

"Clara Grace," my mother immediately leaned forward and assured her. "You are not a parasite. You do a tremendous amount of work around her, and with all this going on, I don't know what we would have done without you. And we certainly don't want to get rid of you by making you enter into a loveless marriage. Do we, Pope?"

She turned to Pop. "Do we, Pope?" she repeated.

"Oh, certainly not," Pop said automatically.

"But Clara Grace," my mother said. "Please, just be kind."

I knew she meant Mr. Petty, who still sat looking miserable. Clara Grace closed her eyes briefly and sighed. Turning to Mr. Petty, she said tonelessly, "Dolly taught me how to make buttermilk pie this afternoon. Would you care for some?"

"Yes, ma'am," he managed to squeak out. "I reckon I would."

"I'll get it," my mother said, jumping up. Clara Grace rose, "I will help," she offered.

My mother handed me a huge slice, which made me feel even guiltier for making her cry. Pop was still upset, not only because he wasn't able to solve the identity of the killer, but because he had criticized the very thing he liked about my mother, her ability to be happy and cheerful. Clara Grace still looked glum. Mr. Petty and Whitey still looked scared. I felt the whole thing was my fault, and I wanted more than anything to cheer my parents up and make things right.

"Pop," I said. "Those farm boys taught Whitey and me a song while you were fishing upstream. Can we sing it to you?"

Pop nodded his head. I thought Whitey would balk at singing

in front of a crowd, but he sprang up beside me, and we plunged, warbling bravely, into "What Shall We Do with a Drunken Sailor?"

My mother smiled and began to chuckle. Pop threw his head back and laughed. Mr. Petty stroked his mustache, smiling underneath it at us. Clara Grace tried to look superior, but the corners of her mouth kept coming up and underneath her long skirt, her foot began to tap.

My parents and Mr. Petty clapped heartily at the end of our song. "I know another verse I could learn you," Mr. Petty said. Startled, he looked around the table and assured the women, "It's an all right verse."

He had a rough, terrible voice, but he was willing. Pop joined in and together they taught us two more verses. Although my mother possessed none of Pop's musical talent and wasn't too much better than Mr. Petty, she joined in later when we sang "Old Dan Tucker," "Turkey in the Straw," and "Buffalo Gals." At the evening's end, she asked Pop if he would do a solo of "My Country, 'Tis of Thee." He did, and at last, Mr. Petty could put it off no longer, and he got up to leave. Pop motioned for me to walk with the two of them to the door. As he opened the front door, Mr. Petty looked back, admiring Clara Grace, and growled like a tomcat. "Grrrr. What a woman!" He jerked his head to Pop and apologized. "Sorry, Pope, I forgot she is your kin."

"Get out of here, Tull," Pop said, not unkindly. "I'll see you tomorrow."

As Pop and I walked toward the back, he put his hand on my shoulder and squeezed it rather hard. "Kit, what we hear in private, stays in private."

Chastised, I nodded. "Yes, sir."

Just before we reached the curtain, however, Pop paused. "You have the makings of a superior voice, Kit. It reminds me of my older brother's. He made a fine singer before being scalped by Indians."

"I didn't know you had a brother scalped by Indians," I said. "But you don't hold that against Asa?"

"Asa had nothing to do with it."

All of us were walking on a happier cloud when we went to bed that night, and homicidal mischief seemed far away. Later, I awakened to hear Pop getting up and going to the back door. I got out of bed and sleepily went to my door. Pop came back in the house, and I heard my mother's voice coming from their bedroom.

"What is it, Pope?"

"I thought I heard something outside," he answered, "but I guess not." I turned to go back into my room when I heard him add, "We really need to get another dog. What is it about a dog that I should be remembering?" he muttered. "Lord have mercy; my back is killing me."

"Now, Pope?" my mother asked. "In the middle of the night?"

"No, Dolly," Pop said. "My back really does hurt. I guess I stood too long doing all that fishing."

"Well, come to bed, and I'll rub it for you," she replied.

I heard his footsteps retreating into their bedroom and the shutting of a door. I was about to enter my room when a noise from the front of the building came faintly to my ears. I turned around and leaned forward. Was it footsteps I heard?

Something touched my arm, and I flinched, almost colliding into the doorframe. But it was just Whitey.

"What's the matter, Kit?" he whispered.

"I think I hear something on the front porch," I whispered back. "Come on."

We stealthily crept forward. Whitey caught his foot on a crock and gave a hop, whispering, "ouch, ouch."

"Shhhh," I whispered. "Come on."

The closer we inched to the front door, the more it became apparent I was right. There came the faint sound of boots stepping against the boards of the porch. We stopped, afraid to go on. A shadow appeared at the door. Through the glass we saw an inky hand reach forward and softly try the locked knob.

Whitey jumped and I did, too. We fell over one another running to the back, all the while screaming, "Aaawwwww!!!"

"What is it? What is it?" my parents called, meeting us at their door, my mother in a nightdress and my father in his long johns.

"Somebody's trying to get in the store," we cried. "Somebody's out there!"

My mother stared at Pop. "Pope?" she asked breathlessly.

"Let me get my gun," he said.

She looked after him as he went to fetch his shotgun. We could hear Clara Grace stirring, and turning around, my mother said, "Kit, Whitey, go put your pants on."

We raced into the room, grabbed our pants, and stumbled back out trying to run and put our britches on at the same time without missing anything. Clara Grace opened her door, wrapped in a robe.

"What is it?" she asked.

"The boys heard something," my mother explained. Meanwhile, Pop came back with the gun and walked to the front with the four of us huddled and creeping behind him. Carefully and silently he opened the door. There was no one on the porch.

Pop looked around, staring into the darkness of the street. I could faintly make out the outline of someone approaching. I moved in front of my mother, closer to Pop.

It was Asa. "Pop, what's going on? What are you doing out here?"

Pop took a deep breath and exhaled it. "Kit and Whitey heard somebody at the door. Have you seen anyone?"

"No, I haven't seen anything," Asa said.

"What are you doing out then?" Pop asked.

Asa paused before answering. "I know this sounds crazy, Pop, but I awakened with the awful feeling of evil around me. Maybe it's my imagination, but I feel like evil is stalking this town."

Pop nodded but didn't say anything. I knew he didn't want to terrify the rest of us. "I'll get my clothes on, and we'll look around," Pop said. "I think we should stick together."

I expected my mother to protest, but ever since the night she prayed so hard for Pop to come home, it was as if she was at peace with God over him.

"Wait here, Pope," she said. "I'll fetch your clothes." She turned and Clara Grace went with her to help. When they came back, my mother held his things while Pop dressed as fast as he could. "Be careful," she cautioned.

He kissed her, patted my head, and left with Asa.

"I'll get my beads," Clara Grace said.

This time four of us sat at the table. Clara Grace silently fingering her rosary, my mother staring at the front door, Whitey and me beseeching God in our childish way to bring Pop back, but mostly we all just waited.

We leapt up in unison an hour later when they returned.

"We didn't find anything," Pop said. "It could have been a drunk thinking we might be playing tonight, who knows."

We said goodnight to Asa and went back to bed.

CHAPTER 22

The sun's rays the next morning began to sweep clear the fear of the night before. Pop, Whitey, and I peed off the back porch before it got too light, Whitey and I trying to see who could pee farther.

"I could have beat you both ten times over in my prime," Pop said.

We went with him as he examined the ground around the house, but none of us found any clues to the mystery of the night before.

"Kit, you boys stay here and help your mother," Pop said. "I want to have a word with Asa before breakfast."

Clara Grace unexpectedly overslept, something unusual for her, so I put off emptying the chamber pots. Whitey and I began filling the wood box instead. After we made enough racket chunking wood into the box to wake the dead, Clara Grace came out of her bedroom and apologized for oversleeping.

"I didn't sleep well last night, Dolly," she said.

"Don't be afraid, Clara Grace," my mother said as she moved pans around on the stove.

"No, it's not that," she said. "It's something else."

Having no interest in how many angels could sit on the head of a pin or a long discussion on predestination versus free will, Whitey and I retrieved the chamber pots from the bedrooms and took them outside.

Just before stepping off the porch, something in the nearby

woods caught my eye. I put the pot I was carrying down.

"What is it, Kit?" Whitey said, putting his pot down, too.

I stared into the woods. "I don't know, Whitey. I thought I saw a flash of something pale moving in the trees."

We stepped off the porch and into the yard, staring, yet afraid to get too close.

Behind me, I could hear the back door open, and my mother came out with Clara Grace at her heels.

"I really need to talk to a priest," Clara Grace was telling her. "I have to make a confession."

"Oh, Kit," my mother said, seeing the chamber pots sitting on the porch. She picked one up. "Clara Grace," she said, slightly aggrieved at both of us. "Just talk to Asa. Confess to him."

She began walking toward the outhouse. I couldn't see anything in the trees, yet I knew someone was there. I turned my head to see my mother put the pot down on the ground in front of the outhouse; it was the expensive one we kept for guests, and she was always afraid she was going to break it. She rose, and as her hand reached for the privy door, I became filled with an awful dread.

"Mama! Don't!" I shouted.

I was too late. She opened the door and stood for a second before sinking to the ground, screaming. "No! No! No!"

Whitey and I raced to her from one direction, Clara Grace from the other. We reached her at the same time and stared into the outhouse.

Maydell sat inside, a rope around her neck. She had been strangled; her head lolled to one side, her tongue swollen black and protruding. Her clothes were torn, and her skirt had been lifted. A broomstick hung suspended between her legs. Next to her was a doll, its head ripped to one side, a piece of rope around its neck also.

Clara Grace slammed the door as my mother continued to wail, hitting the ground with her fists, screaming "No!" over and over.

Pop and Asa reached us. "Dolly," Pop groaned in agony. He opened the door and shut it again. "Take her into the house, Clara Grace," he commanded as he lifted my mother to her feet, murmuring her name and kissing her head. She ceased to scream, but was unable to stop weeping, and she continued to cry as Clara Grace led her into the house while people congregated in the yard.

The men scoured the woods after I told Pop I thought someone had been watching us, but all they found were fresh horse droppings that led nowhere. After the fruitless search, Pop went into the house to talk to my grief-stricken mother who lay on the bed staring at the wall.

"Dolly," he said tenderly, taking her in his arms. "I have to ask you a couple of questions. Can you talk?"

She sniffed and nodded.

"All right then," he said soothingly. "Now, can you tell me if you sold some rope in the past week or so? I know we had quite a bit, and it's gone. Clara Grace said she didn't sell any."

"Rope?" she asked in horror. Her face scrunched in tears again. "Oh, Pope. Maydell bought the rope. Maydell bought it." She buried her face in Pop's chest and began to cry softly while he stroked her hair. "That means whoever killed Maydell talked her into buying the rope? Doesn't it?" she cried.

"Yes, I'm afraid so," Pop answered. "Forget the rope. Do you know if the doll belonged to Maydell?"

She shook her head. "I don't know," she whimpered.

"That's okay," Pop said gently. "I think I know who it belonged to."

She sat up while he continued to hold her and stroke her arms. "Pope," she said. "I'm sorry. I'm sorry I'm all to pieces."

"That's okay, darling. That's okay. But I have to ask you one more thing. Who did you talk to about Maydell having a baby besides me?"

My mother sniffed and tried hard to concentrate and not cry. "Louella Foster. She and Julius and Melvin were in here. But Louella was the one who brought it up! She said someone had told her that Maydell was seen out at night, and she immediately jumped to that conclusion. And then Julius said if Maydell had a baby they would adopt it, and Melvin raised a fuss, and Louella got all mad. It was crazy."

He nodded and lay her down on the bed again. "But, Pope," she cried. "What does this mean?"

"I don't know for sure. But I'll figure it out, Dolly. I'll solve it and put a stop to it, I promise."

"I know you will, Pope." she said.

He rose, stooping to kiss her cheek before leaving. She watched him go, her face a mirror of the faith and trust she had in him.

Chaos ruled in the store that evening. People jammed in, demanding that something be done—what, they didn't know. Men did not talk, they yelled. Women wept. One woman grabbed Pop by the lapels.

"You have to do something!" she screamed. "Do something!"

Pop was too shocked and upset to say or do anything. As she continued to pound on his chest demanding he do something, Clara Grace grabbed her by the wrists and pulled her away.

"Stop it!" she ordered. "Captain Robertson and Marshal Jenkins are doing all they can to find this madman, and they won't be able to with you beating on them."

She looked around the crowd, the hands by her side clenched and her face a whirlpool of ferocity. "Go home! All of you go home! Dolly needs peace and quiet and so do Marshal Jenkins and Captain Robertson if they are to solve this at all!"

She shocked them into silence. Pop went to the front door and opened it. People began to file out, and as they went by Pop, he nodded to them reassuringly. Clara Grace left to check on my mother. Asa and the mayor hung back. The mayor stood hunched as if ill, his face ashen.

"Pope, I need to talk to you and Asa. Is there someplace . . . ?"

Pop nodded and led the mayor and Asa into the storeroom. Whitey and I followed, hoping to be included. Just as Pop was about to tell us we couldn't come in, the mayor said in a tired voice on the verge of breaking, "Pope, let the boys hear what I have to say. They won't understand most of it, but I owe them some kind of apology."

The outside door to the storeroom had been locked, and inside was dark and forbidding, perhaps the best place for a confessional. Pop lit a lantern, but turned it down so only the softest glow shone. The men stood together, while Whitey and I hovered in the shadows near Pop.

"Do you have anything to drink, Pope?" the mayor asked.

Pop nodded and took a jug off a nearby shelf. He blew the dust off, uncorked it, and handed it to the mayor. The mayor's hands shook as he took a swig. He wiped his mouth with his hand and gave the jug back to Pop. "Thank you," he said, while Pop replaced it.

No one said anything, and the mayor gathered his courage to speak. "I knew her, Pope, the first girl who was killed," he said. "She was one of Effie's girls."

Pop and Asa looked at one another, but neither spoke.

"I love my wife, but sometimes a man likes to play a little rough," the mayor said, nervously trying to laugh and bluster his way through. "You know what I mean."

"No, Julius, I don't," Pop said, "but continue."

Deflated, the mayor gave up trying to be the hearty fellow.

"She was willing to do anything as long as the money was right," he admitted. "I paid extra for any little bruise or welt I put on her. Believe me, Pope, she was well paid."

He began to plead with Pop and Asa. "Don't you see why I couldn't say anything? What with the kind of games we had been playing at Effie's, and then she shows up here in Muskrat Hill cut to pieces?"

He began to shake and cry. "I didn't kill her, Pope! I didn't kill her."

Pop remained unruffled by this emotional display, and Asa kept his face unreadable. "Do you have any idea why she was dumped here, Julius?" Pop asked.

"No!"

"Do you have any enemies who are trying to embarrass you?" Pop asked.

"No! No one!" the mayor cried. "Pope, you have to believe me. I did not have anything to do with that girl's death!"

"Julius, calm down," Pop said, looking at the floor and rubbing his fingers against his forehead. He looked up, composed once again. "I have to ask you some questions, Julius, now answer me truthfully. Were you having an affair with Maydell?"

"Good God, no!"

"Why were you willing to adopt an illegitimate child of Maydell's if it came to that?"

The mayor didn't answer right away. He stopped weeping and looked around, as if trying to find the right words. "Do you know what it is to have someone bossing and berating you from the time you get up in the morning until the time you go to bed, Pope?" he said at last. "Do you have any idea what that is like?"

I glanced at Whitey standing beside me, barely able to make him out in the dim smoky light of the coal oil lantern. He stood staring at the mayor with lips parted; drinking in every word he spoke. I turned back to the mayor, but I couldn't forget the look on Whitey's face.

"I thought," he continued. "I thought if Louella had a baby to take care of, she would have something to focus on. That it would soften her."

"All right, Julius," Pop said. "Did Oscar have any connection with this girl from Effie's or with Maydell?"

"Not that I know of, Pope."

"What about Zane? Has he been in contact with either you or Louella?"

"Zane?" the mayor repeated in surprise. "Of course not. Why are you even thinking about Zane? He's in prison."

"Asa wired the warden to make sure he is still in prison, but we haven't heard anything. And Louis? Has Louella heard from him? Has he shown back up?"

The mayor shook his head. "No. She hasn't heard seen or heard from either of them since Zane went to jail, and Louis left. And she doesn't want to.

"But, Pope, you're barking up the wrong tree with Zane. If Zane had broken out of jail, the first thing he would have done would be to kill you. And Louis is almost certainly dead."

"Yes, you're probably right," Pop said.

"Pope," the mayor began, looking uncomfortable. "About that . . . If Louella and I had tried to help, her father would have cut us off without a penny. You know how he felt about Zane. And Louis. Please don't think . . ."

"Forget it, Julius. That's in the past."

"Do you believe me about this woman? That I didn't kill her?" the mayor begged.

"I want to," Pop replied. "One more question, Julius. Do you remember a young woman by the name of Gypsy Schmidt who lived around San Antonio? Dark hair, big breasted, a real knockout? She would be middle-aged by now."

"Gypsy Schmidt?" the mayor said. "No, I've never heard of her. But, Pope, you know my family came here from Dallas. I don't know that many people from San Antone."

"Okay," Pop said, dismissing him. "Go on home, Julius. Just go on home."

"Yes, I will. Louella's not there, though."

"Where is she?" Pop asked.

"She went to visit a friend. She got angry with me for offering to adopt Maydell's baby without discussing it with her and huffed off to the station to take the last train out of town last night," the mayor explained. "She'll be back on the first train in the morning."

It took some time to get the mayor to leave. Now that he had unburdened the load he had been carrying, he wanted to tarry. As soon as Pop shut the door after him, Asa asked, "Who's Gypsy Schmidt?"

"Oh, she has nothing to do with this," Pop said. "She's just somebody from Tull Petty's past who he's terrified will return and queer his pitch with Clara Grace. I was just trying to kill two birds with one stone. It doesn't matter how many people get murdered, Tull will still be pestering me to death to find out something about her."

"Pop," Asa said. "I feel terrible I couldn't find Maydell to question her yesterday. I might have saved her life."

"Don't feel that way," Pop said. "It's not your fault, and I doubt if it would have made any difference."

Asa nodded. Tugging on his collar and looking uncomfortable, he blurted out another question. "Pop, a few weeks ago, I never would have dreamed to ask this, but do you think whoever Maydell was seeing on the sly might have been a woman?"

Pop pondered on it. "She always referred to this person as 'he' to Dolly, but then she would in any case. The young woman in the meadow was probably in a doped condition when she was killed. Oscar's death blow was a stab in the back, but it would have taken an extremely strong woman to put him on a meat hook. That is, if we are looking for one murderer and not two or three."

"Oh, Pop," Asa said in an anguished voice, looking more like a perplexed white man than a stoic Indian. "I can't make heads or tails of this."

"It's late, Asa. Let's sleep on it and start again tomorrow," Pop said.

"Sulfur City?" Asa questioned.

"Yes. We'll have to talk to Effie," Pop said in resignation.

That night, Pop came into my bedroom to say goodnight. In an age when parents took their children to public hangings, it still worried Pop that the horror around us would be too much for us. Our resilience seemed to relieve him.

"Pop, who are Zane and Louis?" I asked, propping myself up on one elbow.

"And Gypsy?" Whitey said.

Pop paused before speaking. "These are all people we used to know, and it's best not to talk about them. I don't want you boys upsetting Dolly or Tull."

"Okay, Pop," we promised.

My mother pulled herself together the next morning and rose before anyone so she could prepare Pop a big breakfast. He left to find workmen who would tear down our old privy and build a new one in a different place. When he came back, Asa was waiting for him in the store, and my mother informed them of the gossip cycling through Muskrat Hill.

"It's all over town that Netta Crenshaw received a message from the grave saying Julius Foster had been having an affair with Maydell," she said. "She said Wilford left her a note on her back porch."

"Blast that woman!" Pop said. "Did anyone think to ask her

if it was from Wilford, why didn't he leave it on her pillow instead of the porch? These cursed old scandalmongers."

My mother shrugged her shoulders, and I was glad to see she was once again trying to let things roll off her back. I asked, "Pop, can Whitey and I go to Sulfur City, too?"

I could tell Pop was about to say no, but to my surprise he stopped and looked at my mother inquiringly.

"Dolly? What do you think?"

Asa grew agitated and opened his mouth to protest, but my mother, looking at me, said slowly, "It might be better for Kit further down the road if he did go now, Pope."

Whitey and I stared at Pop, waiting for his answer. He nodded to my mother and turned to us. "Whitey, you are welcome to ride along, but at one point you'll have to stay at the jail there with the sheriff while we go to interview a woman. We can't let you go where we are going."

"Pop," Asa interjected.

Pop turned to Asa. "You'll understand soon enough, Asa."

Whitey and I didn't understand; we only knew we were going to the big city.

Before we left, Pop again complained that his back hurt.

My mother found the metal corset the salesman left and brought it to Pop.

"I'm not wearing that thing," Pop protested. "My God, woman, do you know how hot it is?"

"Pope, please wear it," my mother pleaded. "If you have to ride in a buggy all day with a back already hurting, you'll be so crippled and stove-up tomorrow, you won't even be able to get out of bed. Please, Pope. Try it."

Pop argued for another minute or two. "Well, help me in the darn thing, Dolly, if you are going to insist," he said, giving in.

At the livery stable, he had to go through another argument with Tull Petty.

"Pope," Mr. Petty said. "Don't take Smokey. Put Gastor on the buggy and let Asa ride his bay."

"Why can't I take my own horse if I want to, Tull?" Pop asked, exasperated.

"I don't like the looks of Smokey today. He's restless and something is bothering him. Listen to my advice you hardheaded old mule and take Gastor."

"Tull," Pop said. "Do you just dream up this stuff to try to impress people with your so-called secret horse sense or do you really know anything?"

"Hellfire and damnation, Pope!" Mr. Petty cursed. "Take the mule and leave Smokey here. He don't need to be around those good-for-nothing whores you are going to see anyway. Those worthless bitches might do something to him."

"He's already been emasculated, so I don't think they can do anything else to him, Tull," Pop grumbled. "But all right, just to shut you up, put Gastor on the buggy then. Asa, do you mind riding your horse?"

"No, Pop," Asa said, laughing. "I wouldn't dream of forcing Smokey to go if Tull says he doesn't want to."

CHAPTER 23

Whitey and I squeezed in on the buggy seat next to Pop while Asa got on his mahogany bay. We were almost beside ourselves with excitement. We didn't know the woman Pop was going to interview and didn't care. Just the chance to see a sprawling metropolis like Sulfur City thrilled our little souls.

As we were about to leave town, Tull Petty stopped us, holding a letter in his hand.

"Postmaster had one of the boys bring this down to try to catch you before you left, Pope. He thought you'd want to see it. It's from the warden at Huntsville," he said. "Durn fool addressed it to Beaver Dam instead of Muskrat Hill."

Pop murmured his thanks and opened the letter, reading it. He looked at Asa and sighed in disgust. "Zane's there, all right, darn it. And this had his sadistic hand written all over it, too."

"Does it say anything else, Pop?" Asa asked.

Pop looked at the letter again. "He's had two visitors in the past few months. The first he's ever had. One was a male he talked to for some time, and a week later, a female. The warden said Zane burst out laughing when he saw the female, and there was nothing conjugal about the visit."

"What the hell woman would be visiting him except a prostitute?" Mr. Petty demanded.

"I don't know, Tull," Pop said. "We've got to be on our way. We're running late as it is."

On the way out, we rode by Melvin Foster's tiny house, looking empty and deserted. "I suppose Melvin is at Julius's office already," Asa said idly as he rode beside us. "No sign of the housekeeper."

"She's probably peeking at us through the windows, thinking we are going to attack her at any minute," Pop groused. "Did Louella come in on the train?"

Asa nodded. "I saw her get off and head for her house. She claims she's visiting an old friend in the next town, but lately these little overnight trips of hers have increased."

Pop shook his head. "She and Julius are headed in two different directions, I fear. What about Horace? Did he get on the train?"

Asa nodded. "If Horace never comes back, then we'll know we let a murderer slip out of our hands."

"Don't worry," Pop said. "He'll come back to those horses if he has to break out of jail to do it."

Sulfur City had a café, two millinery shops, three general stores, and half a dozen saloons. We found a place to water and feed our animals before walking to the café. Asa received a few curious looks, and Pop got several "How you doing, Pope? Been a while," variations as we walked down the sidewalks.

We found a table in the crowded café and sat down. Tobacco juice that had missed the many spittoons littered the sawdust-covered floor. The chairs were mismatched, the tables scarred and crumb covered, and the whole place smelled like old grease, but Whitey and I thought it was wonderful. Pop ordered for us and told us to "eat up boys; it may be a long time before you get to eat again." Whitey dug into his food and ate like a little piglet that hadn't sucked on a teat for two days, but I was used to better fare and had to force myself to get the somewhat rank-tasting food down my excited gullet. Pop ordered pie and that made up for it. "It's hard to make a bad pie," Pop murmured as he ate.

When we finished, Whitey and I followed as Pop and Asa paid and walked onto the sidewalk into the bright sunlight again. We wrinkled our noses at the smell. More people meant more horse and animal manure on the streets, and true to its name, Sulfur City did have a slight sulfuric odor, caused by a nearby spring. The people jostled us on our way to the sheriff's office, and it seemed strange to be in a town where you didn't know the name of every person you met.

"Here we are," Pop said and opened the door to the sheriff's office.

It was much larger than the one in Muskrat Hill. A big man with grizzled hair sat with his feet up on a desk, whittling on a stick. He saw us and leaned over to spit into a nearby spittoon.

"Pope, Asa, what brings y'all to the big city?" he asked.

"We had another killing, an old maid this time," Pop said. "But we received information that the first murdered woman worked for Effie."

I became aware of odd noises above our heads. It sounded like boots scraping, bars clanging, and men talking. I realized the jail cells must have been on the second floor.

"Miss Effie didn't tell me nothing about it," the sheriff said.

"We know that," Pop said. "But we have to check out every lead. Can you keep one of these boys here with you while we go to Effie's?"

"Just one of them?" the sheriff asked, mulling us over.

"Yes, sir," Pop said. He placed his hand on my shoulder. "This is my boy, Kit. We'd appreciate it if you'd keep his friend Whitey here. His parents might not take kindly to us if we took him to Effie's, even if it is just for an interrogation."

The sheriff looked Whitey over. "What did you say your name was, boy?" he asked.

"Whitey, sir," Whitey answered like his mama taught him. "Whitey Collins."

"You kin to those Collinses over near Cedar Bend?"

"Yes, sir," Whitey answered.

The sheriff raised an eyebrow to Pop. "He's your boy's pal, is he?"

"Yes," Pop said, getting a little exasperated. "Can you keep him here or not?"

"Sure. I guess I owe you enough favors, Pope." He looked at Whitey. "You want to earn a nickel emptying the slop jars from upstairs?" he asked. "I hate emptying slop jars, and the Mexican who works for me didn't show up this morning."

Whitey and I looked at one another and stifled grins. Whitey helped me do that all the time for free. "Yes, sir," Whitey responded. "I'll do it."

We began to take our leave. The sheriff glanced at the revolver and gun belt Pop wore. "You think you have to be packing a piece of iron in my town, Pope?" he asked with a grin.

Pop didn't smile back. "If you'd seen what we have, you'd have every able-bodied man in this town carrying a gun," he said.

I was used to people talking almost exclusively to Pop because they knew him better, or because he was older and had seniority, but as we left the sheriff's office, I couldn't get over the impression that the sheriff was intentionally slighting Asa in some way.

Leaving Whitey behind, I held Pop's hand as we walked back to the buggy.

"When we get to where we're going," Pop said. "I don't want to hear a peep out of you the entire time. No questions, nothing. You understand?"

"Yes, sir," I said.

We got into the buggy, and with Asa riding beside us, we left town and were soon heading down a narrow country road. We came upon a large Victorian-style three-story house, painted a puritan white. It had a wraparound front porch and looked almost like a prosperous farm, except there weren't any crops, and despite a big barn, it lacked farm critters. As we drew up in front, an old black man shuffled from the barn to take charge of our horse and mule.

"Captain Pope, I hadn't seen you in a long time, sir," he said. Although he kept his eyes down, I had the feeling he was scrutinizing Asa and me all the while.

"Hello, Ira," Pop said. "You're looking well."

"Tolerable, tolerable, Captain Pope," he said.

"We've come to have a few words with Miss Effie," Pop said.

"She be here," Ira said. "Florence will let you in."

We left our animals in Ira's care and walked onto the porch. Pop knocked, and the door was opened almost immediately by a middle-aged woman with smooth skin the color of polished walnut, an hourglass figure hidden by a starched, blazingly white apron, and black hair almost covered by a matching starched white mop cap. She looked at us, and when she saw Asa, she stiffened perceptibly and her eyes grew haughty.

"Florence," Pop said. "This is Marshal Asa Jenkins from Muskrat Hill, and this is my son, Kit. We need to have a talk with Miss Effie, please, ma'am."

"Yes, sir, Captain Pope," she said. "Come this way, please."

She led us into a foyer unlike anything I'd ever seen. Even the mayor's house was not so richly appointed. Thick flocked wallpaper, even thicker carpet, brass urns, and elaborate vases with little naked shepherdesses filled the entryway and bespoke of luxury and opulence.

"Wait here, please," Florence said.

We stood with hats in hand, Asa looking distinctly uncomfortable. In a minute, Florence returned.

"I'll take your hats," she said, hanging them on an ornate hat rack. "This way, please."

She opened a door, and we followed her into a hall. Before us was a magnificently wide and intricately carved staircase. To our left I peered into a sort of opulent parlor, but this one was filled with indolent, half-dressed women, all of them young.

Pop took me by the collar and pulled me through the door on the right that Florence held open. The room we entered was unlike the rest of the house except for the feel of money spent. With its flowery hurricane lanterns and stiff-backed horsehair chairs and sofa, it looked like the drawing room of a prudish, but prosperous, old maid. In the center sat an elderly woman, her white hair pinned up in a plain style without a wisp out of place. Her hands rested properly in her lap, clasping a silk and lace handkerchief. She wore dark blue, with a cameo pin holding a lace fichu around the high collar of her dress. On her hands were fingerless lace gloves.

"Pope," she said in a prim voice, not unlike the sound of dry, stiff paper crackling. "It's been a long time since we've seen you," she said.

"Miss Effie," Pop bowed. "This is Marshal Asa Jenkins from Muskrat Hill, and this is Kit, my and Dolly's boy."

"What a handsome child. I'm sure Dolly is very proud of him. He looks like you."

I was used to being told I looked like Pop, but there was something about this desiccated old maid schoolteacher that frightened me.

"Please, sit down," she said, motioning to the sofa and chairs in front of her. Asa, blinking nervously, took the chair while Pop and I sat on the sofa.

"May I offer you refreshments?"

"No, no thank you, ma'am," Pop said. "We just ate."

She turned to the maid. "Tea for me, Florence, and bring the boy some lemonade and cookies," she said.

Florence left the room, shutting the door silently behind her.

The room must have been soundproofed, because we heard nothing from the rest of the house. Miss Effie turned back to Pop.

"And how is Dolly? Well I hope?"

Asa's eyes got as round as bois d'arc apples, and he swallowed visibly. Pop, however, remained calm and natural.

"Yes, ma'am, she's fine."

While Pop explained about the murders at Muskrat Hill, Florence returned with a tray. With quiet, smooth motions, she placed a fragile tea set on a small table next to Miss Effie's chair and poured a minute amount in a flowery cup so thin I could almost see the brown tea through the china. She offered me lemonade in a crystal glass wrapped in a linen napkin and a small china plate containing half-a-dozen delicate cookies. I set the plate of cookies carefully in my lap and took the lemonade just as gingerly, terrified I would drop it.

When she finished serving us, Miss Effie said, "That will be all, Florence."

Florence gave a small nod and murmured, "Yes, ma'am." As she left the room, she shot Asa a look of unveiled contempt.

"Why didn't you report the girl missing?" Pop asked, taking the plate of cookies and holding it on his thigh so that it wouldn't slip from my lap and break while I was trying to cope with the glass of richly sugared lemonade.

"I didn't know she was missing," Miss Effie said, taking a sip of tea. "She was a fairly new girl; she had gone to town with the others and not come back. I assumed she had decided to try her luck elsewhere; they sometimes do."

She turned from Pop and gazed at Asa. "Perhaps I'd better explain to the marshal how things are run here."

Asa shot Pop an uncomfortable glance, keeping his head lowered. He appeared embarrassed and was having a hard time looking at Miss Effie. He gave a nod, and after she set her teacup down, she spoke directly to him, carefully enunciating her words.

"I keep my girls on a tight leash, Marshal," she said. "They are allowed into town twice a week to shop, from one to four in the afternoon. It avoids any unpleasantness for the towns-women. They are expected to dress and act appropriately while they are in the stores and on the streets. If there is trouble, the sheriff is quick to resolve it. If it was caused by one of my girls, she is promptly requested to not only to leave my establishment, but the county as well. I tolerate no trouble or insubordination."

"What about this girl?" Pop asked. "Was there anything special about her; did she have any unusual customers?"

"No," Miss Effie replied promptly. "The girl was a little lazier than most, perhaps, but it is a trait that is to be expected. I'm sorry, but there is nothing more I can tell you about her that would shed any light on your murders."

She turned her head to address Pop exclusively. "We have missed seeing you, Pope. I assume Dolly has made you a good wife."

"Yes. Yes, she has," Pop said. "She sends you her regards."

I thought Asa's eyes would just about pop out of his head. Sitting stiffly and without turning, his eyes rotated to Pop.

"Dolly always was a tenderhearted woman," Miss Effie commented. "I often tried to hire her to be one of my girls, although she was older than I prefer them. However, she had a sweet, obliging nature that appeals to many men such as yourself, Pope."

She looked at Asa and allowed herself a small smirk in response to his shock and curiosity. "Dolly was my washer-woman for years," she explained. "She had an abusive husband who stayed gone much of the time, only to return periodically to hound her. Pope met her here."

She glanced at Pop, again letting a small knowing smile break through the old-maidish demeanor she had apparently so assiduously cultivated. "Pope would pay to watch Dolly wash and hang up clothes, and then after she left for the day, he would have a dalliance with one of my girls. The time came when that no longer satisfied him. Unable to pin a murder charge on Dolly's husband that the man most assuredly deserved, he did the next best thing and caught him cattle rustling, an offense that carries much the same sentence."

"I should have killed Zane when I had the chance, but I was afraid Dolly would hold it against me."

"You could have killed him, all his relatives and half of hers, and Dolly never would have held it against you, Pope," Miss Effie replied.

"Have you heard anything about Zane lately?" Pop asked.

"No, he's still in prison, isn't he?" she asked innocently.

"I believe so," Pope said. "What about his brother, Louis?"

"Not a word," Miss Effie said, beginning to rise. "And now, if that . . ."

"There's one more thing, Miss Effie," Pop interjected. "This girl was using morphine; do you know who was supplying it to her?"

Miss Effie frowned and sat back down. She remained silent for several seconds. "My girls are not allowed to use drugs," she said. "They get a little laudanum during the time of their cycle and that is all." She paused briefly before continuing. "If this story should be circulated, I would deny it, and I'm afraid in any case it would look bad for the undertaker who prepared her body. People would begin to wonder how closely he examines the bodies that are brought to him."

"It won't get out," Pop said.

Miss Effie nodded. "Good." She rose. Pop and Asa immediately got to their feet. I rose, too, but still didn't know what to do with the empty glass. Pop set the plate by Miss Effie's tea things, so I put the empty glass there too, relieved to be rid of it.

Miss Effie turned to Pop. "Pope, can I offer you one of my girls for the afternoon? The twins are still here."

"No, thank you," Pop said politely. "But I thought the twins would have married and left a long time ago."

"No, if Mattie finds a man, it upsets Hattie and vice versa," Miss Effie said with a sigh. "I warned them that they are past their prime, and as soon as I find another set of twins, they'll have to leave."

Pop paused, thinking for several seconds. "There are some old bachelor twins on Turtle Creek. What if I explain the situation to them and ask them to come fetch the girls?"

"Turtle Creek," Miss Effie closed her eyes and muttered. She opened them and said, "Yes, two farmers. I remember them. They came here once when they were young, but took one look and fled." She shrugged philosophically. "It happens now and then with shy farm boys." She looked at Pop archly. "Other times, a man sees another man here he doesn't wish to see so he leaves."

It was as if she was throwing him a hint, yet when Pop opened his mouth, she cut him off. "Yes, that would be satisfactory," she said. "You were always good at solving problems, Pope." She turned to Asa.

"I am sorry; I cannot offer you one of my girls," she told him. "It is nothing personal. The men who frequent my establishment do not wish to be with a woman who has had relations with someone outside their race, especially an Indian. It is nothing to me . . ." she said, dismissing it with a wave of her hand. "It's just business."

"That's all right," a red and embarrassed Asa managed to stutter out.

We began to walk toward the door. Pop stopped before opening it. "Miss Effie," he said. "Did you ever have a girl by the name of Gypsy Schmidt work for you here? It's nothing to do with this case; it is another matter."

"Gypsy Schmidt?" she asked, giving Pop an odd look. "No, she never worked for me."

"Thank you," Pop said, and opened the door for her. She disappeared up the wide staircase as Florence appeared with our hats. The girls in the other room were watching us with a sort of languid curiosity. I had never seen women dressed that way, with satiny chemises under fancy striped corsets and feathers wrapped around their necks. I could have looked at them longer, but Pop once more pulled me away from the door, courteously nodding his head and saying, "Good afternoon, ladies," to the women in the room.

My brain felt so overloaded with new information I knew it would take some time to sort out everything I had seen and heard. Florence closed the door behind us, and I was standing on the front porch again before I could even realize what was happening.

Gastor and the buggy, along with Asa's horse, were waiting for us. Asa took off his bandanna and wiped perspiration from his forehead. "Whew! What a tartar!" he exclaimed.

"Don't let her get to you," Pop said, putting on his Stetson. "She's made so much money playing that prim and proper role for so long she believes it herself. I don't think she even remembers that she used to work up and down the Mississippi, selling her pussy to buffalo hunters for two bits a pop."

Unbelieving, Asa asked, "Her? That woman in there?"

"Oh, yes," Pop said. "Before a town gets settled and women and children come in, these old-time whorehouses were wild and woolly and a lot of them still are in the red-light districts of big cities. But Effie knows she has to run this one like a pretend convent to stay in business in a small place like this. Like she said, it's just business—and a lucrative one at that. She has customers come from all over Texas."

Asa retied his bandanna. "I'm ready to get out of here."

"Wait," Pop said, looking at the barn, and he began to walk toward it.

CHAPTER 24

Inside, Ira was polishing a fancy buggy built to hold nine fat people or twelve skinny ones. Pop's questions were polite, and he treated the old man with the same dignity and respect he did everybody. Nevertheless, Ira responded deferentially, his body language and answers giving off an aurora of well-mannered subservience.

"Yes, sir, Captain Pope," Ira said. "I took her to town with the rest of the girls, but she disappeared."

"Had she done that before?" Pop asked.

"Yes, sir, but then she would come back to the buggy when she was supposed to. Miss Effie figured she was making some money on the side. She wanted to get rid of her, but that girl, she kind of wild, she do things with the menfolks other girls don't like to do. Miss Effie said she was going to keep her for a while, but as soon as she could, she'd get shut of her."

"Did you see the man she was meeting?" Pop asked.

"No, sir, she just disappeared, then come back, all sleepy like. Sometimes she sleep all the way home. That girl, she wasn't like the other girls; she was bad through and through."

"Well, she's dead now," Pop said.

"You need to be looking for a white man, Mr. Pope," Ira said. "A mean, ornery white man is who done these murders. That girl, she wouldn't have gone off with nobody but a white man with some money in his pocket."

"I believe you are right at that, Ira," Pop said.

As Pop thanked him, Asa was already leaving the barn. We said goodbye and followed Asa, but one of the horses made a sharp noise, and Pop and I turned back to look. Ira stood, no longer the respectful servant but a powerful big man tightly crushing a polishing rag in one hand while staring with something akin to hatred at Asa's back.

Ira saw us watching him and immediately transformed himself back into the deferential liveryman. He waved. "Goodbye, Mr. Pope, you take good care of that boy of yours. He's a mighty fine young'un."

Pop nodded. "Thank you, Ira. Goodbye."

Asa wasn't saying much, so once in the buggy and on the way back to town, I began to question Pop.

"Were you the sheriff of Sulfur City?" I asked.

Pop shook his head. "No, thank the Lord," he said. "I was a Texas Ranger for a long time, and then I took a job as sheriff in a bigger city south of here. I disliked being a sheriff; I was too old to be a Ranger anymore. So, I thought about opening a store. My grandpap used to have one in Virginia. I get darn sick of being a grocer sometimes, but a man has to do something."

As he held the reins loosely in his hands, he looked down at me. "I brought you here for a reason, Kit. I wanted you to see for yourself exactly how things are, so if anyone ever said anything, you'd know the real facts."

"What do you mean, Pop?"

"Well, for one thing, your mother used to be married to a really bad man. He ill-treated her and left her alone for long periods of time with nothing to eat in the house and no firewood to heat it with. She got a job washing and ironing clothes for Miss Effie and the girls who work for Miss Effie. But, Kit, your mother never did what they do. She worked hard for the money she made in an honest way. Those girls are lazy and take what they can get from a man with no real feelings attached."

I didn't answer because I was still hazy on everything. Except that Pop was trying to tell me what I already knew, that my mother was a good person who disliked using or hurting people and tried her best not to.

"I sent the man who was her husband to prison and paid for her divorce so I could marry her," Pop said. "Everything was done legal and by the book, so your mother had no need to ever be ashamed.

"But," he continued. "That's why some of the women in town don't like to be around your mother too much. They know she knows whose husband went to see those girls and whose didn't. She's seen things that they don't even want to think about, and it makes them uncomfortable to be around her."

Asa had been riding close by, listening. "I knew you put Dolly's ex-husband, Zane, in jail, Pop," he said. "But I didn't realize she had to work at Effie's. And why did you ask the mayor about Zane?"

Pop's eyes widened in surprise. "Zane is Louella's twin brother," he replied. "But I never really knew Louella until I opened the store in Muskrat Hill."

"Her twin brother?" Asa asked, shocked.

"Yes," Pop said. "Their father disinherited Zane and the younger brother, Louis, because of their behavior. He gave everything to Louella. As long as he was alive, she and Julius wouldn't lift a hand to help Dolly for fear of making the old man mad, that's how bad he hated his own sons."

"And Louis?" Asa asked questioningly.

"Louis was the youngest boy," Pop said. "I arrested him at the same time I arrested Zane, but my case against him wasn't quite as strong. But while Zane was a big strapping, dark-haired man, Louis was just the opposite. He was just as bad as Zane, if not worse, but he had such an angelic looking face, the jury couldn't believe he'd so much as spit on the sidewalk. Anyway,

Zane went to prison, and Louis disappeared. Louella would like to forget they ever existed."

Asa shook his head. "Pop," he said. "I didn't realize Muskrat Hill had so many tangled threads running through it."

"They're not tangled," Pop replied. "They are just not all pleasant."

After a while, when Asa rode ahead, I asked Pop why the man and woman at Miss Effie's had given Asa such dirty looks and why the sheriff had almost been snubbing him.

"Is it because he's part Comanche, Pop?" I asked.

Pop was still distracted, thinking about the murders, but he answered me automatically. "The man and woman at Effie's had relatives massacred in the same Indian attack that killed my brother, and they haven't forgotten it. Just looking at Asa reminds them of it. As to the sheriff," Pop said. "It isn't that Asa is part Indian. He is jealous that Asa is a young, muscular, good-looking lawman on an exciting murder investigation in an otherwise nice little town, instead of being fat and old and having to kowtow to a vinegary, greedy old woman."

Whitey sat waiting patiently for us in the sheriff's office, but I could tell from his expression that his experience emptying the slop jars of prisoners had not been a good one.

"Captain Robertson," he timidly asked Pop, "may I go across the street to the dry goods store and buy something with my nickel?"

"Yes, Whitey," Pop answered. "I'm sure you earned it." Pop reached into his pocket, took out a penny and handed it to me. "Kit, you had a rough afternoon, too, but you got lemonade and cookies."

I would have gladly traded that syrupy lemonade and those cookies I had inhaled in one whiff for a nickel to spend with Whitey, but I didn't tell Pop so.

"Don't be running all over town," Pop said. "We've got to be heading back soon."

"Yes, sir," we answered and left the sheriff's office. On the sidewalk, Whitey asked me how the lemonade was.

"Yucky," I answered. "And there wasn't nothing to those cookies. I've seen cigarette papers thicker than they were. How was the jail?"

"Awful, Kit," Whitey said, shivering. "The men upstairs hollered and cursed at the sheriff, and one of them tried to throw the stuff in his slop jar all over us. The sheriff had to take out a blackjack and hit him." Whitey shook his head. He knew what a blackjack was because Pop had one under the counter. "I didn't know being a sheriff was so hard," Whitey said. "I don't ever want to go back up in that jail again."

Instead of being happy to have missed it, I felt slightly envious of Whitey. But I told him how pretty the girls were in their scanty clothes and that made me feel better. As we crossed the street to go into the store, a man in a loud checked suit appeared out of the alley beside it.

"Hey, kids," he said, friendly-like. "You can't go in that store unless you have some money."

"I've got a nickel," Whitey informed him. "He's got a penny," he said, pointing to me.

"Really now?" the man said. "Ain't that something? How'd you like to turn that nickel into a quarter?"

Whitey and I looked at one another and shrugged our shoulders.

"Don't be scared now," he said, smiling. "Come over here by this barrel, and I'll show you how easy it is."

He placed three walnut halves on the barrel, and then showed us a small pea. "See this pea?" he said. "All you have to do is guess which shell the pea is under. Here, we'll try it for nothing first. Watch now."

He placed one of the shells over the pea and moved them

around while Whitey and I watched carefully. "Which shell is the pea under?" he said when he stopped shuffling.

"That one," Whitey said, pointing to the one in the middle.

The man lifted it up, and there was the pea. "See how easy it is? Now we'll play for real. You bet your nickel against my quarter that you can tell which shell the pea is under. If I win, I get your nickel, but if you guess right, you get my quarter. Just think, kid, you'll have thirty cents."

Whitey looked at his nickel, and then he looked at me. "Whitey," I said. "One time a man just like him came in the store and tried to shortchange Pop. Pop had to pull a gun on him, take his money, and put him on the first train out of town."

Our "friend" now turned snarly. "Shut up, kid," he said. Turning to Whitey, he said, "Don't listen to him; he's jealous because he only has a penny."

"Let's go ask Pop," I said. "He's right over there in the sheriff's office."

"All right, you little monsters. Get lost!" He threw us another angry look and disappeared into the darkened alley.

We entered the store and looked around. I couldn't believe how dusty and dirty it was and resolved then and there to stop fussing so much when my mother handed me a cleaning rag and told me to get with it.

"What can I help you boys with?" a man behind the counter asked. I couldn't stop myself from staring at his hair. It didn't look natural; the texture was more like horse hair than human hair.

I thought for sure Whitey was going to say he wanted to buy a nickel's worth of candy, but he surprised me. "I have a nickel," he said. "And I'd like to buy my mother something with it."

"Well, let's see now, what have we got here," the man said, and as he showed Whitey different items, I gazed at his peculiar hair. The air in the store was stifling hot, and sweat beaded up on the man's face. He took his handkerchief and rubbed his forehead. To my surprise, his whole head of hair moved backward.

"I can let you have this comb for a nickel, and I'll wrap it, too," he said.

"That's what I want," Whitey said. "My mother has real pretty hair."

The man took the comb out of the display case and wrapped it in paper for Whitey. "For an extra penny, I can put a pretty bow on it," he said.

I looked down at my penny. I didn't have enough money to buy my mother anything she didn't already have access to anyway. Would she want me to buy a stick of candy with my penny to share with Whitey, or a bow for his mother?

"Here," I said, pushing my penny across the counter. "Put a pretty bow on it."

"Thanks, Kit," Whitey said.

With Whitey clutching his package carefully under one arm so as not to crush the bow, we walked out of the store.

"I think that man was wearing a wig, Whitey," I said.

"Hey, you little bastards!" a rough voice called, and Whitey and I looked up to see the town's ruffians in front of us. "What are you doing in Sulfur City?" a short stocky boy challenged.

"What business of it is yours?" I demanded.

"It's our town, that's what," the boy said and spat on his hands, rubbing them together. "Answer or I'll give you a licking."

We were roughly the same size, and I thought I could take him and get in some good licks before his friends pounced on me.

"Kit!" Whitey hissed. "Don't get in a fight. Your pop might not never bring us again. And besides, if you go home beat up, you'll make your mother cry again."

Pop wouldn't mind me fighting much, but I didn't want to cause my mother further tears. "My pop's investigating some murders that happened in Muskrat Hill," I said, forcing myself to sound calm and sensible. "He's over at the sheriff's now."

In a sudden turnabout, they wanted to be our friends so they could hear all the tittle-tattle about the murders. I remembered Pop's orders and only repeated what everybody in Muskrat Hill already knew. Once they had pumped us for all the information they could get, they got a little uppity with us before leaving.

"Don't forget, this is our town," the short stocky one reminded us.

By now we were close to the sheriff's door, so I felt safe in answering.

"Oh yeah? Well, be careful if you ever come to Muskrat Hill. Because I'll wipe the streets with your blood if you give us any trouble," I said, doing my best Tull Petty imitation before diving into the sheriff's office, closing the door behind us, and flopping against it.

Like the liveryman who switched personas faster than a flicker of an eyelid, Whitey and I became two quiet, innocent boys who blended as invisibly as we could into the background.

". . . and she's given money for schools and orphanages and all kinds of worthy causes, Pope," the sheriff was saying.

"Yeah, just keep telling yourself that while you're putting her payoff money in the bank," Pop responded.

The sheriff looked sheepish and ashamed. "Aw, Pope, I know you don't have a very high opinion of me," he said.

"No, it's not that," Pop answered. "My God, I've had to deal with that situation enough times myself. Just don't be trying to convince yourself that a selfish snake is a faithful dog, that's all."

"Look, Pope," the sheriff said. "I ain't never forgot the times we rode together and how many of those times you covered my back. That day at Bandera—if you hadn't come along when you did, I'da had my balls ripped off in two shakes of rat's tail." He paused for a minute, breathing heavily and sweating. "Look Pope, don't let this get out I told you, because Effie will have my job if I go blabbing about what goes on in that whorehouse. I'm too darn old to go to work now."

Pop nodded, while like us, Asa stayed in the background listening. "Yes," Pop said. "What is it?"

"You know that big Norwegian butcher who got killed? Well, he saw that girl with one of your leading citizens."

Pop's nose stiffened and quivered like a terrier's on the scent. "What do you mean?"

"It's this here way," the sheriff said. "None of the other girls really liked that gal, the one who got killed. One of them told me how she laughed about that big dumb Norwegian accidentally opening the door and being horrified to see the mayor of Muskrat Hill buck naked humping her with a cat-o'-nine-tails in his hand."

Although on the surface Pop and Asa remained unruffled, I knew they were about to jump out of their skins. "Did the mayor know that Oscar had seen him?" Pop asked calmly, but the fingers on his hands tensed.

"I don't know," the sheriff said. "The butcher, this Oscar, got so embarrassed he left and never came back. The mayor, now, returned several times after that."

We stayed for a while longer, but the sheriff had told us all he really knew. When we walked out the door onto the sidewalk and were alone, Pop rubbed his forehead. "Julius, Julius, Julius," he muttered. "What does this mean? What does this mean?"

He walked blindly toward the spot our animals stood. Once there, Asa untied his horse, while we climbed into the buggy. Pop took the reins automatically, still muttering to himself. "It will come to me. It will come to me," he said. He looked at

Whitey and me and forced himself to concentrate on something else.

"What have you got there, Whitey?" he asked.

"It's a comb for my mother," Whitey said, showing off the package. "It cost me a nickel."

"They put that bow on for you?" Pop asked, ever the entrepreneur, regardless of how tired he got of it.

"It cost a penny," Whitey admitted.

"A penny, eh?" Pop said. He looked at me and grinned, ruffling my hair.

Once away from the sulfur fumes, Pop and Asa relaxed. Whitey and I told them about the man with the shells and the kids who wanted to fight us first, then later be friends to pump us for information.

Pop and Asa laughed. "I guess you went to town to see the elephant and you did," Pop said.

"I didn't see no elephant, Pop. What does that mean?"

"It's just an old saying," Pop explained. "It just means you were excited about seeing something, but you got disillusioned by it."

"I wish we'd seen a real elephant," I grumbled. "It would have been more fun."

Pop and Asa talked about Sulfur City a while, but they couldn't stay away from discussing the case.

"Pop," Asa said, keeping his bay near the wagon. "A cat-o'-nine-tails can tear a person up really bad."

Chapter 25

"Yes," Pop agreed. He handed the reins to me. "Here, Kit, you and Whitey take turns with the reins. This blasted thing Dolly has me strapped in is so uncomfortable, I can hardly stand it. I've got half a mind to take the wretched thing off and throw it in the bushes."

I eagerly took the reins and tried to emulate Pop's effortless control of the mule. What looked easy for Pop, however, wasn't for me, and I had to watch my business. Nevertheless, I kept my ears on the conversation as my eyes watched the mule while we bumped along a dirt road not too far removed from the cattle trail it had once been.

"In Julius's case," Pop continued, twisting in the seat to try to get more comfortable. "I think that whip was used more or less for show." He leaned back and grimaced. Forcing the soreness from his mind, he continued.

"For one thing, Effie never would have let him damage her merchandise too much. And for another, it would have been bad for business to see a beat-up whore walking the streets of Sulfur City. They tolerate Effie because they think it keeps men and boys from turning out like Melvin, but they would get riled if it started to look like crime."

"It looks bad against him," Asa said.

"Do you honestly think Julius is capable of something like this?" Pop asked.

"No," Asa said. "But is Louella?"

"You're just mad because she gives you so much hell on how to run the church," Pop laughed.

"Maybe," Asa grinned.

"I don't believe Julius knew Oscar had seen him," Pop said, speaking out loud the thoughts running through his mind. "He continued to go to Effie's, trusting that his fun and games were a secret."

"But that puts us right back to a homicidal maniac bent on destroying anyone he or she thinks is sinning," Asa said.

"What are our options?" Pop said. "A single murderer or more than one killer?"

Growing tired of being so tense over the reins, I gave them to Whitey so I could watch Pop.

"Who are our suspects?" Pop asked, and began counting people off with the fingers of his hand. "A spineless mayor who thinks he likes to play a little rough with women and probably doesn't even know what rough is. A disgruntled wife who might be trying to pin a murder charge on her faithless husband because she is having an affair of her own out of town. A religious fanatic who claims he only rode with the Klan once and may or may not have had something to do with his wife's death. A man who tells us he was disfigured in an explosion, who very well may be lying and out for revenge. A seemingly mild-mannered undertaker who doesn't blanch at killing. Oh, and an unpleasant bookkeeper who hates his brother because he was their father's favorite," Pop said. "Who am I forgetting?"

"A man whose daughter had been molested by one of the victims, who it seems, would also be capable of carrying on an affair with another one of the victims without a qualm," Asa answered. "Pop, to tell you the truth, it could be anybody in Muskrat Hill. Even Tull Petty has a violent temper and a demented hatred of loose women."

"Granted," Pop said. "Okay, let's look at the victims. An unliked and unloved drug-using prostitute. A well-respected butcher who had begun molesting a little girl. A big-titted housekeeper who may have dreamed up her attack to get sympathy. An old maid turned adulteress."

"Miss Maydell was a thief, too," I blurted.

Pop and Asa had forgotten Whitey and I were listening. Pop turned to me and said, "What do you mean?"

I reddened. "She took a pencil from the counter when Mama's back was turned," I said. "I didn't say anything about it, Pop, because it happened so fast I thought maybe I dreamed it."

"A woman who steals a pencil, then breaks into a house to steal paper," Pop said, almost to himself. "Why? Who was she writing?"

"Netta Crenshaw claims she got a note from Wilford, Pop," Asa reminded him.

"But Maydell wouldn't write that note about herself," Pop said. "She must have gotten the pencil and paper for her killer."

Whitey poked me with his elbow and whispered, "The cigarette butts. Did you tell Pop?"

I shook my head. "Pop," I said, turning around. "When we visited Old Man Miller with you, Whitey and I found cigarette butts on top of the hill overlooking his house."

Pop stared at me. "Cigarette butts?" he said, forgetting to reprimand me for saying Old Man Miller instead of Mr. Miller. "And Fergus said his dog was missing. A man intent on watching a house would kill the dog guarding it. But why watch Fergus's place? Fergus never did a wrong thing in his life."

"The mayor wants Fergus's land, Pop," Asa said. "We've heard him talk about what he'd do with it a hundred times."

Pop shut his eyes, rubbing his fingers against his temples as the buggy bumped along the rough road. Whitey handed the reins back to me. We were nearing Muskrat Hill and would soon be passing by Melvin Foster's place. Gastor, sensing how close we were, picked up his pace.

"I don't know," Pop said, shaking his head in disgust. "Nothing is coming to me."

He looked so dispirited; I wanted to chatter about something else to get his mind off murder. I searched around for something to talk about and said the first thing that came into my mind. "I don't much like Sulfur City," I said. "Everybody there is pretending to be something they're not. That old lady pretended to be nice, and she isn't. The maid and the liveryman pretended they were better than Asa. The sheriff pretended what was bad was good. The man with the shells pretended he was our friend. Even the grocery man pretended to have hair, and he didn't."

Pop stiffened and stared at me. "Kit," he said. "I think you've just solved the entire case."

"I did, Pop?"

Pop stared off into space. "Does it fit?" he murmured. His face lit up with excitement. "Of course, it fits." He turned to Asa. "Asa, we are looking at this entirely the wrong way. These murders all have two things in common."

"What, Pop? What?" Asa urged.

"First, they were all meant to scare the living hell out of everybody in Muskrat Hill so they become a terrified mob, ready to kill."

"Yes," Asa said. "And the second thing, Pop?"

We were nearing Melvin's house. Pop was about to answer when his attention was captured by the scene next to the house. The mayor's palomino stood outside the fence that ran by the road. A body lay on the ground, and next to it, the mayor knelt with a knife in his hand.

Luci, the housekeeper, jumped out of the bushes and began waving her hands up in the air, sobbing and screaming. "*Er tötete* Melvin! *Er tötete* Melvin!"

Asa sat up in the saddle, shocked. "She's saying he killed Melvin!"

She began to run away, all the while screaming and crying. Pop yelled at Asa, "Don't let her go! Grab her!"

Asa looked at Pop in shock with wide questioning eyes, but after a second's hesitation, went after the fleeing housekeeper, spurring his horse to hurry. Pop snatched the reins from my hands and popped them as hard as he could. "Giddyup," he hollered at Gastor. It shocked the mule so much, he took off. Pop had to rein hard to get him to stop next to Julius. He jumped from the wagon, with Whitey and me scrambling after him.

Melvin had been mutilated like the others. Miraculously, he appeared to be breathing, although he was obviously bleeding to death. Pop knelt down and gently held Melvin's head and shoulders up. The mayor stared at his brother in a daze, looking at the knife as if he didn't know what it was. Pop tenderly wiped Melvin's mouth with his handkerchief. He stared at Pop with large eyes, an expression of surprise behind the broken glasses on his face.

"Melvin," my father said kindly.

"Pope," Melvin breathed, gasping for his final breaths. "Pope . . . I just wanted . . ."

"I know, Melvin. I know you did," Pop said as Asa brought the hysterically struggling housekeeper back to us, holding her tightly by the arms.

"But who did this to you, Melvin? Who did it?" Pop asked.

Melvin looked at the housekeeper and tried to talk. "L . . ." he began, but his eyes rolled back in death. Pop placed him gently down.

"Julius," Pop said, making it a question.

"Pope," he said, looking and sounding disoriented. "Pope, I . . ."

"Julius! Get a hold of yourself! Tell me what happened," Pop commanded.

The mayor swallowed hard. He dropped the knife as if it were a snake, wiping a blood-covered hand on his pants. "Pope," he began again. "I received a note at the office. One of my men said Luci, Melvin's housekeeper, brought it in. He didn't come to work today."

"What did the note say, Julius?" Pop asked, trying to get the mayor to concentrate.

"It said for me to come to his house right away. I couldn't figure it out. I couldn't figure it out."

"Why couldn't you figure it out, Julius?" Pop said.

"Because Melvin doesn't even keep a scrap of paper at his house," the mayor said, looking at his brother in disbelief. "The handwriting didn't look like his, but the signature did. I knew something was wrong so I came."

"What did you see when you got here?" Pop asked.

"This," the mayor said, motioning with both hands to the body of his brother. He broke down, fell to his knees next to his brother, and began to sob. "Pope, he was my brother. I loved him no matter what."

"I know you did, Julius," Pop said. "Where is Louella?"

"Louella?" the mayor said. He pressed his lips together and tried to focus. "I left her at home this morning when I went to the office. She's at home."

Pop shook his head. "Louella is probably dead, too, then, Julius," he said. "She was probably killed just after you left for work."

Shocked, Asa sucked in his breath. The housekeeper twisted and broke free from his grasp, and in a flash, she had a knife out, jabbing him in the stomach. He went down, and Pop yanked out his pistol. I didn't know it was possible for an old man to move so fast, but even so, the housekeeper had whirled at the same time and grabbed Whitey, clutching him in front of her while she held a knife to his throat. Whitey's face became a mass of white terror as he trembled like a sapling locked in her grasp.

The housekeeper looked at my father and smiled. "Speaka *de Deutsch*, Pope?" she mocked in a harsh, taunting tone as she jammed Whitey closer to her.

"Let him go, Louis," Pop commanded. "Let the boy go. The game is over. If you've been tracking us, you know we spent a lot of time with the sheriff in Sulfur City. He's wiring the Rangers right now."

Louis? I gaped at the half-crazed housekeeper and realized I was looking at a man dressed in women's clothing.

"We know everything," Pop said, staring at him. "We know you planned this down to the last detail to make Julius look like a murderer so you and Zane could inherit his money and land and no one the wiser. But we figured it out, Louis. It's too late."

Louis breathed heavily, his eyes wild, but he hadn't given up hope yet. "Throw your gun down, Pope."

"No," Pop said. "The second I see blood on that boy's throat, you're a dead man. Let him go. Take Asa's horse and ride out of here while you still have the chance. I won't shoot you if you let the boy go and leave. I'm giving you a chance to escape, Louis."

Louis walked backward toward the buggy, still clutching Whitey. His arms shot out, and he shoved Whitey toward Pop with such force, he knocked them both down. With his knife upraised, he whirled and in one swift terrible motion, slit Gastor's throat. Blood gushed everywhere and the mule went down. Louis raced to Asa's horse.

I ran to Pop, trying to get Whitey off of him and help him up. Asa rose up on one elbow and fired his pistol. The bullet went through Louis's shirt, ripping open the pretend breast that really was a bag of sand. With sand spilling everywhere, Louis made it up on Asa's horse, yelling and spurring the horse on, riding so close to the palomino that it fled and raced off toward town. Asa fired two more times, but missed, while Louis disappeared into the woods.

Pop got unsteadily to his feet, glaring at the trees Louis had disappeared among. He stomped furiously in a circle and began to weep tears of frustration. "Hell and damnation," he cried. Enraged, feeling impotent, it took a moment for him to constrain his anger. He turned to make sure Whitey and I were unharmed. Asa was trying to get to his feet, and we went to help him.

"I'll be all right," he gasped, still bent at the waist. "I think he missed the vital organs." He looked up at Pop. "Pop, how did you figure that out?"

"Hellfire," Pop said, still seething in anger. "I should have figured it out a lot sooner than this."

He calmed somewhat and went to Gastor, but the mule was dead. He stroked Gastor one last time, while I began to weep. Whitey was still shaking so hard, he couldn't even cry. Pop turned to us.

"Boys, go look in Melvin's barn and see if his mule is there."

Holding Whitey by the hand, I pulled him with me, but when I reached the barn, I was sorry I had brought him along. Melvin's mule had suffered the same fate as Gastor, except the blood was drying and covered with flies.

We went back to Pop. "He's dead," I said, and I didn't have to explain.

Pop looked around. "Louis must have another horse hidden around here somewhere. We'll have to find it."

The mayor was still sobbing over the fallen body of his brother. Whitey looked at him for a minute before going over and patting him gently on the back, standing next to him with his hand on the mayor's shoulder. Pop stared at them and then

Asa. He looked ruefully at me.

"I'll have to try to patch Asa up first, Kit," he said. "I don't dare let you out of my sight with Louis anywhere in the vicinity."

"He's probably long gone, Pop," I said. "I can look for the horse."

"No, son, wait for me," Pop said, going to Asa and beginning his examination.

He had me run back to the barn for spiderwebs. I made a mad dash inside, trying not to look at the mule, grabbing great handfuls of webs out of the corners. When I got back, Asa had his shirt off and Pop was slashing it into strips.

Pop peeled the webs from my hands, instructing me to run back to the barn for more.

"No," Asa said breathlessly. "That's enough. It doesn't take many." He remained stoic while Pop plastered the wound with the webs and wrapped the torn shirt around him.

"Kit and I will look for Louis's horse," Pop told Asa. "Fire a shot if you need us back."

With his gun drawn, Pop and I began searching the woods and brush, working in a wide circle. Although we saw plenty of signs, they led us nowhere, and Pop grew increasingly frustrated over the time we were wasting. Having covered almost all the ground near Melvin's house, Pop paused, turning his ear toward town. "Is that the sound of horses coming?" he said.

I listened and thought I heard the beat of hoofs, too.

"Let's go back," Pop said.

As we grew closer, the sound of hoofs hitting the road grew louder. Both Asa and Pop had their pistols ready, but relaxed when they saw Tull Petty coming into view, leading Smokey and the mayor's palomino. Bruno rode next to him on Ace. Catching sight of us, they urged their horses to move faster.

"Pope," Mr. Petty cried, jumping off his horse when he

reached us. He glanced at Melvin, made the sign of the cross, and immediately turned back to Pop. "All hell has broken out in town. Somebody threw a stick of dynamite in the telegraph station, blowing it all to hell. I thought my horses were going to go crazy. It took me a while to get them calmed down."

He stopped, took a breath, and plunged on. "Bruno come by in a state because he didn't know where Dolly and Clara Grace had gotten to. One of my lazy stable hands got around to telling us that when Dolly and Clara Grace had come out on the porch to see what happened, that crazy fool housekeeper of Melvin's rode by, threw a piece of paper at them, and then took off riding like hell's fire was at her heels. They read the note, and then Dolly started to leave with Clara Grace just a arguing with her. Clara Grace had to let her go, and Dolly went off down the road as fast as she could. A few minutes later, Clara Grace comes busting out of the store, screaming, 'but Dolly, he can't write,' and she goes chasing off after her.

"Bruno and me, we figured that dynamite was just a diversion to get them women out of town," Mr. Petty said, taking a large gulping swallow of air. "We don't know where the hell they're at, Pope."

"I know where they're at," Pop said with a groan coming from deep within his gut.

"Fergus Miller's place?" Asa said.

"Yes," Pop answered. "Tull, have you got your gun? Bruno? Louis is trying to lure Dolly to Fergus's."

"Louis! At Fergus's? Why?"

"I don't know! Ransom money, revenge. We have to hurry," Pop said. "Julius! Get a hold of yourself and take Whitey back to town. Warn everyone that Louis is the killer and on the loose. He may be dressed as Luci the housekeeper or as a man. Don't let Whitey out of your sight, and don't go into your house."

"I'm going with you, Pop," Asa said, his breath coming out in short spurts.

"You're wounded," Pop said.

"I can make it," Asa said. "I'm going. Let me have a horse. The mayor can walk."

Pop got on Smokey while Mr. Petty and Bruno helped Asa onto the palomino. Like Asa, I was determined to stick with Pop. He must have felt he didn't want me out of his sight either, because he let me climb on the back of Smokey with him without protest.

"Will Louis go after the mayor?" Asa yelled weakly.

"No," Pop shouted spurring his horse. "He's after Dolly now."

CHAPTER 26

With Pop leading the way, we rode toward Fergus Miller's cabin, and this time, the race was for my mother's life. From the back of our galloping horse, I turned and looked at Pop's posse. Instead of hardened young Rangers, it consisted of a wounded half-breed, a nearsighted old man, and another blind in one eye and unable to holler a warning of any kind. Yet even as the wind dried the silent tears on my cheeks, I trusted them with my whole heart to save my mother.

Pop slowed and led us to the hilltop where Whitey and I had found the cigarette butts. In the clearing at the bottom of the hill, and directly in front of us, we could see Clara Grace catching up with my mother, both of them about to walk into a trap.

"Dolly!" Pop screamed. "Stop!" He put the spurs to Smokey to try to reach her.

She and Clara Grace turned. "Pope!" she cried in relief when she saw us racing toward her.

Louis, shorn of his female camouflage, burst out of house, running toward them, gun in hand. My mother turned, her face becoming a mask of horror as she recognized him. "Run, Clara Grace, run!" she cried, pushing Clara Grace away.

Pop aimed his revolver but the women were in his line of fire, and he dared not shoot. Clara Grace tugged at my mother, and although she tried, her game leg couldn't keep up. She kept stumbling, pushing at Clara Grace and screaming at her to run. All the while Pop kept Smokey weaving, trying to reach a posi-

275

tion where he could safely fire at Louis.

Mr. Petty, Bruno, and Asa had fanned out and shot toward Louis with a hailstorm of bullets. He shot back and with the devil's luck continued running toward my mother. In one leap, he was upon her, and the men were forced to stop firing. Louis shot toward Clara Grace while dragging my struggling mother back into the house. His bullet missed Clara Grace, and turning, she was on him like a panther, clawing at his face and arms. He gave her a vicious slap on the side of her head with the butt of his pistol as he pulled my mother across the threshold of the cabin, slamming the door behind them, leaving Clara Grace lying unconscious in the dirt.

Pop whirled Smokey back into the trees just seconds before Louis began firing out the window. I heard for the first time the whistling sound men talked about when they recalled hearing bullets sing past their heads. Pop urged Smokey back toward Asa and the others. Asa and Tull Petty met him on the hilltop.

"I'm going down behind the corncrib and sneak up to the window to get a shot. Tull, you go to the other side," Pop ordered. "There's no back door." He gave a quick glance around them. "Bruno?"

Mr. Petty gave a slight shake of his head, and Pop went on. "Asa, you stay up here and shout to Louis. Pretend you're me. Talk hoarse, whatever it takes, but keep him distracted."

"Pop," Asa said. "We've got to get Clara Grace away from there."

"I'll do a belly crawl and risk it," Mr. Petty said. "You ain't got no strength left."

Asa had to agree. Pop forced me off the horse. "Kit, you stay up here with Asa. Lie low, boy."

I nodded and went to Asa. While Pop and Mr. Petty rode in opposite directions to try to get as close as they could to the house before dismounting, Asa found a fallen log for us to get behind.

"Louis!" he called in a hoarse voice. "You're surrounded; you might as well give it up."

"Pope!" a voice called from inside the cabin. "Is that you?"

"Hell, yes," Asa called. "You hurt my dad-blasted throat when you knocked me down, you son of a bitch."

I had never before heard a curse word cross Asa's lips, but he gave an almost perfect imitation of one of Pop's infrequent cuss fits. Lying flat on my stomach, I lifted my head slightly over the log so I could watch Pop and Mr. Petty dismount and thread their way closer to the cabin. Asa continued to talk to Louis, pretending to be Pop, but Louis began to get suspicious.

"I don't know, Pope, that don't sound like you," he hollered.

"You know good and well it's me," Asa popped back.

"I don't know," Louis said. There was a long pause. With laughing derision, he put Asa to the test. "If you're Pope, tell me who your favorite dove was at Effie's."

Asa blinked and shook his head in frustration. He looked in desperation at the cabin. "You talking about Mattie, or are you talking about Hattie?" he yelled.

"I reckon it's you then," Louis sang out with a laugh. As he and Asa continued to exchange words, I could tell something was going on in the cabin. Louis's voice would move, as if going from one part to another and back again, one time sounding as if he was upright, another time sounding as if he was bent low.

Outside, Pop was getting closer to the corncrib. My breath quickened; a fire began burning in my chest and without stopping to think, I got up and took off after him, trying to run like the wind without sounding like a four-hundred-pound buffalo crashing down the hill. At the same time, Louis was hollering at Pop to send me back to town to get all the money in the store's safe. He wanted it in exchange for my mother's life.

"How do I know Dolly is still alive?" Asa called. "How do I know you haven't already hurt her?"

The cabin remained ominously quiet for what seemed a long time, but in reality, was only seconds. I heard my mother's muffled cry, and her voice near the window shouting.

"Pope, you say you love me!" she called. We heard a stifled cry and silence.

Of course, she knew he loved her. I couldn't figure it out, and then I remember the song Pop was always singing—she was trying to tell him she was in the corner of the cabin.

Asa kept talking, but as I scurried along, it came to me that Louis wasn't responding. I could see Mr. Petty snaking his way on his belly to Clara Grace, reaching her and pulling on her feet, trying to get her out of harm's way. I caught up with Pop behind the corncrib, and I wanted to tell him what my mother had been trying to get across to him, but realized as soon as I neared, he would have known immediately what she meant. He whirled and saw me, his eyes widening. "Get down," he hissed.

I dropped to the ground and no sooner smelt the dirt than heard a noise behind me.

Louis stepped out from the side of the corncrib. Both he and my father fired their revolvers over my head at the same time. Pop went down. "Pop!" I cried. I looked back at Louis. One arm had been ripped by Pop's bullet, but the other hand still held a six-shooter. He walked to me, pausing at my feet. Anyone looking at him might have thought he was glancing down at an annoying dog. As I stared, he raised his pistol to kill me.

A deafening roar rang past my ear, and Louis crumpled to the ground. I looked in front of me to see Pop struggling to rise from his knees. Filled with indescribable relief, I leapt to help him. Once up, he shakily reloaded his pistol, and walking over to Louis, fired another bullet into his skull.

I hugged Pop, burying my face in his chest, realizing why

Louis's bullet hadn't killed him. Pop hugged me back, raising his head and hollering, "Asa, Tull, he's dead!" He gave me another quick squeeze. "Come on, boy!" he urged, "we have to see if your mother is all right."

Although Pop tried to hold me back, I ran into the cabin ahead of everyone. My mother lay in the corner, tied and gagged, surrounded by a pool of blood. Pop burst in behind me.

"Dolly!" he cried and ran to her.

Louis had slit her wrists. Pop jerked his handkerchief from his pocket and tied a tourniquet around one arm as fast as he could, doing the same thing with his string tie, all the while murmuring my mother's name.

She stared at me, and then at Pop, refusing to take her eyes from him. She looked so weak and frail, I began to cry. I felt Tull Petty's arm around my shoulder, squeezing it while he told me not to worry; she would be fine. He bent down and helped Pop minister to her wounds.

Old Man Miller was dead—Louis had slit his throat, too. I wondered why he hadn't killed my mother the same way.

"He wanted her to go slowly, suffering with the knowledge that before she died, he was going to kill Kit and me," Pop said in a low tone to Tull Petty when he voiced the same question. "She had rejected his brother for me, their worst enemy."

In only a little while it seemed all the men of Muskrat Hill were there and armed with more iron than a freight train has tracks. As they roamed with guns and knives drawn, their faces mirrored the intense relief of having the mysterious killer of Muskrat Hill dead, and that he had never been one of us. Those faces also scowled in disappointment when it became apparent they had missed the fight.

"Jumping Lucifer, I wish I'd been here," one man after another muttered to his neighbor.

We got my mother bundled into a wagon. On the way back to town, we had to go by Bruno's body. One of Louis's bullets had stopped what appeared to be a headlong charge. My mother, looking down from the wagon, begged my father to stop.

"Please, Pope, help me down," she insisted despite his warnings that she was too weak.

She knelt by Bruno, touching his scarred cheek with her fingertips. Her hand paused, and she stopped to stare at Bruno intently.

"Pope," she said, looking up in surprise. "This is Thomas. This is my brother, Thomas," and she fainted.

Two weeks later, my mother was back to being her lively and irrepressible self. "I think it's good for a person to lose blood," she said at the table in the back of the store with Pop and me beside her. Asa and Mr. Petty stood nearby, smiling and listening. "A body needs to get rid of some of that old bad blood and make some fresh," she said with a grin.

My father just smiled and shook his head. "Your mother is hopeless, boy," he told me, but his eyes went back to her. He couldn't stop looking at her.

"Pope," she said, "I still don't understand what all of this was about. Tell it to me again, please."

Pop gave her another smile that said he loved her almost as much as God. "Louis and Zane felt cheated and wanted their sister's land and money," he explained again. "Louis came back to Texas to visit Zane in prison, where I imagine they cooked up this scheme together. The second time Louis visited Zane, he dressed as a woman. That's why Zane laughed and didn't pursue a conjugal visit."

Pop paused before continuing. "Louella came over here with a garbled plea not to stir up the past. She kept saying brothers, and I thought she meant Julius and Melvin.

"Louis began his plan of trying to throw subtle suspicion on Julius without being too obvious. He didn't want anything pointing the way back to him. With Louella dead and Julius hung by an angry mob, he and Zane would inherit all their property. They probably thought they could buy Zane a pardon."

"You mean all this torture we went through was just because Louis and Zane were so greedy? It had nothing to do with who did what wrong?" my mother asked.

"Never," Pop said. "We jumped to that conclusion, and it was totally false."

"It was a brilliant plan, though," Asa said, "but you thwarted him at almost every turn, Pop. For instance, you found out about the handkerchief being left at the scene but managed to keep it a secret."

Pop shrugged his shoulders. "Louis didn't realize how well we all understood Julius. Even the Tabor boy grasped that it was probably planted there. And Louis took too many things for granted. He thought Effie would send the sheriff here looking for one of her girls and immediately put the finger on Julius as her customer. Louis didn't realize Effie was only too happy to be rid of her and had a mouth like a miser's purse when it came to saying anything about who paid her money for what.

"He also thought people would jump to the conclusion that Julius was the man Maydell was seeing. But we knew that while Julius might play around out of town, he would never do that here in Muskrat Hill where Louella would hear about it, especially not with someone like Maydell who would be bound to cause complications."

"And y'all never recognized him?" Mr. Petty questioned.

"No," Pop said. "It had been years since either of us had seen him, and he was always careful to come in the store when we were tied up in the back, or else be seen outside when it was almost dark. The day we insisted on talking to him at Melvin's house, he made sure the sun was in our eyes. I should have given that more consideration at the time."

"Everyone suspected Horace and Bruno because they had just come to Muskrat Hill," Asa said. "But we never stopped to consider that Melvin's housekeeper was new to town, too."

"That's just a lot of 'if onlies,' " Mr. Petty said. "What was Louis planning on doing at Melvin's after he hollered that the killer was Julius? Hightail it back into town and spread the word so a mob would form to hang Julius?"

"Yes," Pop said. "The 'housekeeper' would supposedly be hysterical with fright and run away."

"The note said you were at Mr. Miller's and needed me there right away, and I wasn't to tell anyone," my mother said. "I was panic-stricken thinking something had happened to you, Pope. Clara Grace realized it couldn't have been written by Mr. Miller because he didn't know how."

"Well, Dolly," Pop said, patting her hand. "Don't let it worry you now."

"I guess he thought he would make one last-ditch effort to get money by kidnapping me, then taking our money and killing us all," my mother said, being unexpectedly realistic. "I wish I'd never met Zane or Louis. But they were so charming when they were young."

Pop nodded. "It was a gift Louis especially had. He could get people to do what he wanted. Maydell and Melvin were both so starved for love; they would have done anything for him."

"Pop," Asa said. "How much do you think Melvin knew?"

Pop shook his head. "I think," he began slowly, "that Melvin enjoyed putting one over on the people of Muskrat Hill. There he was living with another man and no one realizing it. But Melvin was not a fool. That's the reason Louis had to stage that phony attack. And that it was Maydell he got to steal pencil and paper for him, not Melvin."

"He was so evil," my mother said with a shiver. "Poor Maydell, telling all those lies to protect him." She turned and shook her head. "And when I think about poor Thomas . . ."

She put her arms around Pop's neck and snuggled her head on his shoulder. "Dolly," Pop said, trying to comfort her. "Thomas wanted to be close to you, but he just couldn't bring himself to let you see how his life had turned out. Don't dwell on that; Thomas died feeling he was atoning for his sins. Just be thankful Kit met your brother and made friends with him."

"I know, but I still feel like all of this is my fault. I regret ever having anything to do with Zane," she said.

"Everyone makes mistakes, darling," Pop said. "Just look down the road to the Widow Crenshaw's house, and you'll know that you are not alone with your regrets."

My mother sat up and started laughing. "I don't think that's quite the same thing, but it's nice of you to try to make me feel better, Pope."

"In many ways, Dolly," Pop said dryly. "It's worse."

We heard footsteps and looked up. At the back of the store, the curtain pulled aside, and Clara Grace came out from behind it wearing a new dress covered in ruffles and lace, along with a fancy new hat and parasol, courtesy of Pop. She stood looking primly at Asa, although one of her eyes did not entirely focus with the other. Her right eye had been blinded by the pistol slap Louis gave her.

"I'm ready, Marshal Jenkins," she said, looking more gorgeous than ever, even with a bad eye.

Asa tried to put his own eyeballs back in their sockets. He held his arm out self-consciously for her. As they strolled by us to the front, she said, "Marshal, don't you even think about trying to kiss me on this buggy ride."

Asa turned red and stuttered, "Uh, yes, ma'am, Miss Clara Grace."

After a few more steps, she spoke again. "You may, however, hold my hand."

"For everyone to see?" Asa blurted in shock and disbelief. That she even consented to ride in a buggy with him was almost more than he could take in.

"Marshal," Clara Grace said sternly. "I am not in the habit of behaving one way in private and another in public."

"Uh, yes, ma'am, Miss Clara Grace," Asa stuttered again, holding the door open for her.

As the door behind them shut, Pop looked up at the ceiling and muttered, "Thank you, God."

Mr. Petty stared after Clara Grace and Asa, his mouth in a deep frown. "Ain't that just the way it is?" he complained. "Save a woman's life and then she promenades off with another man. I tell you, women ain't nothing but a . . ." he stopped and looked at my mother. He gave a sheepish grin. "A real blessing. A real God's blessing," he finished lamely.

My mother smiled back at him before looking ruefully toward the door. Pop, knowing she felt dreadful about Clara Grace's eye, too, took a firm stance with her. "Dolly," he said sternly. "Don't you think another thing about Clara Grace losing sight in that eye. No one could have done anything to her to make her happier. She thinks it's a sign of Christian martyrdom."

"Maybe you're right," my mother said with a smile.

"I know I'm right," Pop said empathically.

Mr. Petty gave a sigh. "I guess I'd better be moseying back to the stables," he said. "Those dang idiots I got working for me can't do nothing right without me being right there telling them what to do."

Pop said goodbye, and I followed Mr. Petty to the front, opening the door for him. "Say, Kit," he said, pausing. "Will you teach me some of them there sign signals?"

"Sure, Mr. Petty," I said, surprised he wanted to learn.

"It's like this," he said. "Horace's mother is a widow woman see, and I thought if I could communicate with her daughter, it might put me in her good graces, don't you know?"

I nodded sagely. "That would help," I said. "We can start tomorrow."

"No, no, come over later," Mr. Petty, as impatient as ever, said.

"Yes, sir, Mr. Petty," I replied.

Mr. Petty paused and looked back at my parents sitting side by side at the table, my mother listening as my father stared into her eyes and talked. "You know, Kit," Mr. Petty said. "Horace told me he and Bruno felt sorry for you when they first come to Muskrat Hill because your pa is an old man. But Horace told me before he left that there was no need for anyone to ever feel sorry for you. Horace can be full of horse manure nine-tenths of the time, but he was right about that, squirt, so don't forget it."

"I won't, Mr. Petty," I said and wished him goodbye.

I walked back to the table and stood on the other side of Pop, leaning against him.

"Darn," Pop said. "I still have to find out where Gypsy Schmidt is."

My mother looked at him in shock. "Gypsy Schmidt?" she said in surprise.

"Yes," Pop said, dismissing it with a wave of his hand. "She was Tull's first wife. He wanted me to find out what happened to her. I guess now that Clara Grace has finally admitted which way the wind is blowing, it doesn't matter."

"Pope!" my mother exclaimed. "I thought you knew!"

"Knew what?" Pop said. "What are you talking about?"

"Pope," my mother exclaimed. "Louella was Gypsy Schmidt. I thought you knew that. I never said anything to you about Louella being Tull Petty's ex-wife because neither one of us liked to talk about Zane and Louis, and I just thought you knew."

"How could Louella Foster possibly be Gypsy Schmidt?" Pop demanded. "I saw her once in San Antonio, and she was a knockout with the morals of an alley cat."

"Oh, Pope," my mother fussed. "People change. And you know how women like that are. They go from one extreme to the other."

"I still don't believe it," Pop said.

"It's true. After Tull beat her so badly, her father paid for an annulment and sent her back East to live with cousins. They changed their name to Smith. And Louella dropped that silly nickname and went back to using her real name. Her father bought all this expensive land out here hoping to use it to catch a decent husband for her. When Julius met her, her father knew quite well he was more in love with the farm than with his daughter, but he encouraged them to marry and settle down. By that time, Zane and Louis were getting so bad none of them wanted anything to do with them."

"Dolly?" Pop questioned, still unbelieving.

"Pope, I know what I'm talking about. When you and Julius brought Mr. Petty here, she went into a tizzy, because she didn't want Julius to know anything about her first marriage.

"When Mr. Petty didn't recognize her, it was a huge relief, but at the same time it hurt her deeply that he didn't even know who she was. That's the main reason she hardly ever stepped foot in this part of town. Not because she didn't want to be reminded of her awful brother by me, but because of Tull Petty. I just thought you knew, Pope."

Pop shook his head. "No wonder Effie looked at me like I was crazy when I asked. Well, I'm not telling Tull," he said. "I'm not going to ruin that memory for him."

Pop put his arms around both of us. "You know what I am

going to do?" he asked.

"What, Pop?" I asked.

"I'm going to build my family a brand-new water closet with one of those washout trap bowls so they don't ever have to go into a scary dark privy or empty a slop jar ever again," he said.

"Pope," my mother questioned. "Are those things sanitary? Everyone will think we are just being too highfalutin."

"Of course, they are sanitary, and I don't care what other people think," he said. "And," he added, giving me a squeeze. "I'm going to buy my son a guitar of his own, but first, I'm going to teach him to play mine. We've had enough misery around here; now we're going to have some fun."

He looked lovingly at my mother. "How would you like to go to Paris, Dolly?"

"Paris? Whatever would I want to go to East Texas for? We don't know anybody there," she answered.

"Not Paris, Texas, Dolly," Pop said. "Paris, France."

"We don't know anybody there either," my mother said dubiously. "I think we should take a train ride and see these mythical wonderful relatives you keep talking about."

"They're not mythical," Pop said. "If I can swallow that story about Louella Foster being Gypsy Schmidt, you can swallow mine about my wonderful relatives."

"Can I go get your guitar, Pop?" I asked.

"Yes, yes, yes."

"What about Whitey?" I asked. "He said he wished he could play the harmonica."

"Yes!" Pop said. "You boys are going to drive me crazy. I've got an old harmonica around here in a drawer somewhere. Find it and I'll teach him. Where is he, anyway?"

"He dropped by to visit Mr. Julius," I said. I looked at Pop and the nightmarish events we had lived through together overwhelmed me. I ran to him and hugged him as tightly as I could.

"There, there, Kit," Pop said, stroking my hair. "Don't worry, son, Pop is right here with you. Pop is right here with you, boy."

CHAPTER 27

The hotel room Kit and I sat in had grown dark. A tear dropped down my cheek as I stared at the Big Chief tablet I had long ago ceased to write in. One dim light shown from an ancient floor lamp in the corner, and the room seemed filled with shadows from the past. I thought of my poor mother being raped, of my grandmother, who had given up a stately home occupied by generations of ancestors. And my Uncle Horace, who had risked imprisonment to bring us to Muskrat Hill so we could have a better life.

Kit sat in the chair across from me, staring. "You're Horace's niece, aren't you? Giselle Thibodeaux," he said. "Why didn't you tell me?"

I sniffed and raised my head. "I wanted the truth, and I was afraid you wouldn't say it."

"I probably wouldn't have," he admitted.

He deserved some kind of an explanation from me. Taking a deep breath, I began, trying to tell the mess my life had become in a few brief sentences. "My marriage has been crumbling for years. Our son died. We lost everything. My husband took us out on the road to look for work. Yesterday, he left me a note saying goodbye.

"I don't blame him," I blurted. "I've kept one part of myself shut away from him for years. And lately, I've been consumed with thoughts of the past."

A deep sigh escaped my chest. "I realized from the time I was a little girl the stories about my father weren't real. I knew there were only two people left from the old days who could probably tell me the truth—you and Whitey. When I looked out the hotel window and saw you get out of your car, I knew my chance had come." I looked away in embarrassment.

He leaned forward. "I hope you don't hold the lies people told you against them."

I jerked my head back. "Of course not," I said. "I know they were acting out of love. Your mother went out of her way to help give me a normal and happy childhood."

I stood up to leave. "I'm sorry I pretended to be a writer. I appreciate your talking to me."

He jumped up and grasped my shoulders. To my surprise, I saw tears in his eyes. "Giselle, please don't go." He softened his grasp but his hands remained on me. "I'm not going to leave you stranded here and helpless under any circumstances. But could you see your way to maybe hooking up with a fading old country singer?"

I stared into his eyes. "No," I said. "But I think I'd like very much to hook up with Kittrell Robertson, the bravest boy in Muskrat Hill."

He shut his eyes and hugged me to him. I responded and knew I had come home at last.

ABOUT THE AUTHOR

Easy Jackson is a pseudonym for author Vicky Rose, who also writes under the name of V. J. Rose. Born in a small Texas town with a wild and woolly past, Rose grew up listening to enthralling stories of killings, lynchings, and vigilantes—excitement she tries to add to her writing so the reader, too, can experience the thrill of the Old West.

The employees of Five Star Publishing hope you have enjoyed this book.

Our Five Star novels explore little-known chapters from America's history, stories told from unique perspectives that will entertain a broad range of readers.

Other Five Star books are available at your local library, bookstore, all major book distributors, and directly from Five Star/Gale.

Connect with Five Star Publishing

Visit us on Facebook:
https://www.facebook.com/FiveStarCengage

Email:
FiveStar@cengage.com

For information about titles and placing orders:
(800) 223-1244
gale.orders@cengage.com

To share your comments, write to us:
Five Star Publishing
Attn: Publisher
10 Water St., Suite 310
Waterville, ME 04901